Path of the Guiding Light

Sharon K. Middleton

Black Rose Writing | Texas

ISBN: 978-1-68433-601-2
PUBLISHED BY BLACK ROSE WRITING
www.blackrosewriting.com

Printed in the United States of America
Suggested Retail Price (SRP) $18.95

Path of the Guiding Light is printed in Caslon

Acknowledgements

Once again, I thank my wonderful husband of over 45 years for his love, patience, and consideration when I am writing. What would I do without you? I pray I never find out.

I also give special thanks to my friends and beta readers, Sylvia Kirklin Simpkins, Judy Steckman Broussard, Maureen Maskell, Venita Henson, and Joan Capaiu Greene, for their help.

I also give special thanks to my Cherokee consultants, Venita Henson, Cheryl Schuman, Megan McDonald Smith, and if course, our heroine's namesake, Baylie Smith, for their many helpful tips and suggestions.

Special thanks again to Angela Wollom, Brazoria Country Law Library, for putting up with me hours on end.

And last but not least, special thanks to Reagan Rothe and Black Rose Writing for their continued faith in me as we publish this fifth book in the *McCarron's Corner* series.

This book is dedicated to the brave women who carry their differently abled children to term and love their perfectly imperfect children. God bless each of you.

Path of the Guiding Light

Prologue

I made it. I still cannot quite believe it, but I finally made it.

I tried last Saturday again. It was the month of the bony moon, as the old stories said would be the time when she would arrive. I hoped it would work this time. After all, my divorce was finally finished, after four long, hideous years. My house sold and closed. I quit my job. I decided I had it with my career when my opposing counsel made the salacious proffer of what I could do with him in the conference room. I decided I would not go to Oklahoma to be another paper pusher. I was ready for my Grand Adventure. It was now or never.

I hated to go now on one level. I would miss my family. Heck, I already miss my family. And I will miss my young friend. Fancy Winslow taught me much about Before. Her baby is due any time. I hate missing the birth of her child. He was due shortly after I left. I never gave birth to a child of my own. I was always too busy with work, and my ex held no bones that he did not want a child. Let's face it; he was the child in our relationship from the 'get-go.' But if I stayed, Fancy wanted me to be her baby's godmother. If I ever held her baby in my arms, I would never be able to leave. I would have stayed. I went then because it was 'now or never,' and I could not stay.

My destiny lies elsewhere.

I hiked the four miles from the trailhead to the meadow the week before Valentine's Day. It was cold, but not too bad. I have hiked in colder weather many times. I love to walk with the crisp feel of cold against my skin. It wasn't cold enough to snow when I started, although I could taste snow in the air by the time I reached the meadow.

I shivered and pulled the hoodie on my puffer jacket over my head. I was glad I wore my long john's, wool socks, and my well-worn Timberland boots. I slapped my gloved hands together and kept walking.

In my old life, Beyond, I was known as Baylie Smith. The Cherokees call me Guiding Light. I always thought I was named for the first Guiding Light who helped lead the Cohutta Cherokees to safety before the Trail of Tears. Of course, my grandmother always swore she named me after an old soap opera she loved back in the day. However, I know where we are supposed to go. I traveled the Trail of Tears more than once in the future. I memorized the route of the Trail. With the help of the Great Spirit, I will guide my people safely west to the far distant, isolated protection of the Arbuckle Mountains, as the prophecy foretold. I am not merely a woman named Guiding Light. I *am* the Guiding Light, sent from Beyond to guide my people to a new land, a safe land, where our people can live forever in peace and harmony.

It felt strange to hike along a path I know so well and to hear The Big Noise. I realized at once what the sound signified. Unlike Fancy, I did not fall. I stopped, face uplifted, arms outstretched, as I savored the sound. It rang out loud and true, like a beacon summoning me home.

I smiled when it stopped. I adjusted my pack and said a quick prayer to the four directions. I pulled sage from my pocket and blew it into the air to give thanks to the Great Spirit for guiding me here. I walked on to the springs above the falls, where I knew I would meet Bright Star.

Arriving there first, I bent to drop my pack and scooped a handful of the fresh, clear spring water into my hands. I said a quick prayer of thanksgiving for pure water, untainted by pollution. Sipping the refreshing liquid from my cupped hands, I closed my eyes, exultant as the crystal-clear, ice cold fluid slid down my throat. I never tasted water so pure and clean before.

I heard her before she arrived. Her deerskin moccasins did not make much noise, but I knew what to listen for. I looked up to find a beautiful young woman clad in deerskins who carried a baby on her back. She hesitated as if stunned when she saw me. "Welcome, my sister. I wondered when you would come."

I felt a surge of delight when she realized who I was before I uttered a word. I smiled and arose, crossing quickly to the petite woman. "I came as soon as possible," I said, as I gathered the Bright Star of Hope into my arms for a big hug. "It is good to be here, my sister. My friend, Fancy Winslow, sends her greetings."

I fibbed. I know Fancy well, and she is my dearest friend, but she did not realize I came.

Star kissed me on each cheek, and I kissed her the same way, in the standard greeting among our people. Her face broke into a smile. "She found her Richard? I am so glad. They were meant to be together. She deserved to find some happiness. She suffered much sadness in her life here, Before. However, I did not expect her to send the Guiding Light to us."

I laughed, a bit embarrassed by her unrestrained recognition. "I am not sure Fancy realized who I am or that she gave me the way to come. But yes, they were meant for each other. Yin and yang, we say Beyond. Rick and Fancy fit together perfectly and make each other whole."

Bright Star and I talked as we strolled back to the village, where she took me into the warmth of her snug and cozy *asi*. I pulled out maps to show to her when the men rushed in.

I knew at once who they were. There was a tall, slender, red-haired man who could only be the son of Marcus and Lily McCarron. He must have been as tall as Marc. He is known as Red Wolf among my people. I knew he married Star, and he vigorously protected the woman and the tribe he loved.

I blinked at the sight of the other man as my heart began to sing with joy. *This is him,* I thought. *Who else could it be?* Richard Winslow showed me photos he secretly took of many people when he was here before. It could be no one else, although there was grey beginning to show at his temples in his ebony hair which was not in the photos Richard took. His dark, almond-shaped eyes shone like obsidian. His skin shone like burnished copper. His long, aquiline nose was straight and well formed, and his high cheekbones chiseled handsome planes on his handsome face. He wore red face paint on the lower half of his face as did Red Wolf, so I knew the men trained to go to battle soon. His ears were pierced in the way of our people at that time, with his head shaved back to a topknot from which several feathers extended, one a golden eagle tail feather and the other a bald eagle tail feather. I knew only great warriors or chiefs could wear eagle feathers. His brow was tattooed with grey footprints of a wolf to reflect his name. He was tall, but not too tall, with a broad, well-muscled chest and bulging, bronzed biceps.

My breath caught in my throat. He was everything and more than I ever dreamed. This was a man worth fighting to gain his heart.

I reminded myself to breathe and took a deep breath. I stood up straight and held out my hand. "It is a great honor to meet you, Chief Shadow Wolf."

His gaze never wavered. He nodded slightly as he took my hand into his. "I am glad you arrived at long last. We feared you would never come."

I smiled and lowered my eyes in the way girls do to flirt, letting my eyelashes flutter across my cheeks. "I understand you thought Sassy Selk was the Guiding Light?"

He blushed and glanced aside as if embarrassed. "At one time, yes, I thought Sassy might be the One. How do you know that?"

I tilted my head as I studied his face, looking up at him through my eyelashes. "Fancy Winslow told me. Let me ask, do you still play stickball?"

I never was one to dilly dally about. I guess working as an attorney made me pretty straightforward.

Stickball is a game played among the Cherokees, especially the young ones. It is a way to learn and hone fighting skills, and an opportunity for boys and girls to flirt. A girl knows a boy possesses good warrior skills based on his ability to play stickball. She also learns if he is a man with a sense of humor and strong self-worth without undue ego if he can be beaten by a woman and not become angry or bitter at the loss. It shows if he is a man who is able to withstand teasing and jokes.

I stopped, suddenly self-conscious. It had been a long time since I flirted with a man. At 40, I was no longer young. Brian and I tied the knot fifteen years ago. What a waste those years were! Would Shadow Wolf know I flirted with him? How could he not know I played the coquette?

Would he care?

He stared at me for a moment before answering. "I have not played stickball for many years now, since I won the hand of my Ginny playing the game long ago. It is a sport for young warriors. I might play again for the right woman. Perhaps a woman who came from afar."

"I had to wait until the Great Spirit showed me the way, until it was the right time." I held my head a little higher.

"Timing is important. Yes, I would play stickball for such a woman," he replied.

Then he smiled, and as his smile warmed my lonely heart, I knew I was in the right place. And no, he did not seem to mind that I flirted. He seemed pleased, perhaps even flattered.

Fancy told me Hemingway wrote "the world breaks everyone, and then some become strong at the broken pieces." The Japanese repair broken things with a special process they call Kintsugi. They repair broken pottery with a strong adhesive and sprinkle the adhesive with gold dust. The resulting, repaired piece is stronger, more beautiful, more interesting, for having been broken and repaired. Fancy wanted to be a living piece of Kintsugi.

So, do I.

I am determined I shall be bonded with spiritual epoxy sprinkled with gold. With each passing day, I become a better living example of Kintsugi. I realize this process is not about being perfect, but I work hard every single day to be the best person I can be each day. That's when the transformation occurs, when the change happens. That is how it occurs. Some days, it is hard to effectuate change. I must remember to keep going, to embrace the struggle and let it make me stronger in the places where I was broken. With each passing day, I intend to be stronger. More interesting. Maybe even more beautiful.

I must continue because I now know I am *the* Guiding Light. I found my Wolf. I shall lead my people to safety.

No, let me correct that. *We* shall lead *our* people to safety.

Last Saturday, I found my destiny among the Cohutta Cherokees. Now, I must fulfill the tasks I have been sent here to accomplish.

Chapter 1
Before - 1787

A snowstorm hit the night I arrived at the village of the Cohutta Cherokees. I feared we would be cold in the winter *asi* of my new sister, Bright Star. I did not sleep well the first night. Too much ran through my mind. Yet, within a few nights, with the fire burning warm and nestled beneath the furs, I find I now sleep better, more soundly than I ever remembered sleeping when I lived Beyond in the future I fled. Now, my future lay Before me. Literally.

Star, her husband, Red Wolf, her father, Shadow Wolf, and I talked late into the night.

"Wait. What year did you say it is?" I asked.

"1787. Why?" Red Wolf looked puzzled by my question.

"Hmm. Fancy has been in the future four years, but it's only been three years here."

Shadow Wolf smiled. "Time does not flow in a straight line. Sometimes, it seems to move at the same pace, here and there. At other times, it bends, sometimes in one direction, sometimes the other. Three years passed here while Lily went back to learn medicine. Eighteen years passed there. She left here a child. When Lily came back to us, she'd become the woman needed for our clan and for Marcus."

Shadow Wolf talked at length about the process by which they would introduce me to the tribal elders to seek their acceptance of me. I leaned towards him as I listened with patience, although I already knew the process well. I worked with the Eastern Band of the Cherokee Nation for almost sixteen years. The Eastern Band of the Cherokee Nation descended from the persons listed on the Baker Roll of Cherokee

Indians. They gained recognition as a tribe in the early 20th century. They are one of the three federally recognized Cherokee tribes, the others being the Cherokee Nation and the Keetoowah Band, both in Oklahoma. I understood tribal politics and the historical division of job functions within the tribe, based on the Cherokee construct of gender, a concept with ancient roots among our people. I understood it would be especially crucial for the women leaders of the tribe to accept me and recognize me as the Guiding Light. Without their support and acceptance, I could not succeed.

I read many ethnographic studies about Native Americans and Cherokees since my college days. Many ethnographers do not comprehend the importance of the woman in a matrilineal society, such as the Cherokee. I always found it amusing and irritating they understood one's lineage passes from mother to child but failed to grasp the crucial roles women traditionally held in Cherokee society. For instance, many ethnographers failed to recognize there were women warriors. They thought women were second class citizens in Cherokee society. In reality, nothing could be further from the truth.

Women are the creators of life. They bring forth new life. In the eighteenth century, it was not understood among the Cherokee exactly how men contributed to the creation of a child, but no one could deny the baby was born of the mother. They were the keepers of their bodies. They chose their spouses. They could accept or reject a man who offered for them. Many women set their eyes on the men they wanted and pursued them. Europeans perceived Cherokee women as promiscuous because the women, not the men, were the keepers of their bodies. Cherokee women were not promiscuous, but they were in control of their destinies.

Once married, the man had an obligation to build her a winter *asi* and a summer house as well. Those homes were hers. If she later kicked him out – divorced him – the houses were still hers.

A different rule with a similar result for me applied Beyond among the Cherokees when I divorced my husband. Brian expected to receive half of the equity from the sale of my house. He was unpleasantly surprised to learn among the Eastern Band of the Cherokee Nation, the home in the Qualla land trust was mine. I was a member of the Eastern

Band. My Caucasian husband was not qualified to be a member of the Eastern Band of the Cherokee or of any Cherokee tribe. Only members of the Eastern Band can own land within the Qualla land trust. He appealed the decision. It took two years to get the final ruling, but in the end, the house and all the equity was mine.

It felt good to kick Brian out of my house after the Qualla denied his appeal. As it was, he got half my government retirement account from the Bureau of Indian Affairs. I still came back in time with a veritable buttload of money to help my people relocate to the west.

"Your greatest strength is that you come from Beyond. You know the path to safety and brought the maps to guide our way. But your greatest weakness will be that you come from Beyond. I can tell you know the division of work in our society, but the lines blurred for you. You worked too long in a job that traditionally belongs to men. I fear the beloved women of our tribe will find you are out of harmony." I noticed a worried frown marred Shadow Wolf's handsome features.

I bristled at his words. "Why would they think that?"

He smiled. Almost. "You never had a child."

I felt flabbergasted. "You are joking. Will you judge me based on my fertility? My ability to procreate? Well, that's pretty old fashioned."

He laughed. "We are old fashioned. That is our way. Women are the bringers of life. You never created a new life. However, you bring corn and potatoes. You know how to plant, sow, and reap. These skills will help the beloved women accept you."

"I can do more. I can hunt. Fish. Shoot with both a gun as well as a bow and arrow, and I can hold my own in a fight—"

He shook his head. "In our society, the men hunt and fish. Hunting is man's work. You know this. But your other skills may qualify you to be a warrior woman."

I blinked. "I am a very skilled negotiator."

That time, he roared with laughter. "I see you more as a warrior woman than as a peacekeeper, and we are a warring tribe, not a peacekeeping tribe. The trick will be to keep you out of the hands of the Chickamaugas. They would kill for one with the skills you possess."

My eyes narrowed as I studied him. "I knew this is a warring tribe before I came. I would know it now by the red face paint if I did not know it before I arrived here. Why do you say the Chickamauga tribe would want me?"

"They would kill all the whites and drive them out of our lands. Plus, you speak both English and Cherokee. You were born to be a warrior woman. Such women are rare."

I shook my head. "I have no desire to kill whites. I want us to get to a place of safety before the bad times arrive. I know Lily and Marc. Lily was my friend. I met them Beyond."

He looked both surprised and pleased. "Really? That may help. Our villagers greatly love our Red Moon Woman and Lone Eagle. She is one of our healers. We are blessed to have a healer as skilled as Red Moon Woman amidst us. I will send word to them you arrived. But you must realize we do not focus on the individual and their rights. We are, what was it that Sassy called us? Comm…ut…tarian? Our community is most important."

"Communitarian. The community is first in importance before the individual," I answered by rote as I reflected upon the Cherokee philosophy, which emphasizes the connection between the individual and the community. Cherokees believe a person's social identity and personality are primarily molded by community relationships, with a smaller degree of development from individualism.

I sighed. Dammit, I had to admit he was right. It might well be difficult for me to fit into such a culture with rigid gender-based roles without considerable effort. I had been an independent, modern woman for many years, perhaps too many. I felt more than a twinge of concern.

Yes, I slept poorly that first night. For the first time, I worried whether I could fit into life in the village in 1787. It was also harder than I expected to sleep in the crowded *asi*. With four adults and four children, the cozy accommodations in the winter *asi* were tight and confining, almost stifling. The room was dark and smoky, the tang of the smoke both comforting and irritating. The sleeping ledges were narrow, hard, and unforgiving. I sorely missed my queen-sized Sleep Number mattress. It would take some adjustment to sleep upon this ledge as comfortably as did the Cherokees surrounding me. I wished I had brought a memory foam, twin bed topper with me. It would have significantly enhanced my comfort sleeping on the dratted ledge. Oh well, a day late and a dollar short, as the old saying goes. The fire and the furs kept it warm and snug. In fact, the asi felt almost too warm for me. It hit me hard that a single room house like this would be my home for the rest of my life. I have been camping lots of times in my life, but at the end of the trip, you always went home to your modern house with all the amenities. Even as a child on the farm, we had indoor plumbing, a fridge, a cookstove, flushing toilets, and toilet paper. Those basics which seemed so inconsequential as a child now were penultimate luxuries. Thanks to the Great Spirit that I brought a dozen rolls of Charmin double-ply, sans the cardboard rolls. Lily warned me toilet paper would be one of the things I would miss the most here. No wonder Fancy was so impressed when she went forward in time to live in Rick's exquisite home! After hours of sleepless worry, I arose with a sigh and slipped outside the doorway to watch the silent snowfall. I must have stood there for the better part of an hour watching the village turn white beneath a blanket of snow when Wolf moved up beside me to wrap me in the comforting warmth of a bearskin.

"Thank you," I murmured. I pulled the warm bearskin close around my shoulders.

Shadow Wolf stood there beside me, silent as the snow I watched falling, with his hand lightly resting upon my shoulder. Finally, he spoke. "It may not be easy, but they will come to accept you."

My smile must have been wry. "Be patient, hmm? I'll try. I came too far not to give this my all."

He nodded. "Yes, you have. You must help us put our pieces back together before we are shattered so badly by the outside that we cannot repair ourselves."

I looked at him in surprise. I had not expected him to tell me I was supposed to be the epoxy to fix the whole village. They were supposed to be the epoxy to fix me. "That's asking a lot of one woman. Do you think I can do it?"

He studied me before answering. "I suspect you can do anything once you set your mind upon it. Otherwise, you would not be here."

Wow. Fantastic insight from a man who just met me. My ex knew me for years and never figured that out about me. I smiled as I pulled the bearskin close about me.

We watched the snowfall in silence until sunrise. Wolf slipped back into the *asi* as I made my morning oblations to the four corners, and then I noticed the sky looked red that crisp, cold morning. I remembered Fancy saying "red skies at night, sailors delight, red skies in the morning, sailors take warning." What did the warning concern?

Danger, danger, Will Robinson. Do not proceed. I smiled as I remembered the robotic warnings to young Will from the old television series, *Lost in Space.* I felt like the Robinsons must have felt when lost in space. So many great adventures ahead, but so many unknown risks and dangers as well. *Danger, danger, Baylie Smith. Proceed with caution!*

I took a deep breath. Time to get into the mindset of the gender-specific job functions I would be allowed to perform here and an attitude of communitarian ethos if I wanted to succeed. So why was my mind rebelling against those concepts?

Oh, yeah, now I remember. I hate weeding, and the women are in charge of the crops. I hoped all those treatises that said Cherokees did not weed were correct. Somehow, I had my doubts.

Star took me with her as she worked that day. We began in the small, family garden and then moved on to the large, communal fields. In both, I could see the women preparing the earth to plant the three sisters come springtime, so they could grow in harmony. Beans, corn, and squash comprised the fundamentals of the Cherokee diet. As other women came to join us there, she introduced me, making sure to identify me to the Beloved Women of the village.

My back soon ached from the unaccustomed manual labor. This was not what I had expected or hoped to be doing, if my life was to dig row after endless row of plants. That day, we worked manure into the rich soil to prepare it for spring planting. I knew next month we would plant some of the corn and potatoes I brought with me in both places. Star commented she was glad I thought to bring seed potatoes and corn. We completed the farming work by noon, and then we sat outside the *asi,* weaving baskets. As much as I dislike farming, I always loved basket work and weaving. I worked on one which would eventually be a long tray, useful for carrying vegetables from the garden. Soon, I became lost in the rhythm of weaving the reeds in and out of the basket I was creating. Star began preparing corn soup as well as roasting potatoes and ears of corn for dinner. My mouth began to water as she added a haunch of venison over the fire. As the sun started to set, the men entered the *asi,* and we all began eating.

"I am due to start my cycle tomorrow. After we eat, I will introduce you to more of the women who you did not meet today," Star said.

I remembered with a start the Cherokee believed menstruating women possessed enormous power and stayed apart from the men while in their cycles. Women were considered dangerous to men while menstruating. The seclusion and avoidance of women at such times signified their power over men while on their periods. They believed this seclusion to be a practical precaution and demonstration of the elevated position women held in Cherokee society.

It still rankled my modern mind.

"I can watch the children while you are secluded," I suggested.

She shook her head. "That would be appreciated but it is not necessary. The other women in my clan will watch my children. They are my sisters."

"What clan are you?" I asked.

"Twister Clan," she replied.

At home, we called it the Long Hair Clan, but I knew the name. It made sense because the tribe adopted her mother. People with no Cherokee clan, such as Ginny Blue Eyes, were often adopted into the Twister clan at that time.

"I'm Bird clan. Eagle sub-clan," I murmured.

She nodded. "That makes sense. You are the messenger and will be teaching us the importance of the move to come and how it will affect our lives. Let me introduce you first to your sisters of the Bird Clan. They are a strong group of women. Like yourself, they are willing to sacrifice themselves for the sake of the tribe."

I blinked. I hadn't viewed my coming back in time to be an act of self-sacrifice. I realized with a start that it was. I intentionally gave up everything I had Beyond to come here and guide my brethren to safety far to the West. I came to help my people reclaim their place in this great land. In the future, a study called "Reclaiming Native Truth" will proclaim "contemporary Native Americans are, for the most part, invisible in the United States." If I could accomplish anything by coming back in time, I would help my people relocate, avoid the Trail of Tears, maintain their dignity and their rightful place in this country, and to never become invisible. I intended to help the Cherokee nation remain visible. Those were enormous goals, yet the survival of the Cohutta Cherokees depended upon my success. It boggled my mind that Native Americans only comprised about 1% of the population in North America when I came here. No longer would I try to ignore the genocide of my people, not merely under Andrew Jackson, but as long as Europeans colonized our beautiful land and strove to push us further and further westward to areas less and less desirable. It had been pretty damned successful in the future I fled. With this new self-awareness, I stood a little taller as Star took me to the council house to meet the women of my Clan.

Word passed through the day I came from Beyond and sought a place in the Bird Clan, of which the Eagle is a subset. Birds serve as the messengers between heaven and earth, or between the people and the Creator. We believe the Creator gave us the responsibility of caring for birds. The Cherokees consider the Bird Clan to be the messengers to the gods. That is why Star said it made sense that I am supposed to be a messenger to our people.

The subdivisions are Raven, Turtle Dove, and Eagle. Members of the Eagle Sub-Clan are the only ones authorized to collect Eagle feathers. At first, only the Eagle Sub-Clan could present Eagle feathers to warriors for bravery.

I met a group of ten women that evening, all eager to hear my story and test my knowledge of our clan. Knowledge of a person's clan is essential for many reasons. First of all, men and women of the same clan were forbidden to marry. Clan members are considered family. The clan members are brothers and sisters. When receiving spiritual guidance or medical help, it is vital to name your clan. People were seated at ceremonies by clan, the *Aniwahiya*, or Wolf Clan, the *Anikawi*, or Deer Clan, *Anidjiskwa*, or Bird Clan, which was my Clan, *Aniwodi*, or Paint Clan, *Anisahoni*, or Blue Clan, *Anigotigewi*, the Wild Potato Clan, and the *Anigilohi*, or Twister Clan. A husband and wife would be seated in different sections, according to their clan affiliation.

I love the music of Native American musician Mary Youngblood. Mary is half-Aleut and half-Seminole. While not Cherokee, she wrote a song entitled 'Eagle Clan.' The song touches my soul. I learned to play it on my Native American flute after I first heard it. As the women assembled that night, I pulled out my instrument and began playing the haunting notes of the song of the Eagle Clan. As the last notes faded into the night winds, Star introduced me to the women.

"I asked you here tonight to meet one of your Clan who comes from Beyond. I want to introduce my friend, Guiding Light. I believe she is the messenger promised to us in the Prophecy. She has come to help guide our tribe to safety. I will leave you women to talk with your sister from Beyond," Star said.

One elder woman motioned for Star to stay. "It is not necessary for you to leave us while we talk, Bright Star. You are sister to all of us."

Star smiled and lowered her head. "If the women of the *Anidjiskwa* will not object, I would be honored to stay, Inola. Thank you. Guider, Inola is the Beloved Woman of the Bird Clan."

Inola struck me as intelligent and tenacious as the black fox for whom she received her name many years before. Her hair was now white with age, and her dark eyes peered into mine as if she intended to peak deep inside my soul. "Tell us about yourself. Where was your fire?"

Other tribes call the Cherokees 'the people of the fire.' Cherokees identified the town or village they came from as 'where their fire was.' I smiled.

"I am *Anidjiskwa*, like my mother and grandmother before me. My fire burned about 100 miles northeast of here. We lived on a farm near a little town called Almond on the Nantahala River. It is part of the Qualla, the land owned by the Eastern Band of the Cherokee, in a state called North Carolina. When I was born, my mother wanted to name me Walela for my grandmother. My grandmother told her I was no hummingbird. I would be strong, brave, and fearless. I would be an Eagle."

The women murmured approval. "Go on, my sister. How then were you named Guiding Light?" she asked.

I smiled. "After seven days, they still had not decided on my name. My grandmother said she had a vision. She named me for one called Guiding Light, who lived long before me. She told me the story many times, of the Prophecy of the Bright Star of Hope and how the Guiding Light came from Beyond to help Star lead their people to a place of safety and prosperity, before the trail of great sorrow to come. It was a great honor to bestow this name on a girl, and the clan held a council before allowing it. As a child, I often pretended to be the one who would guide her people to safety, never dreaming it was me."

Another woman spoke. "When did you realize you are the Guiding Light of the prophecy?"

"Fancy Winslow is my friend Beyond. Her parents came through the time gate searching for her, and I was able to meet Red Moon Woman and Lone Eagle. Red Moon Woman felt sure I was her. She urged me to pray about it. I fasted and prayed, and I believe she is correct. I know this is my destiny."

"But how do you know?" she pressed.

"I am here. The Great Spirit allowed me to travel here, from Beyond. That can only happen if meant to be."

The women nodded assent. "That is true."

Inola frowned. "But what of your family? Your children? What will happen to them since you left?"

I gulped. "I was married to one man. He gave me no children. I believe that will allow me to hold each child in our Bird Clan as my own."

Inola blinked. "No children? And you stayed with such a man?"

I shook my head. "I put him aside. He was a poor excuse for a husband."

A poor husband indeed. That was the politest thing I could think to say of him. The lazy bastard never worked a day during our marriage. He always waited for 'his ship to come in.'

I took a deep breath. "May I show you my marks?"

As Inola nodded assent, I lifted my hair back to reveal my ear. A small eagle feather was tattooed behind one ear. I then swept my hair over one shoulder and to one side so they could see the little eagle in flight on the nape of my neck. A golden eagle's feather with small eagles flying off from the tip of the feather encircled my ankle. I stood up and slipped my deerskin tunic over my head to reveal the large tattoo on my back of a pair of outspread eagle's wings.

The women gasped.

"I have never seen such marks before," Inola marveled as she gently traced the elegant watercolor tattoo of the eagle's wings across my back. "These are the finest marks I have ever seen. How do they do these colors?"

I nodded. "I do not deign to claim the knowledge of how they made the marks. They call it a watercolor tattoo Beyond. I wanted my marks to be of my clan, but also to show I am from Beyond. I am one of the *AniYunwiya*. I am also one of the Eagles of the *Anidjiskwa*. I chose marks that reflect my heritage. I sought out the finest markers I could find to make mine."

That was true. I traveled to London for the water colored wings. Those tattoos were expensive, but they are works of art I proudly bear on my body. All the tattoos could be covered when I worked at the BIA. Now, I would never have to hide my heritage again. The ink on my skin was part of me, and I could show each tattoo - marks as my people called them - with honor, pride, and dignity.

My ex-husband hated them. I smiled at the women.

"I still need a mark to show I am Guiding Light."

Inola's eyes narrowed. "It will not look like the marks you brought with you. We have good markers, but..."

I nodded. "I know. They will show I am here, *now*, marked in *this* era by my new tribe, the Cohutta Cherokee. It will help unite me with my new tribe. If you will have me."

She came to stand by me and traced her fingers across my brow. "I welcome you to our tribe and our clan. Now, we will decide how to make the marks which will show you are our Guiding Light, of the Bird Clan."

"Eagle tracks," said one old woman.

"Yes, eagle tracks should cross her brow, like a path," chimed in another woman.

My throat tightened. I had always avoided facial tattoos. Vanity, perhaps, but I could never force myself to ink my face. However, I knew the Clan would probably mark my brow. I nodded my acquiescence. The marking was essential to be accepted by my clan and the entire tribe.

"It will reflect her true name," said Inola.

I blinked, startled by her words. "And what would that be, old mother?"

She smiled. "As foretold, your true name shall be Path of the Guiding Light."

Chapter 2
Before – 1787

I blinked. "I thought my name was Guiding Light, and my role was to guide my people to the path of deliverance."

Inola's face creased with laughter. "Your role *is* to guide your people to the path of deliverance. But your *true* name from the Prophecy includes mention of the path." Her face softened, and she stroked my face. "We will be gentle, my child. The mark may not be as stylish or artistic as the ones you brought from Beyond, but our best marker will do her finest work for you, my daughter."

Tears welled in my eyes. Not from fear of the tattoo, but because of her words. "Yes, my mother."

She beamed with pride at me. I had understood the significance of her words. She accepted me, not only into the clan but into her heart and her hearth as daughter. I found my home.

Motherhood is not a trite sentiment among my people. Cherokee women invoke motherhood as the source of their power. They use their status as mothers to make public appeals. Mothers also convey tribal and clan membership. No one can claim to be of the *AniYunwiya* unless the person had a Cherokee mother or the tribe adopted the person. When she claimed me not merely as one of the clan, but as her child, I knew I could fit in.

Lily and Marc came over the next day, excited I arrived at last. We talked for hours about everything that happened since they came home.

"I'm so glad you finally got here. I fear we must leave soon," Lily said with a nervous glance at Marc.

I frowned. "Why would you leave?"

"The Chickamauga are becoming ever more aggressive towards whites. We have been back a year this time. Marc doesn't want to leave, but the Chickamauga massacred a white settlement not far from here recently. I'm pretty nervous," she said. "Heck, I'll admit it. I'm downright scared."

"I suggested you move into the village years ago," Red Wolf said. "You are our Red Moon Woman, Mother. You are one of our healers. Father is Lone Eagle. He is a great warrior. You will always be welcome in the village of the Cohutta Cherokees."

"It is because he is Lone Eagle that your father will not join the village," Wolf intoned. "And yes, we need them both. If they leave, they will be sorely missed by all of our people, not just us."

In the months that followed, I struggled to find my place among the Cohutta Cherokees. My brow was marked with Eagle tracks, a path, and rays of the sun to light my way. The tattoo was bold and striking. Tribal, as they would someday say in the future. It gave me a feral look that at first rattled me, but I soon grew to like it. It reminded me of eagle tracks I saw in the snow in the mountains of North Carolina. I was home with my tribe and marked for the world to know I was Path of the Guiding Light, of the Eagles of the *Anidjiskwa* Clan.

During the next six months, my skin turned copper from working in the sun, darker than I could remember it had ever been. My nails broke to the quick, and my hands calloused with the gardening. I would never love digging in the dirt. Till the corn, plant the seeds, water the plants, pull weeds when I can't stand it any longer. They laugh when I pull weeds. I try explaining the weeds eat nutrients from the soil, which the three sisters need to grow. Working with the plants always reminded me of my hunger-filled, impoverished childhood on the farm after my dad died. Yet, I began to realize the joy of working with other women, even if it is at what I perceive as a mind-dulling, never-ending task, which I would always loathe.

I realized I had a skill for basketry. The older women, including Inola, were thrilled as I learned to dye the reeds with natural dyes and began to weave intricate Cherokee designs, I learned years before from my grandmother. Inola often examined my baskets. After carefully studying the design, colors, details, and functionality, she would grunt her satisfaction before patting my head. "Good work, Guider."

The tribe quickly adapted to calling me Guider, as Inola and Star did. It's simpler than saying Path of the Guiding Light. It would have been nice if they could have called me Pathfinder, but I learned someone else already received that name.

"To who? I have met no one with that name," I asked Wolf after dinner one evening.

His cheeks burned bright red with embarrassment. "I named Sassy Selk that."

I bit back laughter. I have learned the handsome war chief does not like to be mocked. I knew Wolf 'had a thing' for Sassy years ago. At one time, he thought she was the Guiding Light, I mean, the Path of the Guiding Light.

Star was pleased I knew how to weave, and I could sew a straight line. Soon, I began creating fabric, as well. I urged Wolf to get William Selk to send cotton seed so we could grow cotton. I showed him the cotton fabric I had brought from home.

"Will used to bring fabric like this to Sassy. She made clothing and quilts with it for the settlers. Will said he received money for her quilts up north, too."

I nodded. "I imagine he did. Cotton is strong, washes well, and is comfortable. You can quilt clothing items like petticoats, vests, and even coats made of it for winter warmth. We could make them for our use as well as to sell or trade. In the future, our women will be known for the beauty of our quilts. It would be a blessing if Will would send us some cottonseed."

His eyes narrowed as he studied me. "Marc and Lily brought some cottonseed back the last time they went to Belle Rose. But will it put us more at the mercy of the white eyes? What is the word? More assimlates?"

I was surprised by his insight. "Would it make us more assimilated? I hadn't thought of that, my chief. It was certainly not my goal. If anything, I think it would make us more independent if we were able to grow cotton to make clothing and other items. We trade with other tribes as well as with the Americans. Right now, we trade deer hides, baskets, and even the slaves we capture in wars. We could increase our trade products with cotton. We wouldn't have to trade for cotton. Think about it. Marc could tell us how to grow it. I understand Marc used to work the cotton fields in Virginia."

He nodded but said nothing. I figured he would have to think about it and perhaps talk with the other members of the Council before coming to a decision. I sighed. I understood his desire not to become assimilated, but cotton would not be the determining factor. Slavery would be a significant contributing factor. Who would have dreamed our people might cease to be the *AniYunwiya* of old because we also kept slaves?

No, that was not fair to my people. The change coming in religion would be the most significant component. Christianity would bring different attitudes about gender, work, education, and self-worth. Women would lose their esteemed place in our society as men would take over farming and animal husbandry. Men would lose their traditional roles as hunters as more and more settlers pressed westward, limiting the areas in which our men could hunt. That was why the Chickamauga already fought back.

Perhaps the Chickamauga were right. Maybe if we all fought back, we could curb the westward expansion of colonization by the whites. Yet, even as I contemplated the idea, I knew it would be virtually impossible to stop the hemorrhagic flow of settlers westward-bound. The land was too fertile, too desirable to people long constrained to overworked land and oppressive laws. My heart sank as I realized it was already too late to stop the inevitable changes to come. The best I could do would be to get my people safely out West well before the fateful Trail of Tears.

Soon, it was summer. Crops were growing well under the hot, Georgia sun. One morning, braves rode into our village in a hurry. I heard people talking in quiet but excited tones, their voices heavy with worry. I soon learned a Chickamauga warrior had long been missing. A skeleton had been discovered, which the Chickamauga believed to be his. Don't ask me how on earth they would have known who it was since the skeleton was stripped bare of clothing and weapons. The Chickamauga claimed our tribe killed the man. They killed one of our Bird Clan braves in retaliation. After a council was held of warriors, both men and women, Wolf called me into the meeting.

That all by itself surprised the living daylights out of me.

"Yes, my chief, how may I assist you and your warriors?" I asked.

Shadow Wolf smiled, but the smile did not reach his eyes. "Guider, as chief, I have been asked to invite you to join the War Women. It is a serious decision because we will soon go to war against the Chickamauga."

His words surprised me. He told me months before that I would make a good War Woman, but I thought it was mere talk, flirtation perhaps. Young, athletic, teenaged girls are usually chosen to train for the strenuous job of War Woman. I blinked and cleared my throat. "I am flattered, but I must ask why I am so honored?"

"Before you came here, when you were Beyond, you were a sort of warrior, battling in the courts. Is that, not right?"

"Yes, but that was not a physical battle. It was a war of wits," I replied.

The smile then reached his eyes. "But it enabled you to move between the worlds of men and women. You trained to wage war with men. You performed well at your job, or you would not be the Promised One. A woman such as you who can do that at ease possesses great power. You tell me you can shoot and can hold your own in a fight. I have seen you are wily and strategize well. Such a woman, no matter her age, is welcome to become a Cohutta Warrior. I was a young man then, but I remember well when Nancy Ward became a War Woman during the French and Indian War. She seized her slain husband's gun and joined in the battle against the Creeks when he fell, dead from a gunshot wound. Not many Cherokee women make themselves as important to their tribes as she has. She was not young when she became a War Woman. We believe you could offer us the same central role in both military actions as well as strategy. However, I will not lie. It is a dangerous path. The choice is yours."

No matter my age? I beg your pardon; I am not old. Granted, I wasn't a spring chicken any longer, but I am not ready for the stew pot yet. I didn't know whether to be insulted or flattered by those words, but he correctly stated I am an excellent strategist. Time would tell if I also had the talent in military actions, he accredited me with possessing.

Plus, it felt mighty fine to be given a choice beyond digging in the dirt.

After only a slight hesitation, I nodded. "Okay. What do I do first?"

"You will help us prepare to go to war against the Chickamauga tribe. I will work with you to hone your skills. And before we go to war, we fast, purge, and pray that our efforts be successful."

The next few weeks were a blur of activity. No longer was I expected to work in the fields. Each morning, I trained with both men and women warriors to learn their skills, with Shadow Wolf giving me individual mentoring. Shadow Wolf was pleased I already knew how to shoot a muzzleloader rifle. Fortunately, our dad taught Dan, and Dan taught Bubba and me how to shoot. We grew up hunting for venison and rabbits. I ate a lot of rabbit stew while I lived in the Qualla. We knew it was unlikely I would become proficient in warfare in a few weeks, but the council hoped I would learn enough to survive the battle to come. I intended to survive. I did not travel over 200 years back in time to die before I could help my people move westward. Afternoons were spent weaving cloth and baskets, women's tasks that still had to be done. In the evening, after we ate, we warriors strategized.

As the days passed, I realized Wolf looked at me differently. He still taught me, yet his hands often lingered on my shoulders or my arms after he corrected my aim. Somehow, I learned how to take aim and shoot with the arm of the man I desired above all others laying across my skin. It was not easy to focus as his hand would gently trail down my arm, with his breath warm on my cheek. It is not easy to learn to shoot a musket the way a war chief wants his warriors to perform in battle while his breath caresses your skin, light as the whisper of a secret kiss.

I also realized Wolf was correct. I might have a talent for war strategy, after all. I enjoyed the mental challenge of the strategy sessions, and I loved the way women warriors were treated as equals to the men.

One of the warriors was called Bear Claw. A member of the *Anisahoni* or Blue clan, he had a special gift for making medicines for children. Lily told me he possessed a unique touch with children. I noticed his gentleness with the children, who often flocked around him. I also noticed he often watched my training. I thought it offended him to see an older woman training to be a warrior, especially an older woman like me.

Until the haunch of venison arrived.

I moved in with Inola, a member of my clan who readily took me under her wing. She smiled from ear to ear when I arrived at the *asi* that evening.

"What is it? Why are you grinning like you swallowed a possum?" I asked as I stripped off my tunic to wash off the dirt and sweat of the long day learning to become a warrior.

She pointed to the haunch of venison.

"Who sent it?" I asked, terrified of the answer. *Please, Great Spirit, let it be from my Wolf—*

"Bear Claw. You know the significance?"

I gulped. I could feel the blood draining from my face. I shook my head as I backed away from the side of meat.

"Damn. I can't accept it," I said, my voice tight with frustration the venison was not from the one whose touch I craved. I shut my eyes to squeeze back the tears stinging at my eyes. *Why, Wolf? Why?*

She looked shocked. "Are you sure? He spoke to the council, who approved his petition."

I nodded, afraid at first to speak. I felt physically ill. I blinked at the tears stinging at my eyes. How could I explain this was not the man I wanted?—the man I longed to hold me in his arms? How could I admit the man I dreamed about was one of the same men on the council who approved Bear Claw's petition? I tried to laugh, but it sounded hollow, more sorrowful than glee-filled. How presumptuous it was for me to dare think Shadow Wolf, of all men, might be interested in me. Wolf was an important war chief, the father of the Bright Star of Hope. I felt my shoulders sag as tears welled up in my eyes.

"I'm sure. I married the wrong man once. I refuse to make that mistake again." I blinked the tears back from my eyes, my voice barely above a whisper.

She came to me and put her hands on my shoulders and gazed into my eyes. "You must tell Bear Claw your heart lies elsewhere."

I looked at her, suddenly terrified. "How did you know?"

"Ah, my daughter, you would not be fighting back the tears of sadness if another man did not own your heart."

I struggled to hold back the tears, now finally spilling over. "Old mother, I have never said a word to this man. Do I have to talk to him now?"

She sighed. "It would be kind. I will take the word you want to talk with Bear Claw. Meet him by the stream. I will wait nearby and pray for the right words to form in your mouth. Return the venison. And tell him…"

"My heart lies with another. I can't just tell him this is the wrong time?"

She shook her head. "No, my daughter. That would encourage him to continue to seek you out and continue to court you. If you have your heart set on this other man, you owe it to Bear Claw to let him know you are not interested."

I gulped hard. "So, I have to tell him another man has my heart?"

She sighed and shook her head. "No. You do not *have* to tell him. But you *should*. And you should tell this other man you are rejecting Bear Claw's suit because you have feelings for him."

"I don't think I could do that."

Her eyes narrowed. "Why not, Guider?"

I shook my head as I walked over to the doorway outside. "He's on the council."

She looked surprised for an instant, and then she nodded. "That is… awkward. I understand your reluctance. I am sorry, my daughter."

"If he felt anything for me, I would have thought he would have objected to Bear Claw's petition."

She hugged me close. "Perhaps he did. The vote does not have to be unanimous."

She sent word that I wanted to meet Bear Claw that evening. He met me at the river, eyes alight with excitement until he saw I carried the haunch of venison in my arms. As his face fell, I struggled not to cry or give in. I handed the venison back to him.

"Why?" he asked, his voice hoarse with shock.

I shook my head. "I can't. I don't know you. And…"

"But if we get to know one another? Maybe then?" A look of hope crossed his face and brought a spark of life back to his obsidian-colored eyes.

I ached with compassion for this man. He was a nice-looking man, tall although not as tall as Wolf or my brother, Dan. Broad of shoulders, enormous biceps, altogether powerfully muscled. A strong jaw and handsome, well-made features. Beautiful, well-groomed, black hair. But he was not the one I longed to send me venison. I swallowed hard and took a deep breath. *You can do this, Baylie. Hang tight. You can do this. You are a Warrior Woman of the Cohutta Cherokee. Be strong.*

"No. Another man has captured my heart. He has not offered, but…"

"Then he is a fool," he growled. "Keep the meat. I will honor your request not to court you, but I will not be shamed by taking the venison back home, for all to see."

"I'm sorry," I mumbled, unable to look him in the eye.

"Not as sorry as I am." He thrust the meat back into my hands. I thought for just a minute he would kiss me and try to change my mind, but he wheeled about and strode away without another word. I sagged with relief and hoped I was not a bigger fool than Wolf by my rejection of Bear Claw's suit.

We spent the last days before we went to war in spiritual preparation. Just like the men prepare with fasting, purging, and prayer, so do the women. We purged with specially prepared emetics. Believe me, I was empty at the end of the third day. I understood if any of us suffered an abdominal injury, our chances of survival were higher if our stomachs and guts were clean. This ritual purity would help us survive any injury and would help ensure our success in battle.

The day finally arrived for us to mount our horses to ride to the Chickamauga village. Marc was among the warriors along with Wolf, Michael, and Bear Claw. Lily accompanied us to provide medical assistance in case such was needed. Two scouts went ahead to find well-hidden sites where we could bivouac each night.

"I didn't know you guys would come. I mean, it's not your battle." I hugged Lily tight as I whispered the words to her.

She made a funny sound. I glanced at her face and felt surprised she looked so stressed. "I couldn't stop him. He's determined to accompany Michael. You would think our Red Wolf never went to war before."

"Has he ever fought in a war before?" I asked.

She nodded. "Yes, several times. After all, he has lived with the Cherokee since he was 15, and nearby most of his life."

It was a long journey, longer than I expected, nearly 100 miles. At first, we headed almost due east across the mountains. We camped high in the Cohutta Wilderness, spending the night about halfway to where the town of Ducktown would someday be situated. On the second day, we managed to go as far as where Ducktown was when I came Before. The third day, we headed eastward, in roughly the same path that Highway 64 and 60 would someday head towards Murphy, North Carolina. We got about halfway to where Murphy would eventually be located. On the fourth day, we traveled to about where Murphy is situated. The fifth day, we headed in a northeasterly direction, towards what would someday be called the Nantahala National Forest. On the sixth day, I felt a surge of excitement as we approached the lands I knew as the Qualla. I realized we were close to my old stomping grounds just outside what would someday be the little town of Almond, nestled beside the Nantahala River.

At about six that afternoon, we found the place our scouts selected for us to camp overnight. We ate a cold meal as we finalized our plans for the next day before we turned in early for the night.

Our small group of women went foraging in the direction of the Chickamauga village at first light the following morning. This was probably the most dangerous part of this venture. We women were each armed with knives, but a knife cannot stop a musket ball. We began by picking wild asparagus and purslane in an open field near the shady riverbank. When we spotted cattails, we strolled down to the river to collect armfuls of them. As I looked around while bent down to dig cattail rhizomes from the mud, I grinned. *My old stomping grounds indeed,* I thought. We were at War Woman Creek, named after a victorious battle led in the 1780s by a group of women. I learned the history of the creek from my grandmother long before I bought the land to build my house there in the future.

"Follow me. I know what we must do," I urged the other women.

One of the women grabbed my arm. "How can you know it is safe, Guider?"

"I lived here when I was Beyond, Adsila. I know the story of this creek well. I will tell you all later. Follow me. I know what we are supposed to do," I whispered.

Eyes sparkling with excitement, she nodded. "Come on, Yona. We follow Guider."

We wandered back to the camp, where I explained the Chickamauga village sat on the property where my house would be located in the future on War Woman Creek. I told them the story my grandmother passed down to me about this battle. I drew a diagram of the creek and the promontory overlooking it. I told them the old story that the War Women would creep to the top of the promontory and pelt burning coals on the roofs of the *asi* in the village. As the Chickamauga scramble to the back of the village to save their homes, the rest of the Cohutta Warriors would rush in the unguarded gate. After a brief yet brutal fight, the Cohutta warriors would be the clear victors of the day, taking many captives in the process.

Wolf smiled as he clasped my arm. "See why we needed you amongst us? I knew I was right to ask you to join the warriors."

I beamed at his praise.

Within the hour, the women headed back down the creek towards the promontory. I knew from personal experience the cliff was a pain in the butt to climb, but it could be done, even carrying red hot coals in deer hide slings. I also knew the Chickamauga would not expect anyone to attack from that direction. They built their village there for the presumed protection of the promontory provided from the creek and its annual spring floods, while still being close to the freshwater. That proved to be a significant error in judgment on their part.

We quietly struggled to the top of the cliff as I had done many times in my past life. This area was across from the farm my parents owned when I was a child. The promontory on War Woman Creek had long been a favorite place of mine to slip away and read. That was what motivated me to buy the land when it became available. I showed the women where to put their hands and feet as we climbed up the steep precipice. Once on top, I signaled the men with the small mirror I carried in my pocket. After I received their signal back, indicating they were in place and ready to attack, we pelted the rooftops of the *asis* with the red-hot coals. Since a Cherokee *asi* was made of woven saplings, plastered with mud and roofed with poplar bark, the houses quickly caught fire. As the fire spread and raged out of control, we slipped back down the cliff, across the creek and disappeared into the woods my father would someday clear to plant the three sisters. Fortunately, we managed to slip clean away before anyone thought to climb the cliff and search for us.

We could hear the uproar begin immediately. We heard screams for help and shouts as people came to put out the fires. We slunk low in the copse of walnut trees and held our breaths as one clever Chickamauga brave began shooting across the creek. Fortunately, he did not hit anyone. After a few desultory shots, he returned to the burning village.

And then it sounded like all hell broke loose as the Cohutta Warriors rode into the Chickamauga village. We heard war cries and many shots for the next few minutes, which must have seemed like hours to the Chickamauga. We hurried back to the camp to join Lily.

"Well done, my sisters," she said with both pride and admiration in her voice. She hugged each of us.

A few minutes later, Bear Claw rode into camp, his horse frothing from the fast ride. "Guider, Chief Shadow Wolf wants you to come."

He reached down for my hand to swing me up behind him. I did so and hung on to his waist as he wheeled his horse around to gallop back to the Chickamauga village.

"Why?" I clung tight to his waist as the horse galloped back towards Wolf and the others.

"You come without asking but now ask me 'why'? You never cease to amuse me. You will select prisoners to take back to our village. It is a high honor for a new War Woman, but you deserve it. You made this win easy. Well done, warrior."

I blinked. I had never heard him say so many words at one time to anyone, and I had not expected such high praise from Bear Claw. "Thank you."

In minutes, we rode into the village. Bear Claw swung me down with one hand and then rode his horse to the side where he resumed watching the crowd. It amazed me that a mere ten people, four of whom were women, captured a village of 80 with the fire diversion. *Great Spirit, it worked,* I thought as I looked at the silent, sullen, and shocked crowd of people. *My grandmother's story was true.*

"Guider, well done. Your sage advice brought honor to our people today. You shall select the prisoners for the women. I shall select for the men," said Wolf.

"How many shall I choose?" I asked, my heart beating fast and hard with excitement.

"They murdered an Eagle of the *Anidjiskwa* Clan," came his terse reply. "Take as many of their Bird Clan as you wish. I already claimed the murderer. He shall pay with his life when we return home."

I looked at the Bird Clan and quickly selected eight men and four women. Then, almost as an afterthought, I spotted him. My eyes narrowed, and I pointed to the big man. "Who is that white man? Why is he here? I thought the Chickamauga hate whites."

Wolf's brow furrowed as he frowned, but his eyes followed my pointed finger towards the tall man. His lips narrowed into an angry slash. "You! Did I not tell you to come into our lands no more? Why are you here?"

The big man was dirty, his brown hair hanging in twisted mats down his back. In the future, men would call this style dreadlocks, but I had never heard of white men or anyone else for that matter wearing their hair like this in the 18th century. He turned his angry gaze towards Wolf. "Ye ken full well why I'm here, ye damned red savage. I search for my wife and children."

My skin prickled at the sound of the lilting Irish brogue.

"My God, O'Malley, you're more stubborn than a mule," said Red Wolf. "Where did they find you anyway?"

"Someplace they called Tanassee Bald. Why?"

"He is the *Tsul Kalu.* We found him atop his mountain." The Chickamauga chieftain snapped out the words.

Wolf shook his head as if disgusted.

"Aye, they keep sayin' that. God only knows what these crazy heathens think it means. For the love of God, she's your sister, Red Wolf. Tell me where the hell she went," the Chickamauga captive snapped back. "I'll go after them and be out of your damned hair."

I glanced at Marc, who remained silent. With war paint, the tall Irishman was virtually indistinguishable from the Cherokee, since he wore a turban-like wrap over his long blonde hair. "Is this Kirk O'Malley?"

Wolf nodded without looking at me. "Yes. I warned him many times the Chickamauga would capture him if they caught him near here. Leave him to his fate."

"No, you said I could have anyone in the Bird Clan. This man is their prisoner. I want him."

Bear Claw huffed up in anger and started to speak, but Wolf held up his hand, indicating Bear Claw would wait. "Why?"

"And why should it matter?" I shrugged. "I knew his wife. She was my friend."

"Guider, she's his wife no longer," Marc whispered. "You know she's married to Richard. She thinks Kirk is dead."

"Then don't you think it is high time to tell the man she's gone? And that she thought he was dead and she married another man? Why keep him in this emotional limbo? It's been what? – three years here since she disappeared? Great Spirit, how many times has this man come seeking answers since she went Beyond? This is wrong. I claim him."

Wolf's lips disappeared into a disapproving line. "I don't like it."

"Nor do I, my chief," interjected Bear Claw as he glared at me.

I rolled my eyes but held my tongue.

Wolf held up a hand again and sighed with impatience. "But I told her she could have anyone from the Bird Clan she wanted. So be it. *Tsul Kalu* is yours, Guider."

I blinked. "Why do you call him '*Tsul Kalu*'? I don't know the phrase."

Wolf's laugh sounded like a sea lion's bark, a sound I am sure he had never heard. "Take a good look at him. It means a slant-eyed giant. It is what we call the white devil."

I blinked. I thought the 'white devil' was just an insult indiscriminately applied to whites. And then it hit me. "*Tsul Kalu*. Now, I remember. My grandmother called him *Jutaculla*. The slant-eyed giant who lived atop Tanassee Bald. But why didn't they kill him?"

"They fear his power. Besides, he is a strong man, and women greatly desire the seed of the *Tsul Kalu*." Bear Claw sneered at O'Malley. "Do not ask me why their women would want one like him."

Wolf nodded as he grunted in assent. He wheeled his stallion back around so he could stare imperiously down at the Chickamauga. "Do not think you can attack our village and not face retaliation. This is a warning. Next time, we will wipe out your entire village. Do not let there be a next time."

"Get in line with the others, white devil," I snapped at O'Malley, speaking in English.

He looked startled if not downright shocked. "Why do ye call me that? And how do ye ken English?"

"Don't ask stupid questions. I'm Cherokee, but I read and write several languages, probably better than you. Come, and be quick about it, or Chief Shadow Wolf might change his mind and leave you to your fate among the Chickamauga."

He strode over to join the Chickamauga captives without another word but with an angry scowl marring his face. I recalled Fancy said he was a big, handsome, well-muscled man. I sniffed. He *might* be attractive *if* he were clean. For a white man. Never again would a white man prove to be irresistibly attractive for *this* Cherokee woman, even if he were a 'white devil whose seed was much to be desired.' Sheesh! Give me a freaking break!

The Appaloosa stallion reared as Shadow Wolf let out a war cry and then motioned for the warriors to follow with the captives. A week later, we arrived back at the village.

Since our raid succeeded, the village held a Scalp Dance upon our return. The women circled the fire as we sang about the warriors' courage and brave deeds. We raised our arms and struck out at our imaginary enemies as we ritually re-enacted our vengeance against the Chickamauga. The men joined in the dance and took turns recounting the events of the battle. At that time, we warriors surrendered our spoils of war, including the captives to our nearest female relatives. After the dance, the warriors then retired to the council house for purification. Inola nodded as I handed O'Malley over to her.

We put our captives in the *asis* used like holding cells, where guards watched them. They would also undergo the brief purification process before we began testing the prisoners for the women to decide who lived and who should die.

I had read of the next part of the vengeance but I had never seen it in my life in the future. I worried if I could manage to control myself during it. I knew the women would torture the captives to determine who merited life or death. Could I condemn any of these people to death? We took twenty-nine in total, including O'Malley. Wolf stated the women would be taken to Savannah and sold as slaves. He did not want them in our village, but he realized they were too valuable to be killed. The Cohutta women held the fate of the captured men in our hands. I did not intend to allow O'Malley to be obtained from the Chickamauga only to be killed by us, but must the others die? Somehow, I managed to hold my tongue again. If I were to save but one, I already knew it would be the big Irishman. *You owe me one, Fancy*, I thought with more than a little resentment.

The day on which we enacted vengeance began with the men brought out of the *asis* one by one. Each was stripped and tied to a stake with his arms above his head, and his legs spread wide. It rattled me when the women stretched the men's legs wide. I cringed to think what sort of tortures they would perform. One by one, the tortures commenced on the staked men.

The first was the murderer. I expected his torture would last long hours if not days before he received the final release of death.

The women beat the murderer, head to foot, with thin reeds that left angry, red welts wherever they hit his skin. The man remained stoic, unspeaking, glaring at the women. One woman brought a bowl filled with honey and coated his more tender bits of flesh, and another woman then ladled angry red ants onto him. For the next two days, they alternated between beatings, larding his body with honey, and torture with fire ants.

The next two were Chickamauga warriors, who bragged about martial deeds and showed no fear as they were first thrashed and then larded and seared with flaming torches. I felt nauseated as I smelled their burning flesh. In true Cherokee tradition, they recounted their bravery in battle without evidencing cowardice during the torture.

The fourth fainted from the pain of the thrashing and awakened to the sound of women laughing as they doused him with water. As the women began to rub his skin with lard and slivers of pine, he started begging for forgiveness. The women ridiculed him for being a coward and seared his skin with flaming torches. He howled with pain as his skin scorched. I gagged anew at the stench of the burning flesh. I understood they would show the coward no mercy. As he screamed, one woman continued to pass a torch over his skin, and the other women began beating another man. So, it progressed until they came to O'Malley, the last in the line due to his lowest rank among the prisoners.

Like all the men, first, they thrashed him soundly. He neither bragged nor begged, but remained angrily mute, unwilling to 'give' anything to his tormentors. They then changed their tactic. As O'Malley stood with his legs spread wide, the women began to lasciviously fondle him into a hard erection. He cut angry eyes at me to let me know without words he scorned their behavior. I realized several of the women, including Star and Lily, knew Kirk once owned Fancy and made ill use of her. They intended to pay him back. It shocked me because I saw them behave like this towards no other man. Shocked as I felt, I had to admit he was a splendid specimen with a full, throbbing erection. I refused to let any of them, including the steely-eyed bastard they tortured, see my discomfort at their behavior. I held myself erect and silent as I stood there, watching their abuse of the big Irishman. The women fondled his organ over and over until he would spill his seed. I realized with a start, if he acted as if he enjoyed their attention, they would have clamored for his life to be spared. When he did not, they grew bolder and more sexually aggressive in their treatment of him. I was shocked by their actions.

"Inola, what are they doing?"

"He is *Tsul Kalu*. They pay him homage. Besides, they cannot resist his charms. Aye, he is a devil, that one is. I can barely resist him myself." She cackled.

Funny, but he did not appear impressed by their 'homage' to me. I suspected they were not paying homage as much as they were paying him back for how he treated Fancy. I bit my tongue and made no reply.

Twice that afternoon, a woman climbed on him just as he orgasmed. He would shudder as his seed was spent but never uttered a word. He just continued to glare at us all, myself especially, as if he hated us.

I so wanted to ask if the Chickamauga treated him this way. I figured now he knew how Fancy felt when he kept her as his sex slave for all those long months in Barbados.

Finally, I couldn't bear to watch it any longer. I stood and waved the swan's wing in my hands. "Enough. I claim the life of this man. He shall not die."

The other women fussed as I cut him down. "We aren't finished with our games yet."

"Yes, you are. Come with me, slave," I said with a gentle tug on the rope to his wrist.

He glared at me but followed. Once out of hearing, he finally spoke. "I shall never forgive you for that."

I had not expected their sex games with him, but I would not let him know it.

"Really? My people believe white devils such as you enjoy sex with native women. Besides, you are not the first man used like this when forced into involuntary servitude. Have you never heard the story of how Marc McCarron was sold as a sex slave when he was ten years old?"

He stopped, stunned. He looked appalled. "No. I-I-I had no idea."

"Perhaps. You expected me to treat you differently because I speak English. And I recall you expected Fancy to forgive you when you forced her into indenture as your sex slave until she agreed to marry you," I retorted.

He stopped dead in his tracks, staring at me, mouth agape.

"What? Do you think my friend never told us about the way you treated her?" I snapped.

"You know my wife? Is she here? Where is she?" he asked, his voice filled with an odd mix of excitement and desperation.

I struggled not to cringe at the raw anguish in his voice. I blinked. "You do care about Fancy."

"Aye. More than life itself. Please, help me find her," he whispered. "I beg you."

I glanced about, nervous lest the others overheard our conversation. "Come with me."

He looked confused and then angry. He reached out and grabbed my wrist. "Woman, you must tell me..."

"I am your mistress," I snapped. "Do not touch me unless I invite it. And you do not tell me what I must do. I don't care if the people of our tribe think you are some sort of deity or devil. Let go of me, white man. Now, come."

I jerked on the rope.

He planted his feet firm and grabbed the rope, yanking back as he frowned. "But—"

"No 'but's.' Come with me. Now." I again jerked on the rope tied to his hands, shocked at the barely controlled anger in my voice.

After the slightest hesitation, he nodded and began to follow behind me.

Three days later, Shadow Wolf finally scalped the murderer, and then slit this throat. As the man's blood spilled out onto the ground, Wolf announced, "Retribution is now complete."

Chapter 3
Before - 1787

In the weeks that followed, O'Malley and I entered into an uneasy kind of peace and reliance on one another. He adamantly refused to compete to become a member of the tribe. This disappointed the tribal members because everyone knew he could easily pass the challenges and would make an outstanding addition to the tribe. A couple of times, men shoved him or tripped him to attempt to anger him into a fight. One warrior quickly found himself held in the air by one hand of the angry *Tsul Kalu* he enraged. O'Malley threw another warrior into a nearby tree for teasing him about the women's 'homage.' O'Malley maintained his sole goal was to find Fancy and the children, and he would be happy to leave with his family.

The council held several meetings about his recalcitrance to join the tribe. Several felt he should remain a slave if he refused to leave on his own accord. Several felt they had no right to enslave the *Tsul Kalu*. They worried they might push the Devil-God too far. I thought they should have worried about that before they staked him out for the women's enjoyment.

Others thought we needed to tell him Fancy left and went on with her life when she thought he died. I agreed with them.

Wolf suggested that I could sell or even give him to Lily and Marc, and they could take him out of the Indian Territory. However, we all knew once out of Indian Territory and freed, O'Malley would more than likely head right back here, again demanding to know where Fancy went.

In the meantime, Inola and I often found fish, venison, birds, and rabbits outside the doorway to our *asi*. At first, I thought Wolf left the food, but I suspected Wolf would say something if he began leaving the food. As much as I wanted the food to be from him, I knew in my heart, it came from another. Why could Wolf not see I wanted him? Dammit, I ached for the blasted man. What was it all those old romance novels Mom used to read said? Oh, yeah. Something about 'burning in my loins.' Believe me, my loins burned with unrequited desire for Shadow Wolf. Damn, his voice alone could dampen me with lust. Yes, I had it bad for the blasted man. What did I need to do, put up a billboard? I sighed and then chuckled at the idea of a billboard proclaiming my love for Shadow Wolf, who could not read.

Drat, foiled again. Where was Sequoyah with his syllabary when I needed him?

But seriously, why didn't Wolf want me? At times, I would swear he did. He ate dinner with us many evenings. He would laugh and tease me, and I could see his eyes start to smolder. He would reach over, move my hair from my face, lean in like he was finally going to kiss me, and then, in a flash, he would pull back, suddenly cold and aloof again. Suddenly unfathomable. Unreadable as a Cherokee and totally frustrating to my burning, aching, lust-filled loins.

"He makes me so angry." I slammed down a bowl as I complained to Inola one evening.

She shook her head. "No. He frustrates you. You need to talk to him."

I snorted. "Why bother? His signals are so mixed. I don't know what to think."

"That is why you need to talk to him, my daughter. Perhaps you need to let him know how you feel—"

I snorted again as I had another fleeting thought of my ever-burning loins.

"Fat chance of that," I muttered. I could not forget he was on the Council that allowed another man to court me.

The men allowed Kirk to fish and hunt with them. This comprised special treatment for a slave captured in a war, but of course, they upheld him in that weird *Tsul Kalu* role as well. The tribesmen hoped by treating him like a man rather than a slave, rather than like a devil, the big galoot would decide to become one of the tribe. He would laugh and tell them he still needed to find his wife and children before he could make such a commitment. He would be happy to join the tribe *if* Fancy agreed. Since Marc, Lily, and Michael were there, he believed she might be willing to stay - *if* he could ever find her. Even that tidbit did not motivate the men to tell him she went Beyond, where she married Richard. If anything, it made the men more closed mouth. They were reluctant to tell him Fancy and the children were not planning to return, much less that she married Richard. They feared he would never join the tribe if he learned the truth, and they did not want to lose their slant-eyed, white devil-giant. Don't ask me why not.

Kirk often brought home fish, rabbits, squirrels, and an occasional haunch of wild boar or venison. At first, Inola, Star, and I thought maybe he left the food outside the door. Kirk denied it was from him. "I would bring it in if it were from me. Ye have to face it, Guider. Ye have an admirer."

"An unwanted admirer." If the meat did not originate from Wolf, it was unwanted. I felt sure the meat was not from Wolf. He would bring it to me himself.

When Inola finally asked Wolf about the food, he looked puzzled. "Why would you ask me? Council authorized another warrior to court Guider, not me."

Dammit. It disappointed me to confirm the meat was not from the man I desired.

Based on his comment, Inola and I felt sure Bear Claw continued to leave the tempting morsels as Cherokee courting rituals required. I asked each time to see if anyone knew who left the food. No one claimed any knowledge. Inola and I agreed it would be foolish not to accept the food since Bear Claw had not said anything to anyone, and technically, we were not sure to whom I should return it.

Silly, huh?

I decided not to ask Bear Claw about the meat. I realize I acted in a passive-aggressive manner, but I did not want to legitimate his odd, unwanted courting of me. I made it crystal clear to him that first night my heart belonged to another. I could not comprehend why he would continue to pursue me. The whole situation frustrated the unholy crap out of me.

And, so it went on for months. Furtive, angry, hurt glances from Bear Claw, with never a spoken word between us. Flirtatiousness which led nowhere from Wolf, who always acted afraid to take that next step. No one was playing stickball, that was for sure, but if this pseudo-flirtation demonstrated how Wolf would play for me, I was not impressed.

And then came the bear hunt.

A black bear had been terrorizing the village. It ripped up the cornfield twice and scared the ever living bejeesus out of the older women watching the fields. The men tried to track it several times, but it was a wily old bear. It eluded our hunters. Finally, one older woman who was a watcher was severely mauled by the bear. After old Dorcas was injured, the men went out in a group early one morning to hunt down the bear. Later, we heard them return, exultant their hunt succeeded. As the women went to help butcher the bear, one warrior approached me carrying the skin of the now-deceased animal.

"This is for you, Guider." Bear Claw grinned as he dumped the heavy bearskin at my feet.

I stopped dead in my tracks. Bear Claw offered the bearskin to me in front of everyone, as if he still courted me. As if we had an understanding, which we most assuredly did not have. Shit, no wonder Wolf would not woo me. He thought Bear Claw still wooed me, dammit. I stepped back, shaking my head and motioning I would not accept the gift. "No."

His face reddened with embarrassment. He extended the valuable skin to me again. "It is for you. Take it."

I stepped back again. "No. I told you, I am not interested. Please do not continue to pursue me."

His face clouded with rage, and he grabbed out with one hand to take my arm. "You take all the food I leave on your doorstep, and now you shame me before everyone?"

I shook my head. "I did not know who left the food. I asked, and no one knew. You certainly never said a word to me. Few words have ever passed between us, certainly not of a courting nature. Don't play this ridiculous game with me —"

"This is not a game, woman. This is courtship. You understand that. Do not shame me here."

I began to feel panicked. "I told you—"

He grabbed me with his other hand and shook me hard. "Do not say 'I told you,' woman. I am the man. I will tell you."

I huffed up at that despite the fact the big oaf held me pretty tight at that point with both hands. "I rejected your suit..."

His hand lashed out across my face. Suddenly, the usual noise around us became silent as everyone turned and stared.

Cherokee men do not usually strike their women. It is a matriarchal society. We bear the children. We own our homes. We rule the roost.

Our bodies are our own.

I began to struggle against him. I began to shout, not caring who heard me or who I shamed. "I rejected your suit. You need to take your hands off me—"

Suddenly, his hands went around my throat. I began struggling harder against him, desperate to get loose from his grasping hold. I felt my feet slip out from under me, and I fought harder against him, panicking when I could not catch my breath. He cut off the air to my windpipe. I continued to struggle, clawing at his face and his hands until my vision grew dark as the spots grew together, filling to a vast, black nothingness. *Great Spirit, he's going to kill me—*

And then, as I began to lose consciousness, someone began to rail on Bear Claw. The maniac who claimed to love me let out a bellow of rage as his hold on me lessened, and Bear Claw wheeled about to face my defender. I staggered away and collapsed into Inola's arms in time to see Bear Claw and O'Malley square off to fight, as I began to breathe in big gasps of oxygen.

"No one attacks a member of the Eagle Clan and does not face retribution," Kirk growled, low and menacing.

"Bring it on, slave," taunted Bear Claw. "You mean to fight a warrior of the Blue Clan? You are a bigger fool than I ever suspected."

I began to scream as they rolled to the ground, my voice hoarse and rough from his ill use of me moments before. As they rose to a crouch, Bear Claw pulled his knife, and my screams turned to sobs. "Stop them! Please, someone, stop them!"

O'Malley threw handfuls of dirt into Bear Claw's eyes and lunged for him. Bear Claw roared with fury as he slashed out blindly with his knife. O'Malley grabbed Bear Claw around the waist, lifted him into the air, and then threw him to the ground. He then fell on Bear Claw, pummeling him with his fists. Somewhere amid the dirt throwing and O'Malley tossing Bear Claw down like he was a bag of potato chips, Bear Claw dropped the knife, so the men fought hand to hand.

"She ... told ... you ... no..." Kirk grunted.

And then, Shadow Wolf was there, pulling them apart. "What is the meaning of this? Slave, why have you attacked a warrior of this tribe?"

I guess if you attack a member of the tribe, you no longer qualify as the big stud everyone desires.

I still sobbed. Inola held me tight in her arms as she spoke up. "Bear Claw attacked Guider. He choked her. O'Malley came to his mistress's defense. He acted with honor when Bear Claw attacked the Promised One."

"The bitch shamed me," Bear Claw muttered in his defense.

Shadow Wolf looked from the men to me. His anger turned to fury as he gently traced a finger along the darkening bruises in the shape of Bear Claw's hands forming on my throat. Wolf's nostrils flared, and his lips thinned into an angry slash across his face while a vein in his neck bulged out. "He did this to you?"

I nodded as I tried to control my sobs. "Yes, my chief. O'Malley knows I rejected Bear Claw's suit. He came to my defense, and claimed retribution for my injuries."

Shadow Wolf stared at me for a minute before answering. "What do you say for yourself, O'Malley?"

"You don't treat a woman like this. He was choking her. I don't care if you are Cherokee or white, or purple with green polka dots. A real man doesn't treat a woman he claims to love like this. Hell, he damned near choked her to death. The sorry *mhac na galla* could have killed her. She's my mistress. I came to her defense. He will not treat a warrior woman of the Eagle Clan like she is a common trollop."

Shadow Wolf nodded. "No, you do not treat a woman you claim to love like this. Guider, did you say you rejected his suit?"

I nodded as I rubbed my throat. I tried to speak, coughed and tried to get the words out again. "Yes, months ago. I told him that the first night..."

"She lies!" shouted Bear Claw. "She was eager for my suit. She met my kisses with passion."

Inola stepped forward. "No, she does not lie. She told me that day she could not accept Bear Claw's suit, and that another warrior held her heart. She met Bear Claw at the river to return the meat. I stood nearby to witness what transpired. She told him and tried to return the meat, but he implored her to keep it. He told her he would not take it back and be shamed before the village. She made it clear to him that she did not agree with the courtship. She told him she was interested in another man. And he lies about her kissing him. She never kissed him. She has been circumspect in her behavior at all times."

Wordless, Bear Claw began to shuffle back and forth. "But I left meat since then. She never returned it…"

"Did she know you left it?" Wolf asked, his voice low and quiet.

I shook my head. "No. I tried to find out. No one knew who left it. If they did, no one said."

Bear Claw's face turned dark red with rage, but he said nothing.

"Bright Star, my daughter, did she ask who brought the meat?"

She nodded. "Yes, Father, she did, many times. We went from *asi* to *asi*, asking if anyone knew who brought it. No one knew."

"Then O'Malley properly asked for and obtained retribution. Bear Claw, you are a fool. This woman rejected your suit months ago. You continued to try to court her without telling her you still pursued her. You lead us to believe your courtship continued. Today, you wronged her and the Eagles of whom she is a member. O'Malley acted properly in defending his mistress. It was a fair fight. This is finished. Leave this woman alone. I rescind the permission to court Guider. Do you understand?"

Bear Claw nodded and turned to start away. He then turned back and pointed at me. "This is not finished."

"Oh, yes, it is," said Shadow Wolf. "You *shall* leave this woman alone, or the next time, you will face *me* in battle, and we shall fight to the death. Do you understand me?"

"Oh, I understand. You think she wants you instead of me. You are the chief. You are a better catch than I am. But be warned, my chief. She sleeps with the Irish devil. We all know it-"

Kirk's fist lashed out and struck Bear Claw's jaw. "Ye know nothing if ye think she's sleeping with me, ye great, stupid oaf."

"I don't sleep with slaves. Or devils. I have said it before: I was married to a white man once. I will never bed a white man again. You dishonor yourself to make such a stupid claim, Bear Claw. The fact that I rejected you does not mean I would take O'Malley to bed. I rejected you before O'Malley ever came to this village. Now, let me be clear: if I decide to take any man to my bed, it will be *my* decision. It will never be *your* business. Never. Do you understand?" My voice was hoarse, and my words were tight with anger as I rubbed my aching throat.

"Oh, believe me, I understand, bitch." He spat out the words as if they left a foul taste in his mouth.

Shadow Wolf stood beside me until Bear Claw skulked away, and the crowd began to disburse. As I started to turn away, he grabbed my arm. "Is this true?"

I frowned. "Is what true?"

He looked down at me. "Would you only welcome my suit because I am the chief?"

"Are you freaking serious?" I bit back my angry reply. I could not believe how hurt I felt by his unexpected question. I stared at him, my blood again pounding like a loud noise in my ears while tears stung at my eyes. "If you have to ask that question, you are not nearly as smart a man as I thought you were."

I struggled to hold back the tears. I did not want him to see me cry. I jerked my arm from his grasp and turned to walk away from him but he grabbed my arm again. I wheeled back and tried to jerk free.

"Answer me," he demanded.

"I take it back. It's not that you aren't as smart as I thought you were. You're a damned fool to ask me that question. If you have to ask me that, you are a bigger fool than Bear Claw proved himself to be today." I snapped out the words as I fought not to let my tears spill from my eyes. I pulled away from him and ran to our *asi* as my tears began to flow.

Inola shook her head at Shadow Wolf, 'tsk'ing as she did. "She told me the first day when Bear Claw sent the meat that another man had her heart. She told Bear Claw she loved another man that same night. He said a man would be a fool not to pursue her if he knew she loved him.

Oh, foolish man, don't you understand? She did not simply reject his suit. She loves you. She has worried for months about why you showed so little interest in her. Take the Irishman to her bed? Never. But if *you* had asked? You would have been welcomed with open arms to share her sleeping mats. The fact that you are chief has nothing to do with her interest."

She 'tsk'ed again, and then left to follow me back to the *asi* as Wolf continued to stare after me.

I did not see his body relax as he began to smile while I flounced away.

In the next week, I noticed Wolf smiled at me more often. I was still angry at him, and I did not return his smiles. I often felt his eyes on me as I worked. Several times, he hurried to my side to help me with a heavy load. He would lean in to me, to smooth my hair back from my face as his fingers would linger a little longer than necessary as he gently traced the tracks across my brow. I tried my best not to look at him. As days passed, I would look up, wipe the sweat from my brow as I looked about, and would smile before I caught myself when my eyes landed on him. I would feel my cheeks flush with color when he smiled back, often waving to me. I would quickly look away. I fear he would think I was interested only because he was chief.

I wasn't, was I?

And then three weeks after the fight, I came outside the *asi* one morning to find a haunch of venison by the entrance. It terrified me. Was Bear Claw up to his old tricks? My heart pounding with trepidation, I looked about. "Who left this?"

Gola and her husband lived nearby. When I asked who brought the meat, the pretty, younger woman looked up from her weaving and smiled. "Who do you think? Shadow Wolf brought it."

I blinked; my mouth suddenly dry as cornmeal. "Sh-Shadow Wolf brought the venison? For me?"

She nodded with another smile. "I think so. He did not bring it for Inola."

I turned, excited, to Inola. "What do I do?"

I winced. I sounded as inexperienced as a school girl. But then again, in this world, I lacked experience with men.

Inola laughed, the corners of her eyes crinkling as she did. "Do you accept his suit?"

I nodded, eager and breathless with excitement. "Oh, yes."

"Then you can do one of two things. You can thank him for the venison, and ask him to share supper with us this evening—"

"Yes, that sounds good," I said with a tremulous smile. "What would that convey?"

"It would mean you welcome his suit and look forward to getting to know him better in the months to come." She laughed and reached over to pat my shaking hands. "Slow down, my daughter. There is more. Or you can take some of the cooked food to him tonight."

I knew there was a reason I would do that, but for the life of me, I could not remember it right then. All I could think was, he's officially courting me. He wants me, too. "What would that mean? I swear, I can't think. What is the difference?"

Inola laughed again. "And you call yourself a Cherokee? Silly woman, it would mean you accept."

I blinked. "I don't understand the difference. What is the difference?"

She beamed at me. "With the second, if you return some of the cooked food to him, you are willing to cook for him. Not just for one night, but always. It means you agree to marry him right now."

My legs gave out from under me. I sank to the ground, trembling with excitement. "It would mean…"

She laughed as she bent to hug me. "Sending you the meat means he wants to marry you. If you carry some of it back, cooked, it means you accept his proposal. You are ready to be his wife. If you invite him here to dinner, it means you agree to be courted."

I licked my lips. I could not believe how dry my throat had become. "What do I do?"

She looked surprised. "I thought you told me you love this man. Why do you ask?"

I swallowed hard, sure a desert was growing in my dry mouth. "But does he love me?"

She shrugged. "He must. He sent you the meat. That means the Council approved his petition for permission to court you."

My heart clamored in my chest, running ninety to nothing. I pressed a hand to my chest, and took a deep breath. "He sent meat to Sassy, too."

She nodded. "He did. She rejected it when she realized the significance. She did not love him. And, he sent meat long ago to Ginny. You three women are the only ones to whom he ever sent meat."

"What did Ginny do?" I asked.

"She cooked a stew and carried a pot of it back to him that same night."

I frowned. "Did the white girl know what she was doing?"

She nodded. "Oh, yes. She was only fourteen, but she often visited our village in Virginia before we moved here. Ginny knew exactly what the meat meant, and what it signified when she cooked the stew and took some back to Wolf. When her family realized what she had done, that she accepted his proposal of marriage, they threw a fit. Her father, Josiah Selk, ranted for days while Miss Belle wept. Her parents finally relented, but they would not let them marry until the summer she turned eighteen. I remember her mother wept at the wedding. Her tears were not for joy. Her daughter might be marrying a chieftain, but it was not the life Belle Rose Selk long anticipated for her only daughter. She said Ginny could have married a nobleman from Europe instead of 'a damned, worthless redskin.' We understood Miss Belle feared the life Ginny would live as a Cherokee, especially since the treaty ending the war with the French had been signed. Ginny and her family knew the treaty would send us out here, far from Virginia Colony. Her mother seemed to know when Ginny moved west with us, she would never see her daughter again in this world. I think it broke Miss Belle's heart."

I felt my heart calm as I made my decision. "Then I will invite him to dinner. I won't accept the marriage proposal today. I'll be properly courted by Wolf first."

She nodded. "Good. Make the man work for your love."

I smiled and hugged her tight. "He already won my love. But I will make him work for that place on my sleeping mat. Is there any set length for this courtship? I'll be honest, I don't want to wait for years. I'm not a young girl anymore."

Her cheeks dimpled as she laughed again. "No set time. It could be a day, a week, a month, six months. During it, you are expected to walk with him, talk with him, eat with him—"

"Sleep with him?" I asked, again breathless as a school girl.

"Of course, my daughter. Make love with him. See if you suit one another. It has always been our way. How else would a woman know if the two of you suit? You are in charge of your body. You bring him to your sleeping rugs when *you* choose."

She winked.

I frowned. "The English say men won't buy the cow if she gives away the milk."

Inola laughed. "Here, we tell our daughters not to buy the bull unless you know he can service the cow."

I never heard the expression before. I felt my cheeks redden at the bluntness of her words. I gulped again. "And how long does a Cherokee woman wait to learn if the bull can service the cow?"

She shrugged again. "It depends on the bull and the cow. In this case? Probably not very long. That bull never had any complaints about his services before."

I felt my sun-bronzed cheeks redden again at her words, and yet it thrilled me to learn he was considered to be a good lover.

Inola laughed loudly as she pulled me into her arms. "Let's cook that stew."

Chapter 4
The Wooing

The days moved quickly after that. Wolf ate with us every night and often brought meat for us. We began walking together in the evenings. At first, we walked along, awkward and uncomfortable, as we tried to talk like grown-ups, but sounded like tongue-tied adolescents. Finally, we began to loosen up, laughing and joking with one another. By the second week, he clasped my hand as we strolled by the river, talking more like adults and less like frightened children.

I decided to take things into my own hands at the end of the second week.

I bathed before Wolf came to dinner. I owned no perfume or scented bath oil, so I crushed lavender into a fine powder and scented my body with it after my bath. I put on fresh garments and brushed my long hair until it shone with unexpected luster. For once, I was not self-conscious that my hair was dark brown rather than black, and my brown eyes were not dark as the night. I smiled, confident I looked and smelled pretty damned good for a Cherokee woman in 1788.

When he arrived, I rushed to him. I stopped myself just before I would have thrown myself into his arms.

He laughed and opened his arms wide. "Come to me, my love."

So, I did. I threw myself into Wolf's arms, as bold and impetuous as a schoolgirl in the first throes of young love. As he laughed at my boldness, he lifted me up, and my arms encircled his neck. Without thinking, I kissed him.

It was not the first kiss I long dreamed about. It was more.

He eagerly kissed me back. Still in his embrace, my feet dangling off the floor, he swept me up into his arms.

Inola laughed as she turned from the cooking fire towards us. "I will be back in a little bit. The stew is simmering. It is fine now, but do not forget it, or our dinner will be spoiled, Guider."

Wolf and I both laughed as she left, but then fell into an awkward silence.

Wolf kissed me again. He broke away from our kiss long enough to blow her a kiss as she started to leave the *asi*. "I think she is telling us not to be too long about our love play."

"I think she is telling us she is leaving us alone for a while, so don't waste time." I kissed him again and pulled one of his hands to my breast.

He laughed again, his eyes sparkling like stars on a dark night. He carried me to the sleeping rugs, where he laid me down gently before we began kissing again.

I took one of his hands and placed it back on my breast. "Show me you love me."

Oh, sweet Great Spirit! Believe me, he did.

The light sparked in his eyes as he eased my deerskin tunic up to have better access to my breasts. Soon, I panted with the need for more than mere caresses. I managed somehow to loosen the tie to my skirt, and pulled one of his hands down between my thighs. His eyes widened with lust.

"Are you sure, my love?" His voice sounded husky with desire.

I trembled as I nodded. "Yes. Never more so. I want you."

I slid his hand up under my skirt, guiding it to my most sensitive flesh. Soon, I climaxed from his masterful touch.

He chuckled and pulled back. "Do I please you?"

"Don't ask stupid questions." I kissed him with a fierceness I never demonstrated with a lover before. Wolf's eyes widened with surprise ad I pushed him back onto the rugs. I eased his manhood out of his breech cloth and straddled him. Still clad, I guided his manhood into me and rode him fast and furious. The climax came fast for both of us.

I arose to check the stew. I stirred the pot and added a bit of water and some vegetables before I returned to the handsome warrior sprawled on my rugs. His eyes widened as I pulled my tunic off, dropped it to the floor, and then slid my skirt off as well. "Yes, you please me, except you wear too many clothes."

I dropped to my knees, and helped him slip off his shirt. He quickly shimmied out of his breechcloth, and I climbed on top of him again.

"Again? Are you sure, my love?" His eyes burned through me like hot coals fresh from the fire.

I shuddered as he gently stroked down the side of my naked breasts. I nodded. "Yes. I am not some sixteen-year-old virgin. I am an experienced woman. I know what I want. I want you, again. Now."

He only had to be told once.

He rolled me over and began to shower my body anew with kisses again, as I did him. He aroused me like Brian never could, with wave after wave of crashing climaxes. He then laid back as I pleasured him first with my hands and then with my mouth. When we both could wait no longer, he positioned himself over me and sank his member deep into my sheath.

"I love you," I whispered.

He kissed me again. "I love you as well."

We rode our passion home to one final, resounding paroxysm of sexual ecstasy. I did not know I could feel so fulfilled from sex.

Sex was never like this with Brian.

As soon as I could catch my breath and see straight, I pulled my tunic back on and stepped over to check the stew. Assured anew it was not burning, I pulled my skirt back on as well while Wolf dressed in silence. I did not miss the smile on his face or the twinkle of satisfaction in his eyes. As I passed by him, he reached out to grab me to him for more lustful kisses, promises of more to come another passion-filled night.

Wolf sauntered outside and stretched, sending a quiet word that we had finished with our lovemaking for the evening. I quickly prepared corn cakes over the open fire. When Inola came back in a short time later, the dinner was ready. Wolf and I sat eating in pleasant silence.

She looked at both of us and laughed, her eyes drinking in merriment. "So, tell me. Did the bull service the cow satisfactorily?"

I could feel my cheeks redden. Wolf began to laugh at my embarrassment. "Well, did he, my love?"

I nodded, prim as a schoolmarm. They both laughed again. "He serviced her most admirably."

They laughed even harder, but my bull was wise enough to pull this cow back into his arms. "I am quite pleased you believe the cow was well serviced, my love."

. . .

It soon became our custom that I would run to meet him in the evenings. He would sweep me up into his arms, laughing, for a kiss. With my arms wrapped around his neck, my body lifted off the ground, I swear I felt as close to heaven as I ever imagined possible.

After the first night we made love, Wolf often spent the night with us there in Inola's *asi*. He began building my *asi* for us to move into when we married. I began making my wedding dress. I chose a simple design, one I could complete as soon as I need it to be finished. When he would ask how long until our wedding, I would tease him and ask how long until the *asi* would be completed. I wanted us to go to our own home when we were wed.

Chapter 5
Before – 1788

"I never thought I could feel this way about a woman again, Marc." Wolf's voice was filled with awe.

Marc grinned as he shifted the rail into place. He placed a nail and began to hammer it into the log. "Love will do that, ye big lug. But don't blow smoke at me. You thought you were in love with Sassy a few years ago."

Wolf blushed and reached to help his friend hold the split rail. "Ah, the historian did steal a bit of my heart, but I never felt about her like I feel about my Guider. This woman enchants me. Excites me. Invigorates me. Infuriates me. Why is that?"

Marc shrugged as he pulled another hand-hewn nail from his leather carpenter's apron. "Ah, ye've got it bad. Guider brought emotions back to life for you. Oh, no, don't protest. I know you could feel love, joy, anger, and more without her. I have seen you demonstrate many emotions with your family, your friends, and your people. But Guider? She is meant for you just as surely as Ginny was, long ago. So, when will you marry the lass?"

Wolf shook his head. "She has not said. She says I must woo her and she must make her wedding dress first."

Marc stopped hammering and looked at his friend sharply. "Well? Are ye wooing her? Is she making the dress?"

Wolf nodded. "Yes, but how long does it take to make such a garment? I am ready for her to keep me warm in our sleeping rugs this winter. To stay with me *all* the time, as my wife. Now. Tonight. Why should we wait?"

Marc shrugged again and resumed hammering. "You visit her every night. Guider is in charge of her body. She will say when you two marry. You know that. Have you finished building her *asi* yet?"

Wolf winced. Marc broached a sensitive subject. "We already share our bodies. I am working on her *asi*. The house will be finished before the new moon."

Marc chuckled. "Then my guess is her wedding gown will be completed soon after the *asi* is finished. There. Done. Let's get in from this sun. Lee, *mo leannan*, Wolf is here. Is there a bite to eat for two hungry warriors, fresh from rebuilding the fence?"

Lily laughed as she pulled Marc close for a lingering kiss. "Stew is in the pot, on the fire. There is plenty for all of us and then some. So, how goes the courting, Wolf? Any progress?"

"The *asi* is almost finished. Marc claims the wedding dress will be completed soon after the *asi* is built."

Lily nodded as she ladled the rich stew into the bowls. "That would be my guess, too. So, we should expect a wedding in the next month?"

Wolf groaned. "I hope so. I am ready for my own hearth, a private place just for my love and I."

Lily gave him a sharp look. "Just the two of you? What if she has a child?"

Wolf's surprise was palpable. "Could she? She never had a child before. Guider says she is not a young woman…"

Lily shrugged. "She wasn't married to you then. She's not young, I'll grant you, but she isn't too old to bear a child, although I would want to keep a close eye on her. She might surprise you. What would you think, if the Great Spirit send a babe to fill your golden years?"

Wolf laughed. "My golden years? You make me sound like an ancient grandfather, Lily. I would be thrilled with a child, but if the Great Spirit sends none, I would be happy - more than satisfied - with my Guider and our life. Let's face it. The prophecy said naught about children late in life. I shall be happy with my life with my woman. She is more than I dared hope and then some. And we still have much to fulfill." He laughed, suddenly self-conscious. "Did you know she calls Red Wolf and me her Cohutta Wolves?"

Lily nodded. "I've heard her call you two that before. She says you two will be important in the move west." She frowned. "How do you feel about moving again?"

Wolf shrugged. "It was foretold. We knew another move was someday coming. I am pleased to have a part in helping my people avoid the troubles to come. I still cannot get over falling in love and her loving me."

Lily stopped and turned to stare at Wolf. "Why? You didn't think you were lovable?"

He laughed, suddenly self-conscious. "Not really. Why?"

"I remember how dearly Ginny loved you, how her eyes would alight with joy when you came up to her. And your children and grandchildren adore you. Why wouldn't a woman love you?"

"Sassy did not love me." Wolf looked thoughtful.

"Sassy came for William. We prayed for 13 years for God to send a woman for William. You know that." Lily shook her head at him.

Wolf blushed dark red. "You prayed longer than that for the Great Spirit to send another woman for me, my sister. You told me for many years you prayed the Great Spirit would send another woman to fill my lonely heart."

Lily's eyes softened. "Yes, I did. Does Guider fill your heart?"

He smiled. "Yes. I am lonely no longer. My heart is no longer empty. It is filled with great happiness."

Lily nodded as she turned back to her dinner cooking on the fancy wood stove they brought back from France years before. "Good. So, tell us how are other things going in the village?"

"Bear Claw claimed one of the Chickamauga women. They seem quite happy. I suspect they will marry. I hoped it would resolve the problems he had with Guider, but the brute still harbors great anger and bitterness towards my love. Ah, here comes by beautiful bride-to-be now."

Wolf hurried to the door, where he met Guider. He wrapped her into his arms and kissed her deeply. She sighed as he released her, and then tackled the difficult subject of the day. "O'Malley is outside. He wouldn't let me come alone."

"Good. I still do not trust Bear Claw." He pulled her close, and he kissed her again.

"O'Malley worries Bear Claw may still try to pull some stupid stunt. What do you guys think?" She looked worried.

"I do not know, but his actions have been less than honorable. I do not trust him." Wolf's brow knit into an anxious line.

"Marc says you asked the elders to chastise Bear Claw after he choked Guider," Lily said.

He nodded. "I did. They rebuked him privately, but he seems unaffected by their words. I still see his eyes following her. I do not trust the man. He lied too many times for me."

"He glowers at me every time he sees me, and sometimes he spits towards me when he comes near me. I don't trust him either. He scares me." Guider chewed on her lip, nervous and worried.

"So, what do we do about him?" Wolf asked.

"I don't know. And what do we do about O'Malley? I don't want to take him with us to our *asi* after we marry." Guider leaned her head against his shoulder again.

"I agree," said Wolf, as he stroked down her arm.

"He's your slave, Guider. You have no choice as long as ye keep him a slave. And ye know I believe keeping him enslaved is wrong. I believe slavery is wrong." Marcus gave them both a disapproving frown.

Guider slipped off Wolf's lap and walked to the doorway. She looked first at O'Malley and then glanced back at Marc and Lily. "You think I approve of slavery? Let me jump right to the crux of the matter. Do you still think I put the other women up to it, Marc?"

Marc's lips thinned into an angry slash. "They got the idea somewhere, and he was the only one they treated like that. Why did you do it? You're a Christian woman—"

"Am I? Again, say what you mean, Marc. You didn't think I was a pagan savage like the rest of the tribe because I came from Beyond. I am every bit the pagan savage they are. But I did *not* put the other women up to sexually assaulting O'Malley. It was some weird homage to him. They believe he is the entity called *Tsul Kalu*. They view him as a devil-god who makes women crazy for sex. Hell, you know as well as I do, they thought they were honoring the white devil amongst them, not debasing him. Their behavior that day freaked the bloody hell out of me."

"You have to free him, Bay," Lily coaxed.

Guider shrugged. "He's only been here a few months. He knows he has choices he could make which would free him right now. Fancy was his slave longer than that as I recall."

Marc shook his head. "Fancy was indentured. He is a chattel slave. There is a difference."

She laughed, the sound cold and brittle. "Yes, there is. She was his sex toy. He is *not* mine. Never has been, never will be. I told you guys: I was married to a white man before. No offense, Marc, but I don't ever want another white man in my bed. Period. Wolf is the *only* man I want in my bed."

Wolf remained at the table as Guider ranted at Marc. He looked pleased when she returned and plopped down onto Wolf's lap again. He chuckled as she snuggled close to him. "Good, because you are *my* woman."

She nodded. "You bet your sweet little ol' bippy, I am."

"What is a bippy, my love?" Wolf nibbled at her earlobe.

She giggled. "It's hard to explain. Ooh, do that again."

Marc shifted from foot to foot, uncomfortable at the turn the conversation had taken as well as the overt sensuality of their flirtatiousness. He cleared his throat.

Guider sighed. "Besides, O'Malley is a planter. It hasn't hurt him to see firsthand what slavery is like, from a slave's perspective."

"Oh, for God's sake, Bay, you know better than that. You're a better person than that. You have to free the poor man." Marc sounded horrified.

"You know as well as I do, O'Malley can only be freed a couple of ways. Number One: he can compete and be made a member of the tribe based on worth. He would pass any test they throw at him, but he rejects the idea. The Great Spirit knows he earned his freedom and place in the tribe when he defended me against Bear Claw, *but* he refuses to become a member of the tribe." Guider bent around to kiss Wolf again.

"Just free him. You can do it," Marc urged, as Guider and Wolf continued kissing.

Guider winked at Wolf. "You hear that? Can I just free him, my love, like Marc says?"

Wolf shook his head. "You know the answer to that. So does Marc."

She shook her head. "See? Wolf says I may *not* free O'Malley that way."

Marc looked over at Wolf. "Really?"

Wolf nodded. "No, but we do not need him coming to our new home with us."

Marc raked an impatient hand through his long hair. "Oh, for the love of—what difference would that make if he goes to your new home with you? Aw, dammit, never mind. Just tell me exactly what would it take to get him freed?"

Guider shrugged again. "We discussed this before as well. Method Number Two for O'Malley to Obtain Freedom: Wolf wants you to buy him and take him with you. You leave for Virginia soon. Give me a dollar. Hell, give me two bits. He's yours. Free him when you get out of Indian Territory *if* he promises to never come back."

"And you know full well he will never agree not to return. Besides, I'll not own a slave," Marc retorted.

"Fine. Lily, *you* buy him. Get him to tell Wolf he won't come back. If he runs away from you, and returns, it's on his own head. We make it clear we won't save his stupid ass from the Chickamaugas again," Guider said.

"Nay, we won't do that," Marc mumbled.

Guider frowned. "I figured you would say that, dammit. Method Number Three would be to find a woman in the tribe to marry him. I damned sure won't. I have other plans. So how do I get rid of my cross-eyed bear?"

"There are other eligible women in the village. Wouldn't anyone else marry him?" Lily looked worried.

Guider nodded. "Oh, yes, several want him."

Marc walked over to the door and leaned against the door frame as he lit his pipe, still studying O'Malley. "You're not willing to take him to wed?"

I shook my head. "Oh, hell, no. No way, Jose. I keep telling you, I had one white man. No offense, Marc, but I have my sexy Cherokee warrior all picked out. You know that. I'm rather appalled you would even suggest I marry Kirk instead of my Wolf. I mean, why would I give up a man like Wolf for O'Malley? Besides, O'Malley doesn't want me or anyone else here."

Marc turned back to look at me with interest. "Oh, really? How do you know?"

"Four women have offered for him in the months since the ceremony. Each time, he says he is already married. He is not looking for another woman."

"Oh, dear," Lily murmured. "I was afraid of that."

"Oh, dear, indeed. He does not want to be part of the tribe. He won't leave voluntarily. He wants the truth. He needs to hear the truth. I say it's high time we give it to him. Among my people, a woman divorces a man when she puts him out. In my opinion, Fancy divorced him that way." Guider stood up and stretched.

Marc sighed. "Nay, the marriage was annulled in Ireland. He canna come to terms with the fact it ended. He was tryin' his level best to win her back."

"Isn't there anything else we could do?" Lily said as she sat twisting the soft, frayed fabric of the edge of her blouse. "There must be something."

Wordless, Guider stared at them both. They had discussed this subject repeatedly. "We all know the next option. Method Number Four: We tell him where she is. Maybe he will stay on his own accord. Or, maybe he will give up, leave, and he won't come back again."

Marc cast a nervous glance out the door. "He'll try to go after her."

Guider shook her head. "He might try, but he can't go unless he is *supposed* to go. Who are we to stop him if that is his destiny?"

"She's right," Wolf said. "And you both know it."

Marc sighed. "So, you think we should tell him where she went, Wolf?"

Silent, Wolf nodded.

Marc looked aghast. "You know Fancy and Rick are happy. Jaysus, you would really do that? Send him there to disrupt their lives?"

Guider shrugged. "We would be helping him make peace with that certainty. And perhaps, he would find someone else there. Perhaps *that* is his destiny."

Wolf arose and walked over to Guider. He placed an arm around her shoulders and pulled her close to him. "I don't like it, but I agree with Guider it may be the only way ever to get rid of him, short of killing him. We all know O'Malley can't go through the time hole to the future unless he is meant to do so. It is important we tell him what to expect there so he is prepared if he goes Beyond. He needs appropriate clothing and a bit of cash as well. It is bad to go through the door in time without knowledge of what is happening or what to expect there."

"Jaysus, surely he isn't meant to go forward in time and disrupt their marriage," Marc muttered, as he shook his head in frustration and disgust.

"Darling, he can't go unless he is needed there. Or unless there is someone there for him. His own true love, like you are mine. I agree with Bay. Let's tell him. It's time." Lily sidled over to Marc and slipped an arm around his waist.

Wolf and Guider walked over to stand by Marc and Lily. They all stared out at the man dressing the deer.

Guider had to admit O'Malley was a handsome hunk of man, even if he was not her type. His long hair had been oiled and combed out by the attentive, adoring women who flocked around him, and it shone with an unexpected luster. Bear grease will do that. He adamantly refused to allow them to shave his hair back the way Cherokee men typically wore their hair. He did allow them to shave off his facial hair. Cherokee men didn't wear facial hair, but then, neither did most white men. He often worked shirtless, as did the Cherokee men, and his well-muscled back and shoulders were tanned nearly as dark as a Cherokee, a deep, golden brown from the sun. It was a warm autumn day, and he had stripped down to his small clothes to dress the deer, comfortable with his own near-nakedness. As much as she loved her Wolf, Guider had to admit the lean, well-muscled, near-naked posterior on the handsome devil was well worth watching.

"Only four women have offered for him?" Lily asked, a bit breathless, unconsciously fanning herself with one hand.

Guider nodded. "Yeah. So far."

"Perhaps the right one hasn't asked yet." Lily began to nibble on her upper lip.

"Perhaps the right one isn't here," Guider replied, her voice droll.

Lily shrugged as she flicked a speck of dirt from her nails. "Perhaps. Damned, hard-headed Irishman."

"He is that. But is he as hard-headed as your Irishman?" Guider asked.

Lily grinned. "No one is as hard-headed as my Irishman."

• • •

Kirk sat back on his haunches as he wiped the knife with the deer hide. Sometimes, he felt so close to Fancy that it seemed he could almost reach out and touch her. Twice, while on the way to Marc and Lily's cabin, he swore he could hear her, but she was nowhere to be found. He sighed. Perhaps Bear Claw was right. Perhaps he lost his mind. God knew all he had to do was act like he joined these heathen savages and they would give him his damned freedom. He could become a trader and go back and forth while he searched for Fancy.

But where the bloody hell were Fancy and the children?

He could swear Marc and Lily knew. It drove him near mad they wouldn't tell him. At times, he caught looks between them and the damned woman they called Guider. Now, there was an odd duck if he ever met one. The woman had the strangest manner of speech he ever heard. What the blazes did 'bet your bootie' mean anyway? And what in the blazes was a 'bippy?'

In fact, he would swear the whole tribe knew where his wife went. But nay, they all refused to utter a word. He might have a better chance of getting the dead to talk.

Dead. Dammit, he knew Fancy and the bairns were not dead. He would know it if they were dead. But it had been five long years now since the fateful day when he sailed away from Bermuda with nary a word from her save the letter he found later at the house. How long would he have to wait? Would he ever learn where they went?

His shoulders sagged. He shook his head. Should he admit defeat? Give up? Get on about his life?

But, how could he? He needed to know what happened to them. Telling him 'she's gone' meant naught to him. Gone where? To Ireland? Belle Rose? Hell, mayhap they went to Texas. Winslow hailed from San Antonio. Why the blazes wouldn't they simply tell him where she went?

He loaded half the meat onto a willow bark tray Guider made only last week, hoisted it up, and carried it into the log cabin. The people all stopped talking when he entered the room. Silent, he carried the tray full of meat to the kitchen where he sat the tray on the table. He then went back out to load the rest of the meat into a gathering basket with a lid to take it back to the village. He wrapped the deer skin around the basket, put the lid on top, and then went back inside. "It's loaded. I'll take it back to the village—"

"Sit down, Kirk," Marc said, with an unexpected air of resignation.

"I think I'd rather stand," came his stiff reply.

"Cut the attitude. Sit your stupid ass down. Great Spirit, am I to always be surrounded by stupid white men? We need to talk," Guider snapped.

Kirk's lips thinned in anger. He sank to the ground to sit 'Indian style.' "Of course, mistress."

Guider rolled her eyes at Wolf before asking Marc in Cherokee, "And you actually have to ask why I wouldn't want to marry this ass? When I have the choice of Shadow Wolf instead?"

Lily struggled not to guffaw. Marc bit back his own laugh as he replied, "Behave yourself."

Guider took a deep breath before she started again. "O'Malley, you know Fancy is - was – my friend."

"I think this discussion is ill-timed, my love," warned Wolf.

She frowned. "Would you prefer to tell him?"

Wordless, Wolf shook his head.

Kirk nodded, unsure where the conversation was headed. "Yes…"

"I have not explained to you how I met her," Guider said.

He blinked. "I assumed you met her here, but I'm not sure why it would matter."

She laughed. It sounded odd, as if she were annoyed by his question. "Yes, well, humor me. Just listen. I didn't meet her here. In fact, I never knew her here."

Kirk's brow furrowed in confusion. "I don't understand."

"I think this is a mistake, Bay..." Marc began.

Guider held up her hand. "Let me, Marc. This is my responsibility."

"I think the timing is wrong as well, my brother, but she is right. O'Malley is her responsibility," Wolf replied, his voice resigned.

Lily nodded. "I agree. Let Baylie tell him."

Kirk frowned. "Who the blazes is Baylie?"

Guider looked embarrassed. "That is part of my story. You see, a long, long time ago-"

"In a galaxy far, far away," muttered Lily.

"Now, Lily, don't make Star Wars references. He won't understand it and this is hard enough as it is," said Guider. "Please don't distract me."

Lily blushed. "I'm sorry. Please go on."

"Hmm. You must explain this War of the Stars to me later," Wolf interjected.

"Shush, Wolf, don't interrupt. Well, you see, Kirk, a long time ago, I lived about 100 miles east of here, close to where the Chickamauga village is now located. My brother is a doctor. I met Fancy when Dan introduced us."

"So, she's alive?" he asked, excitement rising in his voice.

Guider paused for a minute and cast a nervous glance at Wolf, Marc and Lily. "Uh, yeah. Well, she was the last time I saw her. But you see—"

"Where did you meet her?" he pressed.

"Well, you see, it's not so much *where* is she. That's the easy part. I met her about 40 or 50 miles southeast of here."

He started to arise. "Please, Guider, show me the way."

She reached out to touch his arm. "No, Kirk, you have to listen to me. Oh, gosh, I'm screwing this all up. It's...well, you see, it's..."

"It's not where, Kirk. It's *when*," Lily said.

He stopped. "What on earth do ye mean, Lily? I doona understand."

"It wasn't *where* I knew her, Kirk. It's *when* I knew her," Guider mumbled.

His face fell. "Ah, well. You said twas a long time ago…"

She took a deep breath. "That's right. Well, first of all, my name— my Americanized name— is Baylie Smith. My brother, Dan, is a doctor in a town called Atlanta. He is - was - Fancy's heart doctor."

He turned grey with shock. "So, she's dead."

Guider reached over to lightly touch Kirk's arm. "No, no, no. She was alive and well when I last saw her. But, you see, it was a lot of years ago."

He frowned again. "What are you trying to say, Guider? When did you know her?"

She sat up straight. "It wasn't in the past. It was in the future. It was more than 200 years in the future."

His face fell, first its disappointment which was quickly replaced with rage. "You doona have to mock me, woman. Tis cruel."

"I told you he would not believe you," Wolf said. "He has not been properly prepared."

"Of course, I don't believe such malarkey. Tis ridiculous. Jaysus, ye mean to bamboozle me to believe ye knew Fancy in the future? Well, how did ye manage such far-fetched shenanigans?" he snapped.

"Fancy traveled through a hole in time to the future," said Lily.

"Oh, of course, Lily. I should have known. I reckon you've traveled through this, what did ye call it? Time hole? I never heard such poppycock in all my life," Kirk snapped.

"Actually, yes, I have. I came here from the future when I was a kid. It was the wrong time and I had to go back until I was grown."

He looked at Marc as if seeking someone – anyone—who might not be insane. "She is joking, right? I mean, such things are not possible."

Marc shook his head. "She isn't joking, Kirk. Tis true."

Wolf nodded as well.

Kirk's mouth sagged open. He stared, unseeing, as he tried to wrap his brain around what they were saying. "I'm … flabbergasted. But… how?"

Guider took another deep breath. "The Cherokee have long had stories about people traveling through time. They call the future the 'Beyond.' We believe you can only travel to the Beyond from here, or here from the Beyond, if the Great Spirit means for you to go."

He blinked. "I don't understand."

"Fancy's destiny awaited her in the future," Guider said.

Kirk looked frantic. He stood up and began to pace back and forth as he looked about as if searching for something or someone to help him. "B-but she'll come back someday, right?"

Guider cringed at the note of desperation in his voice. He sounded close to hysteria. "I don't think so, Kirk. I think she will stay there. She was very happy."

He wheeled back towards her. "Happy? How could she be happy? Where are the bairns?"

"It's okay, Kirk. They are with her," Lily said. "We took them to her. Oh!"

She threw her hands over her mouth as Marc sank his head into his hands. "Ah, Jaysus, Lee, I told ye not to open up this can of worms."

Kirk looked puzzled. "Can of worms? What's a can of worms? Hell, what in the blazes is a can?" He scratched his head and sank back to the floor. "I don't understand any of this nonsense."

"I would like to know what a can is as well," Wolf said.

"Okay. Let's try again. This is becoming quite a kerfuffle. You see, there is this time hole. If you are supposed to go forward or back in time, you can access the time hole. Fancy was fighting a Chickamauga warrior and …" Lily began.

"Yes, that's right … hey, wait, would that be the dead guy they found not far from here?" Guider looked stunned.

Marc began to stammer. "Um, well, ye see…"

Wolf held a hand up. "Perhaps you shouldn't tell me."

"No, it's important," said Lily. "This guy came here to kidnap Fancy…"

"Nay, she wasn't with the Chickamauga," said Kirk. "I would have found her."

"Oh, for the love of - this is the biggest cluster fuck I ever tried to muddle through," Guider muttered. "Just let me tell the freaking story."

Wolf struggled to control his laughter. "Having fun yet?"

Guider looked frustrated. "Oh, shut up."

Wolf walked over to the window so Guider would not see him laughing.

Kirk started to say something, thought about it, and then nodded. "Aye, please proceed."

"Sheesh. About time you quit interrupting me. You are distracting me something pathetic. Now, let me start over. Well, she fought this guy, and then she heard the big noise and she was taken forward in time. I met her through my brother and his family."

"Then take me to her," he said as he began to arise from the floor.

"No can do, big boy. Not that simple. You see, you can't go if you aren't supposed to go," Guider said.

"But Lily said they took the children to her. And you knew her there but now you're here."

"He's got you there. Sorry you started this yet?" Wolf asked, chuckling.

"Oh, shut up, Wolf. You aren't helping things. It's high time someone told him. He's been searching for them for years now. You're the chief. You should have told him. Marc and Lily were *supposed* to take the kids there. And I was *supposed* to come here," Guider said. "I'm the Guiding Light. Well, actually, the Path of the Guiding Light…"

"Well, actually, I think yer off yer rocker," said Kirk. "Or mayhap lying, but most assuredly, your tryin' to bamboozle me. Why could she go and you could come but you think I could not go?"

"Yes, my love, how are you going to explain this part?" Wolf asked, his voice dripping with sarcasm.

She sighed as if exasperated. "I swear, Shadow Wolf, you must be the most frustrating man in the entire world. You can only go if you are supposed to go, Kirk."

"You know full well that you can only go through time if the Great Spirit allows it. If you are being sent to find your true love, or to help someone in tremendous need." Shadow Wolf smiled.

"Wolf, you explain it. Perhaps you can explain it better than we can," Marc said.

"I think Old Beaver's mute wife could do better than you three have been doing," came Wolf's droll reply. "But I must admit, it has been rather amusing to listen to your shenanigans. What is this cluster of which you speak, my love?"

Guider's cheeks began to redden as she began stammering. "Uh, it's hard to explain..."

Lily bit back a chuckle. "We have made a bit of a muddle of it."

Wolf nodded. "A bit. Lily came here years ago to help fulfill part of the Prophecy. Next, Sassy came..."

"Sassy Selk?" Kirk yelped. "Ye gods, how many people have come and gone through this mysterious time thingamajig?"

"More than we know. Then, Rick came..."

"Rick? You mean Richard Winslow? Are ye serious?" Kirk asked.

Wolf nodded. "Yes. It was the wrong time for Rick. He went back Beyond after he left Ireland."

"Good. Oh, wait...didn't you say my Fancy went there, too? To this Beyond place?"

Guider smiled. "Now he's got it."

"M' God, she went after Richard," Kirk muttered. "Tis why you kept telling me 'she's gone.'"

"Well, not quite. She didn't go *after* him..." Marc began.

"She was sent *to* him," Wolf said. "By the Great Spirit."

"And then I came back," Guider said, as if it explained everything. "To be the Guiding Light and fulfill the rest of the Prophecy."

Kirk stared at them. "Hell, I think you're all bloody crazy. Or mayhap you've all been smoking the Jamestown weed. Tis a reason they call it the devil's snare."

"What on earth is he talking about?" Guider asked Lily.

"Jimsonweed," she replied. "They call it the devil's snare. The scientific name is Datura. It's a hallucinogenic. Some tribes use it for religious purposes."

"Oh, okay. Huh, that would kinda make sense," said Guider. "But no. We haven't been smoking whacky weed. We haven't even been smoking ganja, although the Great Spirit knows I sure wish I had some about now."

Kirk had his fill of their blather. He arose abruptly and pushed his way past Marc and Wolf to head back towards the village. "I'll keep my ears peeled for this 'big noise', but I think you all need to sober up. Jaysus, Marc, I never dreamed I'd see the day ye would lie to me..."

He shook his head in disgust and started off towards the village.

Wolf shrugged at the others. "We knew it was a risk to tell him. But perhaps you should have waited for me to explain it all to him."

"And the Jimsonweed? I'm not sure that would have helped." Guider looked frantic, unsure what to do, twisting her hands as her eyes darted to and fro. She turned to sprint after Kirk. She caught up with him at the meadow. "Kirk, I swear, we aren't making this up. You have to let her go..."

He wheeled back towards her. "Never. I'll never give up on her. I love the woman. She has my heart. I'll never—"

And then, there was a huge roar and Kirk felt as though he were falling.

Kirk's words trailed off as Guider threw her hands up to her face. "Oh, Great Spirit, what have we done?"

Chapter 6
Beyond - 8 years after last we visited

"Your temp is 101.2. You aren't going anywhere except back to bed," Richard said. "You're sick, sweetie."

I sighed. "I'm sorry. I wanted to go."

Richard chuckled. "No, you didn't. You dreaded this fast trip. Still, pneumonia is a bit radical to get out of a trip to San Antonio, Cessie. You are definitely not lollygagging or malingering. Oh, well. The pharmacy will deliver your antibiotics this morning. If you don't feel better by noon, get Bella to take you to urgent care at the hospital when she gets in from school. I will run over to San Antonio, finalize the contract on the new offices, and look at the houses."

I sighed as I laid back against the plump down pillows. "You know which one you want. It's not like you really even need me along."

Richard frowned. "That's not fair, Cessie. There's a half dozen houses we are supposed to see this weekend."

"Yes, but you and I both know number one on the list is the big house a few blocks from Trinity. The one you used to ride past on your bike when you were a kid."

He nodded with a wistful smile. "I always loved that house."

I must have heard the story at least a hundred times since Richard and Dan were invited to open a clinic in San Antonio to be affiliated with the med school there. Richard lived in San Antonio when he was a kid. His dad taught at Trinity University. In fact, Owen Winslow and Sassy met at Trinity, where she was one of Owen's history students. In the afternoons, Richard rode his bike in the neighborhood near the school as well as all over the campus. He loved this big old house, and used to tell the lady who lived there someday he would buy it. Now, in all likelihood, he would put a contract on the house tomorrow.

I didn't know whether to smile or cry.

I didn't want to move. I loved Ellijay. I loved our life in Georgia. Well, at least I did until six months ago.

It had been a crappy six months. It all started when the dog died. Danny was still a pup when Charlie found him. He had been an integral part of our lives ever since. Charlie grieved especially hard over the loss. "My old dog died," he mourned many times as tears would cloud his beautiful brown eyes. "I know he was just a dog, but he was *my* dog."

My heart ached for my son. "No, sweetheart, Danny was not just a dog. I know he was far more than that to you..."

"People don't understand, Mom. They don't know how many times I had long talks with Danny. How he would sit pretty and tell me 'hello' whenever I came home from school. Or how many nights he slept by me, curled up beside me, on my bed. They don't know how many times when we first came here, I would cry for things to be the way they were before we came here. He would snuggle up close to me and lick my tears away."

"I didn't know that, Charlie." I struggled not to cry, too.

"They don't know how many nights I awaken now, afraid, because my dog is not there. Or how much he changed me when he came into my life." My son sounded bleak.

"I didn't know you wake up at night afraid. Why hadn't you told me?" I could no longer hold back my tears.

It was if he didn't hear me. My quiet son, as introverted as his grandfather, was on a roll, spilling his heart to me.

"They don't know, Mom. No one knows. How many times he was there, right by my side. I was able to face anything with my dog by my side."

I remembered how Charlie always insisted Danny accompany us to his games. Danny was his biggest fan.

"How I was able to face the dark when we first moved here and I was so scared, because Danny was with me." His voice broke.

"I love you, Charlie," I said, as I wrapped my fifteen-year-old son into my arms as we both sobbed for the loss of his best friend.

"They don't know how scared I was when my old dog got sick. How many times I hugged Danny and told him he would get well. They don't know what it was like to pet him and tell him how much I loved him as he lay dying in my arms, Mom. Or how damned scared I am when I wake up at night now, alone and overwhelmed with my grief."

I held him close, stroking his hair. "They don't know that loving a dog, crying for your dog, is one of the most noble, significant, honest, most decent things any of us can do, son."

He nodded. His tears slowly subsided. "I'm sorry. I didn't mean to cry. I'm too big to cry."

"Don't ever think you have to apologize for loving a person or a pet, darling. Like I said, I think it shows your nobility, your decency. Don't ever be ashamed of those qualities."

He wiped his nose with his sleeve and started away from me. At the doorway, he turned back, with a faint smile. "Thank you, Mom."

Next, Gramma O died. Lord knew she was old, but our old gal was robust and nothing ever held her back. We were at a piano recital one Friday evening when Gramma O suddenly collapsed. Thank God Bella had already performed. Richard said the cerebral hemorrhage was massive. She did not suffer, but it's damned hard to have someone you love collapse and die in your arms.

My God, I thought the death of that dear, old dog was hard? It was nothing compared to losing Olathe Roberts. I loved her like she was the grandmother I never knew. When she died, I felt like I lost my rock, my center. I had indeed lost my best friend. Bay was my best friend until she went back in time years ago. My pain of loss is still raw for both of those women.

Gramma O was special. When I came here twelve years ago, Richard's grandmother took me right under her wing. We had many long, philosophical talks. She lived through a difficult period of social evolution in this country. She often talked about the changes in her life before and after the Civil Rights changes of the 1960's. We talked about Ronan Roberts and she marching with Dr. King and the grief they both felt when he was assassinated. She had an important viewpoint from that time, and I was determined it not be lost.

We also talked at length about the difficulties of being a black woman who fell in love with and married a white man, and the challenges Ronan and she faced in a mixed marriage. She told me how hard being biracial was on their daughter, Katherine, who would say she never felt like she fit in with either group. We talked a lot about her grief over her loss of the stillborn son they both wanted so desperately, then of losing Ronan to cancer at 45, and later losing Katherine, to drugs. Olathe felt responsible for Kathy's drug addiction and death. We talked a lot about parental responsibility versus personal responsibility.

I will never forget the day she looked at me, tears in her eyes, and she said, "It's easy to say it's not my fault, but she was my child. My *only* child. My bright, shining star. I can't help it, Fancy. I will always feel that on some level I failed her. God willing, child, you will never feel that way about any of your precious babies."

I held her while she cried for her Kathy. I cried, too.

Fortunately, I recorded many of our conversations. With her permission and her excited approval, our talks became the basis for my third book, entitled *Conversations with Gramma O*. It is due to be released soon. I wish she had lived to see it.

And then, to top it all off, three months ago, The Incident. Literally, the one that is making my hair turn prematurely grey. I mean, your hair should not turn grey when you are thirty-six years old.

We were at a dance recital in Atlanta for Elizabeth and Dara. Liz is the true dancer in the family. She has been accepted to attend Juilliard in dance once she graduates from high school a year from May. Dara loves dance and has some talent but not like her big sister. Of course, no one in the family can sing like Dara. She has the voice of an angel.

Liz had already danced when I was called to the judges table. Three irate dance judges were peering over their dance forms at me. Dara stood in front of them, nervously shifting from one foot to the other. "I need to be with my team," she whispered.

I frowned. "What's the problem, judges? Why did you pull Dara down here?"

One little old, silver-haired biddy pushed her bifocals back up her nose and glared at me. "This girl already danced this morning. With a different team."

"Oh, that's ridiculous—" I began.

The little silver-haired witch pursed her lips at me. "Do not interrupt me. And with a different name. Let me see … here it is … this child danced with the LaFleur Jefferson Dancettes using the name of … Sara Henderson."

She took off her glasses and looked at me as if she had won a prize.

I frowned. "I have no earthly idea who Sara Henderson is, but this is Dara Siobhan Winslow and she dances with the Cohutta Queens. Her team is waiting to perform. This nonsense is going to throw every girl on the team off today. This is insane."

Little old biddy put her glasses back on, peered at me again, and made a motion to a nervous aid. "Go find LeFleur Jefferson. Tell her we need to see little Sara Henderson down here, right now." She smiled thinly and sat back, crossing her arms. "It will be interesting to see *if* said child exists."

I frowned at her. "So, can the team go ahead and perform?"

"Oh, no, no, no, Mrs. Winslow. This issue will be resolved to our satis… fact… what the hell is going on here? Are these two girls twins? Why didn't you tell me your daughter had a twin?"

I started to snap back at her as I turned around. My jaw must have hit the ground. There before us was a second girl who looked to be about the same age as Dara, and who looked enough like Dara to be her sister. Her twin sister.

"Uh…" I began stammering, not sure what to say. "They aren't twins."

The little old biddy looked aggravated by my answer so she got on the loudspeaker. "Will the parent of Sara Henderson please come to the judge's table?"

"My mom isn't here," the child said.

"How about your dad?" she asked.

The child shrugged. "Don't have one."

I began to have a sick feeling. "Where's your mom, honey?"

"She's at work. She's a nurse," Sara said.

Oh, yeah, I definitely felt sick by then.

About then, Richard came up. He bent over and kissed Sara on the top of her head. "Hi, sweetie. Aren't you supposed to be dancing?"

"Uh, Richard, that isn't Dara," I stammered. "This is Sara Henderson. Honey, what did you say your mom's name is?"

The little girl looked up at me with amber eyes I knew so well. "Melanie Henderson."

About then, Richard realized Sara was not Dara. He bent down and peered into the face of the child who looked so much like our own daughter. "Sweet Jesus. Uhm… Honey, I think we better call your mom."

The child frowned. "I'm not supposed to call her at work. She's very important. She's a charge nurse at Grady."

Richard stood up as he began dialing the phone. "Hey, Carol? This is Dr. Winslow. I need to talk to Mellie Henderson. Yeah, tell her to call me back on my cell ASAP. It's about Sara. No, not my Dara. Her Sara."

His hands were shaking as he hung up. "Cessie, I had no idea…"

I took a big gulp of air. "Judge, I think it is obvious there are two little girls here who look a lot alike but dance on different teams. May we proceed?"

Wordless, she nodded. I have to admit she looked more than a little rattled by then. I felt pretty damned shaken myself. The girls rushed off to finish getting ready to perform.

Richard reached out for my arm. "Cessie…"

"Later, Richard. Not here." I shook his hand off my arm as I trembled like a leaf in a high wind. I was deathly afraid I was about to start vomiting. Or screaming. Or maybe both.

Sweet Jesus, my husband had a baby by another woman.

Mellie arrived at the competition about an hour later. I had never seen her so flustered. Sara sat with her grandmother on one side of the auditorium while Dara and Liz sat with me on the other side. Richard went outside to talk to Mellie. A while later, he came storming back inside. "Come on. We're going home."

I nodded and helped the girls gather up their things. As we headed out, Mellie stood by the door talking to her mom, tears streaming down her face. Richard strode over to them. "This isn't finished, Mellie."

She raised her eyes to him, defiant. "Oh, yes, it is, Rick. This was finished years ago when you walked out."

He shook his head. "You should have told me. This was not fair to this child, nor to me. How dare you keep this from me for all these years?"

I tugged on his sleeve as I glanced around at the curious faces eagerly watching the drama unfold. "Not here, Richard. Wrong place, wrong time. This has waited for twelve years. It can wait until we can all meet someplace private. Not… here…"

My voice cracked.

Mellie nodded as she blinked tears back from her eyes. "Please, Rick. Fancy's right. Not here."

He stood there, clenching and unclenching his fists, angrier than I ever saw him before. "Tomorrow then, at 10 o'clock, in my uncle's law office in Marietta."

Mellie bristled. "You won't take Sara from me."

"Of course, I won't, you idiot. But by damn, I'm her father and I *will* be in her life. Do you understand?"

She looked uncertain. Her mother whispered something to her and she nodded. "Okay, I'll meet you at Mr. Suarez's office…"

"You damned sure better. Twelve years, goddammit, Melanie. Twelve freaking years you kept her from me." Furious, Richard snapped out the words.

She pulled a wide-eyed, flabbergasted Sara to her side and they hurried from the building. "Come on, honey. Let's go home," I coaxed.

He stood staring after Melanie and Sara. "Jesus Christ, I can't believe I just called Mellie an idiot. I just feel so damned gobsmacked."

I ran my hand down his back. "It will be okay, Richard."

He shook his head. "I don't know, Cessie. Twelve damned years, and I never knew that little girl existed. Goddammit, how will she ever forgive me? Hell, how do I ever forgive myself?"

His voice cracked, and I realized he was crying. So was I.

Melanie said she realized she was pregnant after he left to go back in time. I personally think she knew before he left, but, hey, weirder things have happened. Like time travel. Ironically, he was there -we refer to it as Before- for about 18 months, during which Dara was born. When he returned here, he had only been gone from here – what we call Beyond - about six months. Sara was born about the time he came back. Melanie was on leave, but Richard didn't realize she was on maternity leave. She never told him she had a baby, much less that it was his.

"Why didn't you tell him?" I asked the next day at Jim's office.

She looked shame faced. "I was going to. Really, I was. I almost did a couple of times. But then you came. And ... I couldn't."

I actually kind of understood. I don't think Richard ever will. He snorted when she told us that in Jim's office. "So, you decided it would be better for our daughter to grow up without a father because I was in love with another woman? Oh, that's priceless. What a load of malarkey."

She huffed up at his words. "Look, I had her. I could have aborted her. I kept her. I could have given her up for adoption—"

"You kept her from me for twelve years, dammit. Didn't you ever think that was abusive of me? Hell, it was abusive of her. You stole her right to have her father in her life for twelve long years, Mellie. And why? Because you were pissed I didn't love you. Good God, woman. How could you do that to your own child?"

She stood up, shaking with anger. "Now, listen up, Rick Winslow. Don't you dare take that attitude with me—"

"Oh, no, Melanie. Don't you dare try to justify this bull crap. You kept her from me to punish me for loving Cessie and not loving you. Don't you cut an attitude with me. Jesus, woman. We broke up before I ever met Cessie. Dammit, I knew you were struggling to make ends meet these past few years. I gave you every special duty assignment I had. I even offered to let you live at the house at Carter's Lake rent-free..."

"It's too damned far from my job, Rick. You know that," she snapped.

"Fine. We offered you a job with our clinic with a pay increase from what the hospital paid then. But, hey, whatever. Jesus, I never dreamed you had a child...*my* child..." Richard's voice broke.

"I didn't want you to know." Mellie's reply spit out with years of terse, pent-up fury.

"You didn't... oh, bull crap, Mellie. Your lives could have been a hell of a lot more comfortable if you told me. You could have been getting child support for all these years—" His voice broke.

She crossed her arms and began to tap her foot again. "This is *not* about child support, Rick. I managed just fine without your damned money."

He shook his head in disgust. "You're an idiot. I never realized it before, but you really are a certifiable nincompoop."

She arose, and pushed away from the table. "That does it. I'm done here—"

I reached out and grabbed her hand. "Mellie, he feels guilty. Sit down. Let's try to sort out this kerfuffle."

Later, after they worked out the details of their shared custody agreement, I went on a three-day bender, the only one of my life. I felt so guilty that this little girl was growing up without a father, thinking some man out there rejected her, assuming that he didn't want her, and I pulled the most stupid stunt of my life. Well, certainly one of the most stupid stunts. The jury was still out whether remarrying Kirk was the most stupid thing, but most days I could forget about that. I got stinking drunk and I wrapped my car around a tree on the way to the Beech Bottom Trailhead. I hiked the last few miles to the cabin, where I drank moonshine until I was totally shit faced. When Richard finally found me, I cried and cried.

He cried as well.

In the days that followed, Sara was legally determined to be Richard's child. Richard set up a trust fund for her, paying into it the money he figured he should have paid in child support for her over all those years, if he had known about her. He wasn't ordered to do it. The Judge commended him when he learned what Richard had done. And then, Richard started paying monthly support as well. He makes good money, and the Smith-Winslow valve and minimally invasive replacement procedures have set us up pretty well financially.

Sara started visiting us, twice a month. She was not thrilled to suddenly have a father and a bunch of half-siblings. Believe me, all we needed was one more attitudinal, hormonal teen in the house. And just like that, we were a 'typical', American, blended family, with one of the kids coming for visits but not living with us. So naturally, we all started counseling.

I gained twenty pounds. Richard gained thirty. But like they say, women get fat and frumpy. Men get portly and distinguished. Yeah, like I needed something else to make me feel worse about myself right then.

And then we got the offer to open the new clinic in San Antonio. Richard and Dan were all stoked up about this opportunity. I realized Richard saw it as a way to separate us a little from Mellie and Sara. She would still come to visit, but he hoped we would regain some of the semblance of normalcy we had in our lives before we learned about Sara. I realized he was trying to run away from the unexpected complication dumped into our laps at dance competition that awful Saturday morning. So now, if he wanted to move to another town, who was I to say no? Maybe we needed this move.

Maybe *I* needed this move.

We planned the trip to San Antonio to be like a second honeymoon. Heck fire, if you got right down to it, we never had our first honeymoon. But I started coughing two days before this trip, and began running a fever last night. That morning, I felt like crap on a stick. I knew Richard was right. I was too sick to go.

Drat. I glumly watched Richard's sleek, sexy sports car pull out of the driveway and nose south towards Atlanta. I sighed and crawled back into bed. He would sign the lease on the offices and probably the contract to buy the big house he wanted since he was a kid while I lay in bed fighting a damned cold. Now I would have no say on the house we would move to in Texas. My throat hurt, my head hurt, my chest hurt. Heck fire, I hurt all over.

Richard might say it was pneumonia, but I refused to accept the diagnosis. I could not imagine I somehow managed to catch bacterial pneumonia. I hadn't been sick in years. Surely, it was just a cold. Okay, maybe it was the flu.

I pushed the nagging thought out of my head: the CDC reports that 56,000 people die from the flu each year. Nope, not gonna happen. I rebuked the thought as quickly as it reared its ugly head.

I dozed back to sleep only to be startled awake as the phone rang. I heard Hannah tell whoever was on the line I could not come to the phone. "I'm sorry, Mrs. Winslow is sick. She is unavailable. May I take a message?" She must have jotted information down because then I heard her say, "I'll be sure to tell her."

I reached over and got a couple of aspirin, and one of the antibiotics the pharmacy delivered, which I washed down with half a bottle of water.

I sighed and laid back down. It seemed every time I dozed off the blasted phone would ring. Finally, I grabbed it. "This is Fancy Winslow."

I cringed. My voice sounded gruff and surly. I tried to clear my throat and coughed a couple of times. "Sorry. I have a bad cold. What can I do for you?"

"Mrs. Winslow? This is Todd Rickert up at the ranger's station. We have kind of a weird situation. There is a man up here hunting for you."

"Tell him I'm sick and I'm not interested in new windows or vinyl siding for the cabin. That ship has sailed," I said. It was a standing joke that everyone wanted to sell us vinyl siding (for the log cabin, mind you) or new windows.

Todd hesitated just a second before he replied. "Uh, no ma'am, he isn't trying to sell anything. But he's hunting for you. He says his name is Kirk O'Malley. He's kind of an odd duck—"

The hairs on my arms were standing up as I bolted up from the bed. "He said what? Are you sure?"

"Yes, ma'am. He's dressed kinda strange, too. He claims he came a long way—"

Suddenly, I could hear a scuffle on the other end. I realized with a jolt I could hear the voice of a man I had long thought was dead. *Oh, sweet Jesus, no! Why now?* "Okay, Todd, tell him I'm on the way. It will take a couple of hours for me to get there. In fact, please put him on the phone."

Please, Kirk, don't freak out.

"Hello?" I heard his voice, tentative and nervous as he spoke into the phone. "Fancy?"

"Kirk? I'm on the way. It will take me a couple of hours to get there. Just … hang tight. I'm coming," I babbled.

"Are you alright? You sound sick," he fretted.

I started coughing again. "No, no, it's just a bad cold. I'll be okay. And don't talk too much to this guy, okay?"

"Okay. I understand, I think. I love you, *mo leannan*, " Kirk said.

"Uh…yeah… Let me talk to the ranger again." I pressed my hand to my chest. My heart was beating ninety to nothing and my breathing was rough and ragged.

Todd took the phone back. "Uh, Mrs. Winslow, you might want to bring him some clothes."

That startled me. "Clothes? Wh-what do you mean?"

"Well, he's in a swimsuit. I guess you could call it a swimsuit. It's the oddest thing I ever saw any man wearing here, and I've worked this trail for fifteen years. I've seen guys swimming at the falls in all sorts of swimsuits over the years, but this one takes the cake, lemme tell ya. The weather has changed and it's getting pretty cool. Bring him some pants and a shirt. Shoes and a jacket wouldn't hurt either."

Sweet Jesus, what happened? How did Kirk get here, in a swimsuit of all things? I pulled on some clothes and ran my brush through my dirty hair. I frowned and pulled it back into a ponytail. I frowned again as my eyes landed on the coffee stain on my t-shirt. I jerked it off and pulled on a clean blouse. I sighed and slipped earrings into my ear lobes. I slapped on some lipstick as I prayed it would somehow give me a healthy glow. I grabbed a pair of Richard's sweat pants, a sweatshirt, and an oversized hoodie. Almost as an afterthought, I grabbed a pair of underpants, socks and Richard's slip-on house shoes. I shoved them all into a duffle bag, threw in my antibiotics, a bottle of NyQuil Extra Strength, a box of Kleenex, a big bag of cough drops and some Tylenol. I slung my purse over my shoulder, grabbed an umbrella, a blanket, and a pillow, and ran to the garage to get the car.

Hannah frowned as I sprinted by her. "Where are you going, Miss Fancy?"

"Doctor's office. Be back later."

I pulled the car out into the downpour of rain. How on earth did he get here? Why now, of all times? What the hell would I do with him? As my mind began playing all sorts of crazy scenes of Kirk encountering 21st-century life, I didn't know whether to laugh, cry, or run away, so I drove like a bat out of hell straight to the high school. I dashed into the attendance office, and told the clerk I needed Bella and Elizabeth ASAP. The clerk shrugged and sent for both girls.

One thing for certain: I damned sure wasn't going after Kirk O'Malley by myself.

Elizabeth slumped into the back seat and pulled her headphones on to listen to her music. As her foot began to tap out the rhythm of the Lady Gaga tune, Bella winked at me. "Where are we going?"

"Beech Bottom Trailhead. They have an urgent problem and need me up there ASAP. Liz, do not tap out the rhythm of the song on the back of my seat. Please."

"Good grief, Mom, it's raining cats and dogs. There's a flood warning out. Do we really have to go up there today? Miguel is supposed to call me tonight." Bella sounded frustrated.

Her words rattled me. I knew it was raining but I had not realized there was a flash flood warning. I shrugged and tried to look nonchalant. "No big deal. That young man calls you every night. Besides, he calls you on your cell phone. The ranger said this was urgent. You want to drive now or later?"

"Sheesh, you know the phone reception in the Cohutta Wilderness sucks toads. I'll let you drive right now. Tell me when you want me to trade," she said with a sigh and a shake of her head. She slipped her own earphones in as she began playing a Chopin sonata, her hands moving as if over the keys to the tune she was struggling to master.

It took almost two hours to get there. I trembled with exhaustion by the time we reached the ranger's shack. The girls tumbled out of the car and hurried inside. I sat there another minute to gather up enough strength to get out of the car and go inside. I grabbed my umbrella, and trudged in behind them carrying the duffel bag full of clothing for Kirk. As I pushed the door open, I saw a startled Bella be gathered into a bear hug by a near-naked man. I struggled to hold back my laughter.

"Ah, *mo leannan*, I thought I would never find you," Kirk said, and then he lowered his head to kiss my shocked daughter full on the mouth.

Bella, initially shocked still for once, began to struggle against him. She balled her fists up and began pummeling his arms. As Kirk pulled back, shocked by her response, she literally slapped the snot out of him.

Oh, hell, it was worth driving here in a thunder storm when I was sick to see this.

"Uh, Kirk, that's Bella. I'm Fancy," I said, my voice little more than a hoarse whisper. "Girls, this is my *ex*-husband, Captain Kirk O'Malley."

He looked up, shocked by my words as his hands dropped from Bella. He stepped back as his face flushed red with embarrassment and he began stammering an apology. "I-I-I'm sorry—"

Bella stood wiping the kiss from her face and then wiping her arms with her hands. "Good grief, Kirk, control yourself."

Elizabeth rolled her eyes and shook her head. "Jesus, Mom. You used to be married to him? What a perv."

I rolled my eyes at Elizabeth and 'shushed' her. "Cut it out. He's your father," I hissed as I shoved the duffel bag into his arms. I pointed to the men's rest room. "You go in there and pull on the clothes. We'll wait for you out here."

Elizabeth shook her head. "Not me, Mom. I'll be in the car. You coming, Bella?"

Bella nodded. "Yeah. You want me to drive, Mom?"

I nodded and handed her the keys. "Please, if you don't mind, honey. You two sit in the front. I'll sit in the back with Kirk."

Elizabeth snorted. "You better. Neither of us want to sit by the old perv."

"Well, in his defense, he's pretty good looking for an old dude. Heck, he looks better than Daddy — Oh, my freaking God!" Bella exclaimed as he came back into the room.

He fit in Richard's sweat pants, but just barely. He's taller than Richard so the pants hung low where they caught on his hips, just above his pelvis, much like the pants he used to lounge in, back in Barbados. The sweatshirt did not fit. He held it out to me. "It was too small for me. I was afraid I might rip it."

Elizabeth's mouth hung open as she stared at the muscles of his well-defined six pack. I guess the girls could enjoy the view once he was no longer clad only in something that best approximated Tarzan's loincloth. Above the narrow waist and firm belly were rock hard pectoral muscles I knew Richard would kill to have again. Kirk's shoulders and biceps were bigger than I remembered, too. Hell, they were humongous. I blinked in surprise at the tribal styled tattoo around one bicep, and blinked again as I realized his facial hair was gone. My God, he looked so young without the sinister-looking mustache and little goatee-shaped beard. As if suddenly self-conscious, he glanced downward as he began to pull on the hoodie, and frowned as he fumbled with the zipper.

I reached over to help. "I don't think it will zip, Kirk. I guess you'll just have to go like this."

"I can stop at the Walmart at Crandall, Mom. I'll run in and get ol' Conan here some t-shirts." Bella's eyes widened with surprise as she surveyed the well-muscled chest of the man who was once her step-father. "Wowza."

"Mrs. Winslow, excuse me, ma'am, you really need to go back the northern route through Ducktown to McCaysville. I'm actually kinda shocked you guys made it coming up from Crandall. Highway 2 is washing out," said Todd.

"Well, shit. That will add at least another hour to the drive," fussed Elizabeth with a frown. "David wanted to go grab a movie when we get back. Some Friday date night this is turning into, Mom."

"Behave, Liz," I murmured and then I started coughing again.

"Liz? Jaysus, ye mean this is Elizabeth?" Kirk sounded stunned. "My wee Betty?"

I nodded. "Yes. Why?"

"How long has it been? You know…" his voice trailed off.

"Twelve years, Daddy Dearest," snapped Elizabeth. "We have not seen or heard from you in twelve long years. Come on. The rain is getting worse. Mom doesn't need to be out in this. Hell, none of us do. We need to head home."

"Watch your language, Elizabeth," I said as I pulled my hoodie up over my head.

"Give me a break, Mom. I think I'm entitled to say 'hell' once when he shows up after twelve freaking years, looking like Conan the Barbarian." She snapped the words out angrily.

We all hustled through the pelting rain to the car. I was coughing again as I climbed into the back seat. It hurt so much to cough that I had to hold my sides. Coughing caused a pain I had not felt in years. My chest felt like it was on fire and it hurt to breathe. I shoved the pillow behind me and pulled the blanket over me as I began shivering in earnest. "Oh, God, I feel awful. Turn the heater on, Bella."

After only a moment's hesitation, Kirk climbed in the back seat beside me. He flipped his long hair back out of his face and then leaned over and touched my forehead before he began rubbing my hands. "My God, Fancy, you're burning up. What's wrong with you? You look like you're on death's door."

"Gee, thanks, Kirk. Way to make a girl feel good about herself. It's just a really bad cold." My voice cracked before I began coughing again.

"Bull hockey, Mom. Daddy said he thought you had pneumonia this morning before he left to go to San Antonio. He wanted you to go to the doctor today. You ought to be home in bed instead of running all over creation to pick up Mr. Macho Man," Elizabeth snapped. "Here. Take some Tylenol and another dose of Extra Strength NyQuil. The Tylenol and NyQuil will at least help ease that cough a little. My Daddy's gonna have a cow." She gave Kirk a look of total revulsion.

She was right. Richard would 'have a cow' when he found out. I gulped, but I didn't say anything. What was I going to say? Oh, yeah, Richard's going to be upset to learn Kirk is still alive? And to realize that Kirk thinks we are still married? I cringed to think of the scene to come. I just took the Tylenol, water bottle and NyQuil from her and swallowed the Tylenol down with a swig of NyQuil. I then drank about a half a bottle of water before Kirk could bat an eye.

"Pneumonia? You told me you have a cold—" He began to stammer.

"She lied. Don't make her talk." Liz stated her position bluntly.

She stuck her earphones back in her ears and cranked up Lady Gaga. I tried not to chuckle as she began to sing the lyrics to 'Bad Romance.' Was that her opinion of my ill-fated romance with her dad? At least her feet were no longer tapping out the dance routine to the song.

Bella put her earphones back in her ears and cranked up Queen. I figured she gave up on Chopin as she started singing. I could not hold the ripple of laughter which ended with another bout of coughing as Bella belted out 'I Want to Break Free.' The image in my head of Kirk going ape when he saw the video with the members of Queen all dressed in drag was more than I could handle right then, but I realized it was a sight I wouldn't want to miss.

Kirk looked rattled by the music emanating from both girls. "How did they do that?"

Bella glanced back to him and shook her head. "You get into the car without a damned word and want to know about the music? Hilarious."

"Guider told me there were a lot of changes," he mumbled. "I'm tryin' to be accepting of those changes. But now that you opened the discussion, what is this contraption? And how fast will it travel?"

"It's a car. It's how we get from one place to another," Bella explained. "It can go in excess of 70 miles per hour. Not that we will be traveling that fast on these roads tonight in the rain and the dark."

"Interesting. Does it run on a steam engine? I'm convinced steam engines are the way of the future." Kirk leaned forward, fascinated.

"No, it's a gasoline-powered engine. Wait ... you know about steam engines?" Bella's surprise showed all over her face.

He nodded. "Aye, I expect steam engines will soon be available in ships. Or, uh, were soon available, back then."

"They were." I winced. My voice sounded little more than a hoarse whisper, and then I frowned. "Who's Guider?"

"She said her name was Baylie Smith when she lived here. She was your friend."

I grabbed his hand. "You know Bay? Is she okay?"

He nodded. "Aye. In fact, she's a far sight better than you are right now. She's supposed to get married soon."

"Really? Anyone I know?" I asked, my interest whetted.

He nodded. "Aye, she's marryin' Shadow Wolf."

My eyebrows must have popped up at that. "Get out of here! Really?"

He nodded, but as I started coughing again, I decided he could tell me more later. I just wanted to stop coughing. If I didn't, I knew I would start to vomit soon. Fortunately, once the NyQuil kicked in, I pretty much stopped coughing, and I dozed off.

We rode on in silence except for my occasional coughing and the faint blare of music and accompanying singing from both girls. I realized what 'silence is golden' meant as we rode along that night without talking more about why Kirk suddenly showed up, a genuinely unexpected blast from the past.

Chapter 7
Richard

I was humming as I came into the house Saturday afternoon. I was so stoked over the new business venture and snagging the house of my dreams that I knew nothing could knock me out of my happy place.

Boy, was I wrong.

We signed the contract on the new offices Friday. I drove to La Fonda on Main for dinner to celebrate. It was always our favorite 'go to' fancy restaurant for celebrations when I was a kid. I felt nostalgic as I sat in the elegant, familiar setting and ate the best cheese enchiladas in the entire world. I knew I would bring Cessie and the kids here soon to celebrate.

When Cessie did not answer the phone Friday, it didn't worry me. I knew she was sicker than a dog and was in bed under the influence of NyQuil Extra-strength for Severe Colds or Flu as well as the antibiotics, which the kids assured me she was taking. Bella told me their Mom did not have much voice, so it didn't rattle me when I couldn't get her on the phone. Well, not too much, anyway.

It thrilled me to learn Mrs. Gravesen still lived in the house. We became friends years ago as I would ride my bike through the neighborhood. I fell off my bike right in front of her house one day as she worked in her garden. When I fell, she ran to the street to check on me. I was more rattled than hurt, but she took me into the gorgeous house to doctor my scraped knee and to give me a glass of ice-cold water.

That was the day I told her someday I would live in her house.

I remember she laughed. "Well, I hope not. That would mean I no longer lived here."

Mrs. Gravesen called Dad and told him I took a tumble, and she brought me inside to doctor my 'battle injury.' I thought it was cool when she described my scraped knee that way. I managed to be pretty brave while she cleaned the abrasion. I remember I grinned at her only to wince as she put some red-colored medicine on my knee. It was far worse than the alcohol my mom used to clean scrapes. I grimaced. "That stuff stings."

She laughed again, that beautiful trill I thought for years epitomized the way a lady's laugh should sound. "Yes, young man, it certainly does, but the monkey's blood will kill the germs and help keep your knee from getting infected."

"What did you call it, Miss Lettie?"

"The proper name for it is mercurochrome, but it is often called monkey's blood," she replied.

That fascinated me. "Why?"

She laughed again. "Ricky Winslow, I never met a lad more inquisitive than you. I think they call the medicine "monkey's blood" because it looks like blood. Now, hold still and let me finish tending to this."

And then she did the most endearing thing. When she finished bandaging my knee, she bent over and kissed it. I guess I looked surprised. She smiled, tousled my hair, and asked, "Want some ice cream? I made it myself."

I was never a boy to turn down a bowl of ice cream, especially homemade. My eyes lit up as I nodded my head. "Yes, please."

She smiled again. "Curious and polite. So, you're going to buy my house when you grow up, are you?"

I nodded. "Yes, ma'am, Miss Lettie. I want to be a doctor. And I want to live right here someday. I think this is the prettiest house in all the world."

"My husband was a doctor here for many years. He died in the Gulf War. I used to be his nurse."

"Oh, that's why you knew how to treat my injury. And won't it be perfect, Miss Lettie? If you can't live here any longer, I'll be the new doctor to live in your house. And who knows? Maybe I'll be lucky and marry a nurse, too."

I stood reminiscing about our conversations as Miss Lettie opened the door for the realtor and me on Saturday morning. "Oh, Miss Cook, I see you are quite punctual. Please come in."

It rattled me to see how old she had grown. Of course, when I was ten, and she was about 45, I thought she was old. Thirty-five years later, she had aged into a beautiful, silver-haired matron who now walked with a cane.

"Mrs. Gravesen, this is the gentleman I have been telling you about."

She looked up to me and beamed as she reached up to stroke my face. "Dr. Winslow, I presume? My, oh, my, Ricky, you're all grown up now and every bit as handsome as I always knew you would be. I will admit though: I thought you would never come to buy my house."

The realtor looked confused. "Uhm—"

And then I heard that beautiful tinkling laugh I loved so much as a boy. "Oh, Cecile, Dr. Winslow and I go way back. Don't we, Ricky?"

I nodded and reached over to gingerly hug her. "Indeed, we do, Miss Lettie."

We chatted a while before she showed us through the house. I told her I was married to a nurse, and we had five children.

"Five? I'm impressed. How does she manage to work with that brood?"

"I am blessed with the best wife in all the world. If she wants something, she makes it work. And we have the world's best nanny. We could not manage without Hannah."

I felt disappointed later when I still couldn't get Cessie on the phone to tell her I signed the contract on the house, but Bella insisted Cessie had no voice and could not talk. She said Cessie grinned and gave a big thumbs up about the house.

I never thought about FaceTime until after I hung up. I felt pretty stupid because I intended to FaceTime with my wife as I went through the house. I was so excited to see Miss Lettie again after all those years and to finally walk through the home of my dreams that I forgot all about FaceTime. But I took about a jillion photos of the house, new offices, the med center, and good ol' Trinity U. I knew Cessie and the children could get an idea about it all from my photos. Cessie teases me sometimes because I take so many pictures. I was eager to show everything to everyone when I got home.

My gorgeous, 'new' house was only a few blocks from Trinity and less than two blocks from Suarez House. I knew Cessie would love that fact. Bella would live at Suarez House this fall, thanks to Uncle Jim. This would give her some separation from Mom, but we would be nearby, just in case.

The house was built in 1920, in the Romanesque style. The ad described the house as a two-story home, 'resplendent with coved ceilings, double moldings, arched windows, Redondo tile and oak floors, Mission-style millwork, three fireplaces, and dual staircases.' A rooftop terrace overlooked the grounds with arbored colonnades and patios edging the 60' long pool and spa. I loved that roof-top terrace the first time I saw it, after I fell and skinned my knee. Landscaping was still impeccable. The views of Trinity and downtown were just as exquisite as I remembered them. The terrace was filled with tropical plants. Miss Lettie told us how her husband and she used to love to bundle up under blankets to watch the stormy sky as cold fronts would blow in. The terrace overlooked the pool. I told her I couldn't wait to swim laps in that gorgeous pool.

"Ricky, did you know this is the home of the famous artist, Mary O'Connor?" Miss Lettie asked.

My eyes must have about bulged out of my head. "No, I did not realize that. She's one of my favorite artists. We own two of her etchings."

Miss Lettie beamed at me. "She painted the stairwell up to this terrace. I love the tropical plants and the whimsical cat. You know, she was also very involved in conservation here in San Antonio. I think that is why I always felt a special obligation to maintain and preserve this beautiful old house. I feel good knowing you will be taking on the project for me."

I reached over and squeezed her hand. "Thank you for waiting for me to come back to buy it, Miss Lettie."

I told Miss Lettie I knew Cessie would love the premiere, gourmet-worthy kitchen. I told Cessie that she could remodel it if she wanted, but I was sure she would love it 'as is.'

There was also a library, sitting rooms, and even a wine cellar. It might only be a half-acre of land, and in the city, but it was most definitely 'all that and a bag of chips,' as our kids say.

As we finished the tour of the house, she asked if it lived up to my childhood memories.

"Oh, yes, ma'am. Cecile, do you have the contract handy?"

Cecile Cook's eyes grew wide with excitement. Realtors don't get contracts signed for 1.4 million every day. She pulled out the contract and quickly reviewed it with me. In less than fifteen minutes, I signed the contract, and we were all eating Miss Lettie's homemade lavender vanilla ice cream on the rooftop terrace, just like in the old days. I trembled with excitement, knowing this rooftop terrace and this exquisite home were now mine.

Bella could live away from home at Suarez House, with her beloved grand piano only a few steps away from her at our house. I hoped the proximity to Bella would help Cessie adjust to the move. Cessie already dreaded losing her beloved first child. She loved them all, but she had a special relationship with Bella, I guess because it was just the two of them for a couple of years. Cessie told me if she had not had Bella, she might not have survived Simon LeGrand's abuse.

Heck, one reason I wanted to move to San Antonio when the opportunity arose was so Cessie could stay close to Bella. I knew it would just about kill Cessie for Bella to be so far away at college if we remained in Georgia, even if it is a mere four-hour flight.

So, as I cheerfully walked into the Ellijay house that Saturday afternoon, I felt like I was on top of the world. No squirrels were running wild anymore as they had for the past six months. Cessie always cracks me up with that line. God knows the hypothetical squirrels ran rampant in our lives for months, but today, our ducks were compliant, in a neat and orderly, well-mannered row for the next part of our lives. I opened the front door and shouted, "I'm home!"

I expected a bunch of kids, a dog, and my wife to rush down to hear about the wonderful trip. I did not expect silence. Finally, Hannah stuck her head out of the kitchen. "Doc, the Missus is in the hospital in Ellijay. Didn't you know?"

I shook my head. "No. No one told me. When did she go?"

She shrugged. "Sometime yesterday. The girls took her. But I swear, you never do know what kind of raggedy ol' rat the cat goin' to drag into this house, do you?"

She shook her head in disapproval and shuffled back into the kitchen.

I bit back the laugh that threatened to burst from my mouth. Hannah tends to take offense if I laugh at her colloquialisms. You never know what gems are going to pop out of Hannah's mouth. I followed after her. "What do you mean, Hannah? And where are the kids?"

"Miss Mellie picked up Dara and Ronan this morning. She said she would bring them back tomorrow night. The others are at the hospital with the Missus." She walked away, muttering something I could not quite make out.

I frowned. "What did you say, Hannah?"

She stopped and turned back to glare at me. "I never dreamed we would have all the craziness I been seein' here these past six months. First, the poor old dog died. Then, dear, sweet, Miss Olathe died, too. She sure enough never told me this house would be so full of craziness when she talked me into taking this job six years ago. And then the whole mess with Miss Mellie and that poor child. I swear Miss Olathe would have died over that mess alone. Heck fire, I feel plumb dab discombobulated over all this malarkey. And, this latest shenanigan? No, sir, Miss Olathe sho' nuff never mentioned anything like this could happen here."

I bristled at her words but was determined to keep a civil tongue. "What are you talking about, Hannah? Please explain."

She lifted her hands to wave a finger back and forth. "Oh, no, Doc. Not my place. You gonna see soon enough." She turned to shuffle off again. "Lawd, I swear, I never dreamed."

Well, that killed my happy buzz.

I hurried to our room and changed out of the business suit into jeans, a button-down oxford, and loafers before I grabbed my wallet, phone, and keys to head back to my Jag. I was pleased to see the diet and running had trimmed me down enough that I could fit back into my favorite pair of jeans. Now, to get my six-pack back. It was still lost somewhere in the extra pounds I gained when we learned about Sara. I had been working hard but had not quite managed to inch all of it off yet. I frowned at the sight of new grey in my hair. Dad was blonde, so his grey didn't show as much as mine, and he damned sure had a full head of hair when he died. I was painfully aware mine was starting to thin at my crown. Still, not half bad for a dude my age. After all, I was 44 now. I couldn't expect to look like I did when I first met Cessie when I was in my 20's.

In minutes, I arrived at the hospital, where I quickly found my wife's room. The charge nurse told me Cessie's condition was stable. "Her fever is down. Her lungs sound better. She is still pretty out of it, but she is much improved. Your kids went downstairs for some food a little while ago, but your friend stayed with her."

I frowned. "My friend? Who?"

She shrugged. "I didn't catch the name, but if he's single, I want an introduction. Ooh, my God, that accent! That man is to die for, Doc. Gosh, he's gorgeous."

I figured she meant Stephan. He's our friend who joined the practice a few years ago from France, and he is one of the best-looking men I ever met. I didn't have the heart to tell her the big, handsome Frenchman would not be interested. He prefers men. I chuckled as I walked into the room, only to pull up short at the sight before me.

"What in the hell are you doing here, O'Malley?" I growled, as I quickly crossed to the man sitting in the chair beside my sleeping wife.

"Well, it's about high time ye got back, Winslow. Yer poor wife at death's door and you've been off roaming all over the country. Tis a good thing the Almighty let me come through that time thingamajig," he retorted in anger. "Tell me, how do ye sleep at night, treating this dear woman so poorly?"

My hands balled into fists. Goddammit, the son of a bitch was wearing my favorite leather jacket. I bought that jacket in Florence, Italy, during our Christmas holiday a couple of years ago. The damned jacket looked better on him than it ever looked on me. I longed to thrash the bastard soundly, but I damned sure did not intend to get kicked out of the hospital, much less arrested, over the likes of Killian O'Malley.

"Naked, in case you want to kiss my ass. Jesus Christ, you got deported for hurting her. Get the hell out of here, Killian. Now."

He tilted his head and blinked. "Killian. Who the hell is Killian?"

And then his words hit me. Time thing-a-ma-bob. Oh, my freaking God. It wasn't Killian. It was Killian's great-great-great-grandpappy, in the flesh. Eff me running. Kirk O'Malley managed to access the time portal to come forward in time after my sweet Cessie. I thought I was going to puke up my toenails.

I pulled a twenty out of my pocket and handed it to Kirk. "Why don't you catch up with the kids and get something to eat, too? And ask Bella to bring me a caramel macchiato."

Kirk frowned, his brow wrinkling as if he didn't understand what I said. "Uh, what?

I shut my eyes and took a deep breath. "Oh, for the love of—ask her to bring me a coffee. Then, the rest of you can go back to the house and catch some z's. I'll stay here with Francesca."

Kirk frowned again. "Why would we go hunting while Fancy is in the hospital? And what the blazes are 'z's'? And where the hell were you anyway?"

Oh, this was going to be fun, I thought as I sighed with unfettered exasperation. "'Catch some z's' means catch some sleep. You look exhausted, Kirk. I went to San Antonio, Texas, on a business trip. My wife planned to accompany me, but she was sick enough yesterday that I felt she should stay home in bed."

Kirk's scowl deepened. "You expect me to believe you went all the way to Northern Mexico yesterday? And back today? Hogwash."

"Oh, for the love of—Texas has not been part of Mexico since 1836. It was an independent nation until 1847 when it became a state. All I had to do was hop on a plane and fly there. It took 4 hours each way. Sheesh, Kirk, give me a freaking break," I grumbled.

"What's a plane?" He scratched his head.

"Like a ship that flies through the sky," I replied.

"Oh, yeah, I'm sure." Kirk shrugged. "I'll believe it when I see it. You still left her when she had pneumonia."

"I left her with a prescription for antibiotics and strict orders for her to stay in bed. I'm a doctor. I can diagnose illness and prescribe medication. I told her she had pneumonia, and she needed to see a doctor Friday if her condition worsened. Did she do that? No. Instead, she has been gallivanting all over creation. Why? Because you showed up."

Kirk looked embarrassed. "She said she had a wee cold."

"A wee cold, hmm? Not so much, Bucky. Now she's in the hospital with acute bacterial pneumonia, which could have been handled at home if she had not gone trucking all over creation after your ass yesterday," I fumed.

Kirk blinked a couple of times as he glanced over at Cessie. "She looks so sick, Richard. Will she live?"

"Of course, she will, you moron. Now, get some food. Bring me some coffee. And then, you guys get out of here for a few hours," I snapped.

"But her heart—" Kirk began.

"Fortunately, we repaired her heart years ago. She's been healthy as a proverbial horse since then. Now, get out of here. Get some rest. We can talk later."

He hesitated for a second, and then his shoulders sagged. He nodded, turned, and left the room.

Bella brought the coffee a little later and told me they were going home for a couple of hours. "Call me if you need me. I'll see if we can keep Kirk out of your hair for a while."

"Why didn't you tell me?" I asked.

Her cheeks reddened with embarrassment. I noticed she couldn't quite look me in the eye. I thought for the umpteenth time how much she reminds me of Cessie. "I'm sorry. My bad. I figured this was not something you needed to hear over the phone."

I felt my brow wrinkle as I frowned. "What? That she was admitted to the hospital? Why did you think that would rattle me?"

She shook her head. "No, that Kirk turned up. And that we went after him. And then, when she was unresponsive in the car, I brought her here. I remembered you said Piedmont is the best hospital in the area."

I nodded. Yeah, Bella was right. That would have stressed the shit out of me. I pulled her to me for a hug. "It will all be okay. Go home and get some rest."

I must have dozed off later. I awoke as fingers gently ruffled my hair. I raised my head, rubbed my eyes, and smiled at my wife. "Hi, Sleeping Beauty."

She smiled. "Hi. Where am I?"

"Piedmont. How do you feel?"

She shrugged. "I've felt better. So, I reckon you were right? Pneumonia?"

I nodded. "Yep. Remember anything?"

She shook her head. "It's pretty muddled. I had some crazy dreams."

I kind of laughed. "Oh? Like what?"

"I was trying to train cats to jump through hoops and to walk on a tightrope."

I roared with laughter. "Now, that's hilarious."

"But Richard, it was so strange. I swear, the cat would turn towards me, and its face would become Kirk's face. Why would I dream about Kirk after all this time?"

That brought me up short. I stopped laughing and gathered both her hands into mine. "Uh, Cessie, you see—"

Just then, the door swung open. Cessie's eyes opened wide in shock or surprise or maybe both. "I brought ye some lunch, Winslow. Ah, Fancy, darlin', I see you woke up. How are ye feeling, my love?"

She paled as he spoke. She cut her eyes at me as if afraid of how I would react. "Uh, Richard…"

I bent to kiss her cheek. "It's okay, sweetie. Thanks, O'Malley. I thought you went back to the house with the kids. How did you get back here?"

"I walked. Tis only a couple of miles," he said.

Three-point-five to be exact, I thought. "Hey, the cute little nurse at the nurses' station wants to know if you're single."

He nodded. "Aye. I told her I'm married."

Cessie turned grey. "Did you tell her who you are married to?"

He nodded as he picked up half a roast beef sandwich and began eating it. "Of course. I told her you're my wife."

"Oh, dear God, no," Cessie murmured, shock and horror all over her face.

"Well, in case you forgot, Bucky, that marriage was determined *void ab initio*," I said. "A long-damned time ago."

O'Malley's cheeks dimpled as he nodded and took another bite of his sandwich. "Aye, it was. Oh, wait. I reckon Fancy never told you we married again after you left?" He looked from my shocked expression to her horrified one and began to laugh. "Oh, this is priceless."

I was wrong. The damned ducks are no longer in a nice, orderly row. Just when I thought I had all my ducks in a compliant, well-behaved queue, one of the fluffy little devils wandered off and caused trouble. Or maybe like Cessie says, the freaking squirrels are everywhere. Again.

Dammit, I think I'm getting a migraine. If shit like this continues, I might figure out why my mother used drugs. Hell, at this rate, I might start using drugs. I took another deep breath and then smiled. "As I said, that was a long time ago. Way more than seven years."

That knocked the cocky grin off Kirk's face. "So what? We're still married."

I shrugged. "Not really, Kirk. You were judicially determined to be dead before Cessie and I got married."

He blinked and stopped eating the sandwich. "Say what?"

Oh, yeah, that felt good. "In an abundance of caution, you were declared legally dead before we got married. Sorry, old man. She's not your wife any more. She's mine."

Kirk's lips thinned into an angry slash. "But it hadn't been seven years..."

"Wrong, Bucky. It's been over 200 years." I smiled.

"I'll sue. On the grounds of fraud and adultery," Kirk said.

Cessie looked horrified. "Oh, no, please, Kirk—"

I patted her hand. "Bring it on, big boy. I can't wait to see the Judge's expression when you tell him you married Francesca in 1783, and you are suing for fraud and adultery because she married me over 200 years later."

Kirk looked shocked as his eyes darted from Cessie to me and back to Cessie again. I noticed she couldn't quite look either of us in the eye. Ol' Tom Selk used to whip her for looking him in the eye when he 'corrected' her. Tom viewed it as 'uppity behavior.'

"You let him have me declared dead?" Kirk asked, his voice filled with dismay.

She was clinging tight to my hand. "It's true, Kirk. I tried to tell you."

"Jaysus, woman, you told me you loved me," he said, his voice cracking with emotion.

I have to admit, between the voice and the tears welling up in his eyes, he almost got to me. Almost.

"That was a long time ago, Kirk," Cessie said, her voice wavering.

"In a galaxy far, far away, Lily said. Well, at least now I have an inkling of what she meant by that," Kirk replied

"She used a Star Wars quote? Oops, my bad, the reference probably means nothing to you," I said with a forced laugh.

"I have no idea what this Star Wars is. I just know Lily said that," Kirk responded.

"Do we have to deal with this right now? While I'm sick and in the hospital," Cessie asked, her voice wavering. "Surely this can wait a few days."

I frowned. "But sweetie…" I began.

"You know he could only come to find his true love or if he was needed urgently. Let it go for now, Richard. We can sort it all out when I feel better. For now, just don't kill each other," she said, her eyes imploring us not to kill each other right there in her hospital room.

Tempting as it was to just lay into him whole hog, I resisted the urge. I bent and kissed her hand. "We can do that, sweetie. For now. Right, Kirk?"

He leveled those cold, grey eyes on me before he answered. I could not hold back the chuckle when he made the 'eyes on you' motion Marc used to make to him. "Aye. For now."

"And you might tell the nurse you did not realize you are no longer married to Cessie," I suggested.

"I'll think about it." He mumbled the words.

I glanced at Cessie. "Kinda like teaching a cat to jump through a hoop or to walk a tightrope?"

"I think training the cat to do those things would be easier than trying to convince Kirk to do just about anything," she murmured.

Kirk and I tried hard not to get into it. The girls took him shopping Sunday afternoon, with my credit card, of course. The plan was they would keep him out of my hair a few hours, not that it helped. He went right back to sniping at me when they returned to the house. Tensions between us continued to escalate Sunday evening as I brought Cessie home from the hospital. I got her settled onto the couch just in time to hear the doorbell.

Kirk said, "I'll get it."

I nodded and kept tending to Cessie. I plumped the pillows for her and tucked her favorite quilt around her.

"I'm fine. Go and see who's at the door. Don't leave the Macho Man alone too long," she whispered.

I nodded and bent over to kiss her. "Okay."

I walked into the foyer in time to see Dara and Ronan come back into the house. Sara stood outside with her mother.

"Thanks for watching the kids for us, Mellie. We really appreciate it," I said.

And then it hit me. Kirk O'Malley looked like he had been hit in the head with a two by four. He looked like he had been gobsmacked, for lack of a better word.

"Kirk, have you met Mellie and Sara?" I asked.

He shook his head. "No. I must have been at the hospital with the older weans when this lovely lady came to fetch the bairns yesterday. I'm fair certain I would remember if I met you, ma'am."

"Likewise," she murmured as she eyed his bulging muscles.

"Uh, Melanie Henderson, this is Kirk O'Malley. Kirk, this is Melanie Henderson and her daughter, Sara. I mean, our daughter, Sara."

Kirk cut his eyes at me in shock. "You mean to tell me you had an affair with this woman after you stole my wife? Well, I'll be damned."

"No, you sorry, rat bastard…" I began.

"Again, Winslow, exactly how do you manage to sleep at night? Does your duplicity know no bounds?" Kirk appeared furious.

I could feel my anger welling up again. "Oh, for the love of—shut the eff up, O'Malley. STFU. And like I said before, I sleep naked in case you want to kiss my hairy white ass."

Sara giggled.

Dara rolled her eyes. "Oh, Daddy, behave."

Melanie finally dragged her eyes off Old Hunka Hunka Burning Love there and frowned at me. "I agree. Behave, Rick. I think it's sweet Mr. O'Malley defends me. Thank you, kind sir. But actually, Rick and I dated several years before he met Fancy."

I gawked as she curtseyed.

And then the damned son of a bitch bowed over her hand and kissed it. "My pleasure, sweet lady. I canna understand why he abandoned such a beautiful woman."

I heard Fancy giggle. I turned towards her to realize Liz and Bella were grinning ear to ear as they watched the whole debacle as well. Hell, just eff me running. Sideways.

"I was pretty skeptical about the whole time-travel thing. We broke up before he took off on his grand adventure. I guess you could say we were not involved when he left," Mellie explained.

O'Malley arched a brow at me. "It appears you had been quite intimately involved, Richard."

My hands balled into fists. "Okay, that does it. You are in my home, enjoying my hospitality. You might be polite and not continually try to stir the pot, Kirk."

He arched a supercilious brow at me. "Stir the pot? I'm not cooking anything. I haven't touched a thing in that kitchen since I arrived. Oh, I take it back. I played with the water taps a bit as I figured them out. What a clever idea: hot and cold running water."

Then he winked at Mellie. She giggled. He grinned, flashing those damned dimples at her as he did.

I groaned and started to say something to Mellie, but she swept past me to go into the den. "How is the patient today?"

"Much better, thank you. How was the dance class?" Cessie reached up to hug her. They had a freaky good relationship, especially considering, well, you know, everything.

"Fine. Sara seems to be fitting in with the new group. I never dreamed she would be able to dance on a team the caliber of the Cohutta Queens. She loves it, don't you, sweetie?"

Dara nodded. "Yes, ma'am. She works us hard, but I love it. And it's fun to be dancing with Dara. Everyone thinks we are twins."

"I could never have afforded for her to dance on that team without your help, Rick. She and Dara make a dynamic duo. Ms. Whitaker is excited about the routine they are learning for competition. I have to admit, they look great together." Mellie smiled.

"Oh, good, I'm glad to hear it. I really appreciate you took them this weekend. Richard or I will get down to pick Sara up on Friday." Cessie smiled back at Mellie.

"No problemo. Let me know if you aren't up to it, and I can meet you guys halfway if you want." She gave a long, sidewise glance at Kirk.

"Sounds great," Cessie said. "You really ought to give another thought to moving into the house at Carter's Lake and to taking the job at the office. Peggy is retiring and we need another good cardiovascular nurse."

Mellie took a deep breath as she glanced at me. "I'll think about it. Sara, how would you like to move to Ellijay? We'd be closer to dance classes and to your Dad."

Sara shrugged. "I dunno, Mom. Maybe. I'll think about it."

Sometimes these two women are so civil to each other that it is enough to puke a mule, as Will Selk would say. It just about puked me right then. I could taste the bile rising. I cleared my throat. "I think I'll go check on supper."

"You do that, Winslow," Kirk said. "I think the old darky don't like me much—"

I wheeled around in stunned surprise. "The old—please tell me you did not call our housekeeper an 'old darky.' I mean, who the hell talks like that, for God's sake?"

Kirk shrugged. "Well, what should I call her? Bella told me twas rude to call her a ni—"

Mellie threw her hand over Kirk's mouth just in time. "Mr. O'Malley, we don't use that word in polite company."

He frowned as she lowered her hand. "What word?"

"The 'n' word you were about to say. It isn't socially acceptable language in this day and age."

I glowered at Kirk. "No, it isn't. And in a house filled with persons of color, I have to say we find the 'n' word especially offensive."

Cessie looked troubled by the whole exchange. "I think Kirk tried to be polite by referring to Hannah as a 'darky' instead of using the 'n' word. I appreciate that, Kirk, but you need to know 'darky' is nearly as offensive. I think Hannah would be hurt if she heard you call her that. She is a human being, just like the rest of us. Kindly remember that language has changed. Please try not to identify people based on the color of their skin."

Kirk looked perplexed. "So, what would I say to describe her?"

"How about you just say 'Hannah' or 'the housekeeper," I suggested.

"And you all might stop and think about how hard it would be for you to suddenly be catapulted more than 200 years into the future, like Kirk was two days ago. The children know. I do, too. He has a lot to assimilate and try to comprehend in short order if he is to survive his sojourn here." Cessie surprised me with her defense of Kirk.

"Assimilate? Sojourn? And where did a girl with your limited education learn words like those?" Kirk smirked.

She smiled. "College."

I bit back my laugh as the one word wiped the smirk right off his cocky face. Damn, I love this woman.

Chapter 8
Back in the Day – Before Baylie

"No!"

I could not believe it happened right before my eyes. O'Malley disappeared as he catapulted through time and space to the Beyond. Great Spirit, had I caused this with my foolish meddling?

I stood there gaping as Shadow Wolf, Marc and Lily ran up. Marc looked appalled.

"My God, woman, are ye satisfied now? He'll cause chaos and discord in their family. Is that what you wanted?"

I turned towards him, filled with rage and anger. "Of course not, Marcus McCarron. You should know that was never my intent. I did not think he could go…"

And then, the tears began to course down my cheeks. As my body began to shake with sobs, Lily wrapped me into her arms.

"It will be okay, Bay. He couldn't go unless he were supposed to go. Leave her alone, Marc." Lily cast a worried glance at Marc.

I nodded as I hiccuped.

Shadow Wolf looked grave. "Why do you weep, Guider? We knew this was a possibility."

I nodded and struggled to control my emotions. What was it that they used to say about 'stoic Indians?' I sure as hell wasn't feeling stoic right then. "I know, but I never thought he'd go through time."

His eyes narrowed. "Is Bear Claw correct? Did you take O'Malley to your bed? Does the blasted man have your heart?"

I cringed. Wolf sounded indignant, no, hurt. I took a deep breath and raised my head to look him in the eyes. "Hell, no. You of all people should know the only man sharing *my* bed is *you*. I do *not* want a white man, any white man, in my bed. If anything, *Fancy* has part of my heart. She was like a daughter to me. The daughter I never had. The daughter I always wanted. I'm worried about what will happen to them."

"It will be as the Great Spirit wills, as will be your future, traveler. Do not cry over the likes of him. I don't care if the elders believe he is related to *Tsul Kalu*. He is not worthy of you or your tears." Shadow Wolf snapped the words out as if they left a foul taste in his mouth.

I frowned. "The slant-eyed white giant? Why do they think he is related to the giant?"

Wolf sighed in impatience. "You know the old stories. The giant came here and took a local woman. The people heard the great noise and the giant and the woman disappeared. They believed someday their children would return."

I stared at Wolf, mouth agape, stunned by his words. "So, this is why the Chickamauga had not killed him."

"Probably. You must admit O'Malley is taller than most humans."

"So is Marc. Does the tribe think Marc descended from the giant as well?" I noticed Marc began to blush, and Lily shifted nervously.

Wolf looked rattled. "Perhaps."

"This is crazy! Marc is your friend. He's been your friend for many years. Is this why some of the elders did not want to tell O'Malley where she went?" I frowned as I pressed for more information.

He hesitated as he looked from Marc to Lily and back to me. "Yes. Some feared he could summon the loud noise and follow Fancy if he descended from *Tsul Kalu*."

Marc's eyes narrowed. "Is that why the village was eager to accept him?"

Wolf nodded. "You summoned the noise to go after Fancy, and then to return here. We feared he could as well."

I exploded. "Why the hell didn't anyone tell me this?"

Wolf's surprise showed on his face. "You are Cherokee. You know our stories. We thought you knew—"

"You *presumed* that I knew. You knew I came from Beyond. No one bothered to learn if *I* knew this story. No one bothered to tell me they thought O'Malley descended from *Tsul Kalu*. Does the whole village believe he was the Indian Satan?"

He nodded.

"So, you think O'Malley as well as your good friend, Marc, who is the Lone Eagle, and his son, Red Wolf, and his daughter, Fancy, and her children all descended from Satan? How could you have brought them into the tribe then? Why would the tribe accept them?"

Hell, was that what he thought of me as well? Did he believe I descended from the Cherokee Devil, also?

Wolf's eyes were flashing daggers at me by then. "Woman, surely you know this. They are strong enough to escape the powers of *Tsul Kalu*. They brought many strong powers with them. O'Malley resisted joining the tribe. His ability to follow Fancy when told of the great noise confirms he is descended—"

"Oh, give me a break, Wolf. The fact that he went somewhere Beyond in no way conveys O'Malley descended from Satan or that O'Malley somehow escaped hell. That is ludicrous."

Wolf raised himself to tower over me. "Do not speak to me like this, woman."

"Why? You told me yesterday *you* were going to tell him. Why are you so angry, *I* told him? You were right there when I told him. Why didn't you jump in and tell him whatever you think he needed to know? Your anger is unreasonable. It is unmerited. It is unfair."

I started to cry again. For a minute, I thought Wolf was going to take me into his arms and kiss me. Boy, I was wrong. He glowered at me as he pushed past me to stride back towards the village. I looked at Lily in silence as tears welled up in my eyes once again. "He doesn't understand."

She nodded as she hugged me again. "No, he doesn't. Give it time. He will calm down and realize your tears were not about losing O'Malley."

I looked at her with what I am sure was desperation all over my tear-streaked face. I grabbed her hands. "Do you think so?"

She nodded. "I think so."

Marc looked utterly bumfuzzled. "What in the blazes is going on, Lee?"

"She loves him, Marc," Lily said.

He looked horrified. "Loves O'Malley? But all this time ye said—"

"She loves Wolf, big dope. They plan to marry soon. You know that. Good lord, you're as bad as Wolf, although I never expected his reaction," Lily replied.

"I never expected to be told they think I'm the Son of Satan." Marc still looked stunned.

Silent, I nodded as my body shuddered with emotion. "Yeah."

I wiped my face with my sleeve and walked back to the village alone.

People stopped talking to stare at me in hostile silence as I entered the village gates. I held my head higher, determined not to be victimized by this. *We talked about this. Wolf agreed O'Malley should be told. He should have told O'Malley if he thought he could do a better job. It is not my fault O'Malley went Beyond. I refuse to believe Kirk or any of us is the Spawn of Satan. I will not be the scapegoat here. It. Is. Not. My. Fault.*

Maybe if I tell myself this often enough, I will begin to believe it.

I stopped as it hit me. *Damn, isn't that what Fancy said she used to tell herself about her mother?*

Tears welled up in my eyes again.

Wolf avoided me all week. With each passing hour, I felt like a little more of my heart died within me. I quit working on my wedding dress and put it aside after I burst into tears as I tried to finish the beadwork on it. Finally, the council of elders summoned me. I would say 'they called me on the carpet,' but there was no carpet in the council hall. It surprised me to see Lily and Marc there. Lily looked nervous. Marc looked more than nervous. He looked downright worried as he gnawed on his thumbnail.

It terrified me. I feared I would be told Wolf no longer wanted to marry me. I struggled to control my shaking hands and not break down in tears.

I never dreamed they would demand of me what they did. I could no longer hold back my shaking or sobs of horror. I stared at the council in shock. "I have to go back to the future after O'Malley? This isn't fair."

"Much in life is not fair. It was not fair for you to send him Beyond with no preparation. It is up to you to fix the wrong. Then you may return *if* it pleases the Great Spirit," said old Yellow Tooth.

"It was not fair for *me* to send him back? Really? Do you people think *I* sent him Beyond? Good grief, I thought you believed him to be the son of *Tsul Kalu*, who could travel through time at will." I wheeled to leave the council. "Fine. I'll go."

But 'fine' was not how I felt. I felt anything but fine. As I started to leave, my mind racing with a myriad of thoughts and emotions, Shadow Wolf spoke. "The council is not finished yet."

I stopped and balled my fists in anger. I swiped my shaking hand across my tear-stained cheek, and I forced myself to take a ragged breath before I turned back towards him. "I apologize, Chief Shadow Wolf. What else would this council like to tell me?"

He tilted his head at me, obviously catching the anger in my voice, or perhaps the tears on my cheeks. I held my head up a little higher, stood a little straighter as if daring him to tell me something – anything – of importance. *Tell me to come back to you. Tell me that you still love me. Tell me you still want to marry me—*

"Lone Eagle, tell Guider what you ask of her," Wolf replied. He sounded tired, frustrated, and resigned to the task at hand.

My heart sank. No words of love from this man. How did I read him so completely wrong for all these months? The Great Spirit knew *he* never played stickball for me, but he brought me meat. He was building my *asi*. We enjoyed the pleasures of each other's bodies many times. He told me he loved me and wanted to marry me. With a lump in my throat about the size of Tennessee, I turned to face Marc.

"Many years ago, this harp was given to my mother in the days when she was known as Meara McCarron. She carried it with her from Scotland to England and from England to Ireland after she married my father. I brought it to the United States when I returned home from our last trip to Ireland to protect it. The English are destroying the small harps when they find them in Ireland. The harp represents the clans and the independent spirit of Ireland. The English intend to break Ireland once and for all. I would like you to take the harp to Fancy, with this letter from me."

He held out a good-sized harp. I had seen it at the cabin, and I had heard Lily play it several times. The harp was a pretty little thing with what looked like a dragon carved along the top and some lettering down one side. Marc had told me it was crafted from ash wood. I knew it was not lightweight. I figured it weighed about 30 pounds. I blinked and sighed. "Are you serious? You want me to take a blasted harp to your daughter?"

"Aye. I would like to have it returned to Waterside someday when it is safe to have it there again. Lily and I plan to leave here soon. I fear I cannot get it safely back to the coast. I realize this adds yet one more burden on you, but—"

"But, hey, what does it matter? Guider can handle it. The harp will only add 30 pounds or so to my load," I grumbled.

"At least you have the opportunity to take things with you, and to wear appropriate clothing as you travel," Wolf said. "O'Malley went near-naked, with not a cent to his name, and unprepared for the journey."

I rolled my eyes at him but said nothing. *Not. My. Fault.* Silent, I nodded and grudgingly took the harp and letter from Marc. Since he was also supposed to be one of the Sons of Satan, with the ability to jump through time at will, I wondered why *he* was not sent to help O'Malley, but I held my tongue. "Fine. Whatever."

I flipped my hand as I said the word. Lily cringed as I did. She knew what I meant, even if no one else did.

I came here to help my people find a way to the new promised land. Now, I was being sent back to the future in disgrace with a freaking eighteenth-century Irish harp. I could care less about what happened to the damned harp. Fabulous. I could not believe this was happening.

A week later, as I gathered my things together to try to go forward in time, a shadow passed over the entrance to the *asi*. I looked up, surprised to see Wolf finally came to see me.

"May I enter?" His voice was low, almost as if he were imploring me to allow him entry.

I nodded and motioned for him to come in the *asi*. "Of course. Come in."

He entered and shifted from foot to foot, as if unsure what to say or do next. Finally, he cleared his throat. "Guider, I have come to tell you – to beg you – to come back to me."

I blinked, unsure what he was saying. "Uh, Wolf, you're the one who is sending me away."

He shook his head. I was shocked to see anguish all across his face. "No. The council sends you. It was their decision. But, my love, this situation is killing me. I cannot survive without you in my life, in my arms. You must return to me."

I frowned. "Wolf, you're the chief. Why can't you tell them what to do? I don't understand."

He tried to smile. "It is the way of our people. We are – what did you call us? Commutatarian? We look to what the tribe wants, not the individual. It is why I could not raise a complaint when Bear Claw asked to court you. I voted against it, but he had enough council votes to gain permission despite my opposition. In the same way, I voted against sending you forward in time, but the votes favored sending you to fetch O'Malley."

"Communitarian community. The village will do what is best for the village, not the individual. Of course. I should have realized." As I rushed into his open arms, he pulled me close.

"It will kill me if you do not return," he murmured to me as he stroked my hair. "I could not let you leave without telling you that you are my heart. A man cannot live without his heart. You must come back to me."

I choked up at his words. I longed to hear him say something like this to me for weeks. I clung to him as I fought back the tears threatening to fall. "I will, but what if he refuses to come? What do I do then?"

"He must not refuse. The council says he must return with you. I shall die if you do not return. You must return to me, my love. I completed building the *asi*. We need to be living there, together, as man and wife."

I choked back a sob. "I know, my darling. I will come back as soon as possible. But Wolf, what if he refuses to come? What do I do then?"

He froze for a minute and then bent to kiss me. "The council says you must bring him. But, if he refuses, you come back anyway. We will work it out somehow. Perhaps we would go west without the rest of the tribe. I believe my children and their families would come with us."

I nodded and reached up to pull him back to me for another kiss. He groaned, and then he swung me up into his arms and carried me to the sleeping rugs. Soon, we were kissing and caressing each other again. As the fire of our passion grew, we pushed our clothing aside, and he entered me one more time.

It was fast and furious. We both came quickly with shouts of ecstasy.

All those wasted years with Brian, I never dreamed lovemaking could be so sublime. Now, I find my paradise when I am in Wolf's arms. We both needed the reassurance the intimacy gave us that we each still loved the other.

Afterward, as we basked in the afterglow of our lovemaking, I asked him once again. "What if O'Malley won't come?"

His hand stilled for a moment before he resumed stroking my hair. "Come back anyway. We will figure out what to do. I will not live without you, woman. You are my heart. I refuse to give you up."

He kissed me again. I clung to him as my tears began anew. "I will, my darling. I promise."

The next morning, I cut bangs to hang across my forehead and cover my facial tattoos. I dressed in my jeans and a t-shirt, carrying Marc's well-wrapped family heirloom and letters, my wallet, and with a bit of money in my pocket, I returned to the time my people call 'Beyond.' I hiked to the trailhead, where I phoned Dan from the ranger's station. My brother hustled to the trailhead to fetch me. A few days later, I met with Fancy, Rick, and of course, the proverbial Son of Satan himself, Kirk O'Malley, who seemed to be fitting in remarkably well.

Wolf was right. Time does not always run in straight lines. While I was away, in what I call the Before, eighteen months passed there. It shocked me to realize I was gone from Beyond for eight long years.

Chapter 9
Fancy - Beyond

The first thing Bay did when she got back was give me the 'blasted harp,' as she called it.

"Oh, my God, Bay, this was my Gramma Meara's harp." I ran my hands over the exquisite carvings with reverence.

Bay frowned. "Why on earth is this harp so damned special that I had to bring the blasted thing to you?"

"This little harp passed down from my great-grandfather, Hewlett McCarron, the original owner, who built it in 1700. Originally, each clan had its own harper, or bard, who held a position of high esteem. This harp was intended to be the McCarron clan harp. She's crafted of ash wood and decorated with Celtic artwork. I did a little research about these old harps after I was catapulted through time here years ago. Not many of these ancient harps survived until today. By the late 1700s, the British outlawed the *clarsach*, which the Irish word for a small harp. They confiscated and destroyed many of them. It was one more way to break the clans of Ireland, to break the Irish spirit."

Baylie looked surprised. "Marc said something like that. He said it was one more way to force assimilation, just like the settlers were doing to my people then as well."

I nodded. "Exactly. I guess that is why the Scots and Irish, with their history of clans, and strong, independent natures, blended so well with the Native Americans. Hmm. Anyway, it's a miracle this one survived, especially in such pristine condition. Other old harps that survived are often black with grime, from exposure to peat smoke, or they have been damaged and are no longer playable. In contrast, the Queene here is still beautiful."

"It's gorgeous. The top piece looks like it was designed to represent some sort of animal. What is it?" Richard reached out to touch the carving.

"I asked my Grandfather that same question when we were in Ireland. He said, 'ah, faith, darling girl, she's a dragon lady, our wee Queene is.' He told me that in the Gaelic, the *clarsach* is a feminine word. French and Spanish cast gender upon objects, too. *La puerta. Los muebles. La casa. La table. Un voiture. La petite. Le coeur. El corazon.* Like that."

"The Cherokee language assigns gender to words as well," said Baylie, with a look of surprise.

"Oh, really? Interesting. The top part where she is carved is called the harmonic curve or the neck. Our Queene is engraved with a design that is traditionally recognized in Celtic art as a dragon. You can see the undulation of the dragon carved into her back in the harmonic curve. It would tell an art historian that this is a 'dragon lady of a harp.' The words stenciled down the side of the soundbox pronounce in Gaelic she is the 'Queene of the Harps.' I remember Tamsin used to play her. This instrument has a rich, otherworldly sound like no other harp I ever heard. Oh, yes, our little dragon lady is a queen. At least, that's what my Grandfather told me." I suddenly felt embarrassed to have been chattering on and on about the harp.

"My God, is that the Queene of the Harps?" asked Kirk as he entered the room. "I remember Micah showing us this harp."

Richard looked surprised. "You remember the harp?"

Kirk nodded. "Aye. Tammy used to play it sometimes. It would make old Micah weep with precious memories of his late wife playing it. There was some story about one of the old Irish harpers and this instrument."

I nodded. "Grandfather claimed an old blind harper made his living traveling about singing and harping. He said the man became pretty well known for the tributes he would draft for his hosts. According to Grandfather, the harper went to the McCarron place, and stayed there a fortnight, during which he wrote my ancestor a tribute called 'Hewlett.'"

About then, Bella spoke up. She pulled a book of sheet music over and opened it to a piece she had been practicing on the piano. "Mom, was this blind harper named Turlough O'Carolan?"

I nodded. "Yes, I think that's the name. Why?"

She ran her hands over the harmonic curve of the harp with reverential respect. "Oh, my God, Mom, O'Carolan was the greatest Irish harper who ever lived. And you said O'Carolan wrote 'Hewlett' for my great-great-grandfather?"

I nodded again. "Yes. And in fact, family history says he played the tune the first time it was played on this little harp in the manorial home of Gramma Meara on the Isle of Skye."

Richard let out a low whistle. "Wow. So how did it get the name, 'Queene of the Harps'?"

"Grandfather claimed when O'Carolan played her, he exclaimed, 'Faith, she has a voice like an angel. She must be the Queene of all the Harps!' With promo like that, the name stuck. Hewlett McCarron had the name inscribed on the soundbox. My Grandmother took it with her to England in 1722. Later, she met and married Grandfather, and the *clarsach* went to Ireland when Micah took Meara to Waterside. Hmm. I wonder if O'Carolan ever visited them at Waterside? In 1781, my Grandfather told me the harp was valuable. I can't imagine the worth of this little treasure today."

Bella looked up from her examination of the harp. "May I play it, Mom?"

"Of course, but you should tune it first."

Bella quickly tuned the old harp, and then pulled it to her shoulder. "I never tried to play a wire-strung instrument before," she said with a nervous laugh.

"You will probably like it since you play a wire strung harp with your nails rather than the pads of your fingers," I answered.

She grinned as she nodded, and then flexed her hands as she put them into position. "Thumbs up, fingers curved."

She played Hewlett in honor of her great-great-grandfather and then moved on to several other Irish and Scottish tunes she knew by heart. As she finished, we all clapped.

"O'Carolan was right. She *is* the Queene of the Harps," Bella said with reverence.

"Oh, I almost forgot. Marc sent this packet of letters as well." Baylie handed the thick packet to me.

I carefully opened it. My heart leaped as I saw the letters from Lily and my Daddy. I clasped them close to my heart and stood up as tears welled in my eyes. "I think I'll just go to my room now and read my letters if you guys don't mind."

"Not at all. I need to talk to O'Malley," said Baylie with a tight smile.

I settled onto the couch in the sitting area of our bedroom as I started reading the letters. I debated whether to stretch the packet out for days, using every ounce of self-discipline I possessed, or to indulge myself and read through everything right then. Finally, with a shrug and feeling a bit bittersweet, I began to read. What did Sassy say? Oh, yes. *Que sera, sera.* Whatever would be, would be.

I started with Lily's letter. She told me they would soon be traveling to Belle Rose before they headed on to Waterside. Marc was ready to return to Ireland at long last. She admitted she felt unsure if he would be able to fit into Irish high society life, but he wanted to try. She caught me up to date on everything at the Corner and in the village. "Bay is so sad. They all condemn her for Kirk going forward in time. I hope he has not caused too much chaos for you guys. Bay is heartbroken over Wolf's reaction to Kirk coming through the portal. They were supposed to marry before this happened. The damned fool man thinks Kirk is the Son of *Tsul Kalu*, who legend says was the slant-eyed, white giant. You have to admit he fits the part. I shit you not. Send them both back as soon as possible. The tribe thinks Kirk is messing with the whole time-space consortium and will create nothing but havoc and chaos there."

I would be more than thrilled to send Kirk back in time, but I had no idea how I was supposed to send Kirk or Baylie back. I shrugged and started to pick up the next letter when I heard a caterwauling in the living room. I frowned as I sat down my packet and strode into the other room.

"What the blazes is going on?" I scowled at Bay and Kirk, who both quit yelling mid-sentence as I walked in.

"This bitch called me the devil's spawn," Kirk roared.

Bay threw her hands up in the air in frustration. "Walk like a duck, talk like a duck, and people think you're a duck. Fine. I'm out of here. Call me. Maybe *we* can have lunch. Without *him*." She looked back at Kirk and waved her index finger at his face. "You have ruined everything. Do you hear me, O'Malley? Everything. Because of you, I lost the man I love."

"I can't imagine how that must hurt," he spat back.

Zing. I flinched at the scorn in his voice as well as in his words.

Bay never slowed down. "And to think I saved you because you loved Fancy. Boy, did I blow that one. You will never know how bitterly I regret I saved your stupid ass that day."

And with that, she wheeled around and stormed out of the house.

I gave Kirk a pointed look. "Care to explain? I swear, I never saw anyone except her ex-husband infuriate her like that. What did you do?"

"Why do you assume the argument was my fault, over something I did? Jesus. Women. You're all alike."

"How's that?" I asked.

"You're all fecking crazy," he muttered.

"You picked me. Oh, let me correct that: you bought me, if memory serves me correctly," I snapped. "No one forced your hand."

He stopped and stared at me in shocked disbelief. "Forced my hand? Is that what ye think I did? Is that what ye think of me?"

I cringed. His voice was hoarse as if he were in pain. Anguish was written all across his damnably handsome face. I forced myself to shrug and tossed my highlighted tresses back over my shoulder. "Isn't that what happened? What else am I to think? You forced me into indentured servitude after you bought me from Tarleton. I was a free woman when he kidnaped and sold me to you. No one forced you to buy me. You chose to buy me. I told you repeatedly the shipping line would reimburse you the cost. You refused it.

"In contrast, you and I both know I had no choice but to sign those Articles of Indenture. When I did, I was your bondswoman for three years unless I married you. And we both know I married you so my Dara would *not* be born a slave for life."

As the twinkle faded from his eyes, I felt guilty. I knew he loved me. I didn't have to be so blunt, but he needed to realize he forced my hand back then. Now? He needed to know I was happy here. I intended to remain here with my husband, Richard.

Kirk's face fell as his shoulders slumped. He rubbed a hand across his forehead before he turned to walk out of the room, shaking his head and mumbling something in Irish I could not make out. At the door, he turned back. "And the second time? In May of '83? Do ye think I somehow forced ye then as well?"

I shrugged as I bit my tongue. I could not bring myself to admit even in my anger, I married him the second time on the rebound after Richard left. I looked away, embarrassed and ashamed by my brash words. "The Cherokee think you're the Son of Satan, and you can make women desire you. Heck if I know."

He looked horrified. "That's what Guider said. You actually believe I could be the Son of Satan?"

I shrugged as I chewed a nail, but I said nothing.

He looked horror-stricken. "My God, Fancy."

I looked away from him as his voice broke, unable to look him in the eyes any longer. After he walked away, shoulders slumped, and his head hung low, I sighed as I shook my head. As my shoulders slumped, perhaps with more than a little shame, I turned and went back to my room.

Heck fire, maybe Kirk is right. Perhaps I am crazy. Why would I say that to him? I'm not usually a mean-spirited person. God knew I, sure enough, felt crazier by the minute with him around. I resisted the strong urge to run after him and apologize for my hurtful words. I knew full well that would take me someplace I did not intend to ever go with him again. My wild Irish rogue, I used to call him. Oh yes, I remembered the nights of wild, passionate lovemaking we once shared, how he could arouse my passion with a look or the slightest touch. I felt my cheeks heat as the sensuous memories flooded my mind. Heck fire, maybe he *is* the Son of Satan.

After all, I met his mother.

. . .

"Hey, Pop! Kirk! Where are you going?" Elizabeth ran to catch up with the angry man as he strode away from the house.

"Walking," he said, his response short and concise. "Why? What difference does it make? You don't want me here, anyway."

He stopped when Elizabeth reached out to grab his hand. "What? Why do you say that?"

He snorted. "Girl, ye've made that clear to me more than once since I came. Everyone has. I'm going walking. I need to clear my head, do some thinking."

"About what? I never said I don't want you here. Why would you say that?" she asked, her voice tremulous, as tears began welling up in her eyes.

He blinked. "You called me a pervert. I swear, I thought Bella was Fancy. She looks so damned much like Fancy did, back then. And you have all made it pretty clear none of ye need me or want me here."

She shook her head. "I should never have said that. I was teasing you. Mom says I'm just like you, and I tease too hard. I didn't mean to hurt your feelings."

Kirk looked stunned as Elizabeth struggled to hold back the threatening tears. He patted her on the back, his touch awkward as if he was unsure what to do. "Ah, lass, don't cry for the sorry likes of me."

After all, your Mam thinks I'm the Son of Satan.

She threw her arms around his waist. "But … but you're my daddy. My real daddy. I thought you left us on purpose. I remember you both argued the day you left. Mom doesn't talk about you much anymore, but I remember how upset she was after the hurricane. It was tough for her to get us all off the island by herself. Then she found Papa with a broken leg, and the doctor wanted to saw it off. And when she heard the ship sank, and you were dead, she fainted, dead away. I swear, Kirk, she thought you were dead. We all did."

He looked surprised. "She fainted? Your mother?"

Elizabeth nodded. "I swear to God, yes, she did. She would say she didn't know why the damned fool man - that would be you - had to go off and get himself killed. She bought news sheets in every town, hoping somehow you survived. Gramma brought them with us when we all came to find Mom. She keeps them in a file in her desk. I remember every time she got a news sheet, she would cry all over again."

"I had no idea." Kirk slowly dropped his hands to her shoulders and pushed her back enough that he could peer down into her grey eyes, so much like his own. "You're not like me, *mo leannan*. You're like your Mam."

Elizabeth tried to laugh, but it came out more like a hiccup. "I'm nothing like Mom. I'm the odd one. I don't look like the others. I... I... "

He pulled her back into his arms as his only child started crying again. "No. You're not like Fancy. I meant your real Mam. Anya was her name, and if there was any woman on earth more beautiful than Fancy or you, it was my Anya."

He bent and kissed her head and then pulled a clean handkerchief out of his pocket and handed it to her. She wiped her face and blew her nose before responding. "Really?"

He nodded. "Aye, really. I loved Fancy. Hell, I still do even though she has moved on. But Anya was the great love of my life. She was a beautiful woman. She was tall, with a voluptuous figure. She had dark brown curly hair, like yours, and an indomitable spirit."

Elizabeth stared at him as if not quite believing him.

"What? You don't believe me?" he asked, and then he ruffled her hair.

She looked around, furtive before she answered. "Mom says Anya was a slave at your plantation. You know, back then. Before."

Kirk could feel the color drain from his face. "Aye, she was. I intended to take her to Ireland. I could free her there, and we could have wed. But she wanted to give birth to you on Barbados with her own Mam nearby. Naught I said would dissuade her of the notion. I offered to take her Mam with us. Tis one of the reasons why I said you are so much like her. She was stubborn to a fault."

Elizabeth gulped. "I ... I didn't know that."

"Tis my greatest regret. Perhaps if I insisted, we go on to Ireland, she might have lived..." His voice broke. "T'was difficult, nay, impossible to secure a decent physician willing to treat a slave in labor. But at least *you* lived. I took you to Ireland, where you could be free. I felt bad to take you from your grandmother in Barbados, but…"

"But what, Poppa?" Elizabeth asked.

She called me Poppa, he thought in amazement. *Like she did when she was little.* He patted her hand and struggled to smile for his beautiful daughter, who had so long been missing from his life. "She was only eighteen when she died."

Elizabeth looked horrified. "My God, she was Bella's age. She was just a kid."

He shook his head. "Not in that day and age. She was a woman, full-grown, when she came to me the first time at fifteen. Many girls her age were betrothed or wed by that age. It was the way of the world. So, when she died, I took you to Ireland, where I thought my own Mam would take good care of you. I was horrified when we went for you, and you were filthy, covered in lice. I couldn't believe it when I heard my mother speak of you, her grandchild, in such hateful terms. It nigh broke my heart. Thank God, Fancy agreed to adopt you. We brought you home with us that same day."

"I remember Mom gave me candy. I never had any before that day. I was always cold and hungry there. I hated being with those people. None of them wanted me there. They made it clear I was a burden on them. That's tough for a little kid to understand." Her voice was low but firm.

Kirk flinched at the underlying pain in her voice. "I know. I realized years ago I was wrong to take you from your grandmother, Dolly. She bitterly missed you. She never once complained, but I could see her grief in her face, in her bearing. But if I kept you there, you would have been a slave. The law in Barbados was clear. No person with even a drop of colored blood can be freed on that Isle, nor can they marry a white. I could never free you there. I had to take you away. Freedom was the one thing I failed to give your mother. I would not deprive my Anya's babe of it. I was determined to give it to you. My child would not live one day longer as a slave than necessary before I could get you safe away and ensure your freedom."

Elizabeth looked shocked at his words. "But Mom is mixed. I thought you two married in Barbados."

He nodded. "Aye, naught but Fancy and I knew she was mixed. No one thought she might be mixed with her auburn tresses, aqua eyes, and fair complexion."

Elizabeth nodded. "In contrast, my skin has more color, and my hair has what Mama calls an 'ethnic texture.'"

"Aye, love, but you're still a rare beauty. You have an exotic look you inherited from Anya, with your almond-shaped eyes and beautiful cheekbones. You could be, what do they call it here? A model? An actress? Your looks would gain you jobs."

The faintest glimmer of a smile began to flit across her face. "I want to be a dancer. I'm going to Juilliard after I finish high school to continue to train as a dancer. Mama and Dad wouldn't let me go sooner. The school wanted me to come next fall. But you're wrong. I get my almond-shaped eyes from you. Mom says, my eyes are just like yours."

His heart lurched at her words. Was the Cherokee right? Was he the son of the slant-eyed, white giant?

"Mayhap they will reconsider since they are moving to Texas. You should ask."

Her eyes alit with unexpected warmth. "Do you think so? Bella said the same thing. I was going to stay here to finish high school. Hmm. I wonder if they would let me."

"There is only one way to find out, lass. Ask them. Perhaps we could all visit the school, and you could see if you feel ready to tackle it yet. Tis an enormous step. Now, to finish answering your question. Fancy was married to Sir Calvin before me. She was a Countess as well as a Duchess when she came to Barbados. No one questioned her right to marry me."

"But wasn't she a slave there?" Elizabeth asked, her voice shaky with emotion.

Kirk looked shocked. "Nay, she was indentured. There's a world of difference. She was my bondswoman. She was *not* chattel for life."

Elizabeth frowned. "I understand the difference, but wasn't she pretty much like a slave while she was indentured? I mean, couldn't you sell her if you wanted to?"

Kirk was appalled. They had reached the end of the lane and were by a little pond. He led Elizabeth over to a bench by the pond, where they both sat down. "Yes, I could have sold her, but I would no more have sold Fancy or Anya than I would sell my soul, child. I loved both of them. It would have been like selling my own heart. Christ Jesus, girl, do you think so poorly of me?"

Elizabeth flinched as his voice broke. She struggled to choose her words carefully before she spoke again. "No. I just don't understand that world. It's like when you called Hannah that awful word, and then called her a 'darky.' I never heard anyone even use the name 'darky' to describe another person before. I know I'm a person of color, but I would be distraught if anyone called me that 'n' word or 'darky.' That's just rude."

Kirk's face flushed with shame. "Ah, lass, I never meant to shame poor Hannah or ye. I reckon I should have said she is colored. And again, no one in Barbados ever suspected my Fancy was a colored woman."

Elizabeth winced at his use of the archaic term. Today, people said "POC," or "person of color," if any reference was made to color. She knew he was trying to be polite – they called it 'politically correct' at school – but he had a long way to go on the learning curve. And, she had to admit the whole discussion was difficult for her. She could vaguely remember people who were slaves from her early childhood. The children had been well versed against talking about their earlier life in the eighteenth century with most people in the twenty-first century. Now, that part of her life seemed like a dream from long ago. It no longer seemed real to her.

Elizabeth sighed. She knew racism still existed in the country. She heard about it every day in the news, at school, in the papers, even on social media. At times, she tried to talk to Fancy about the racism still existing in the United States. Fancy would tell her people today had no real idea what racial prejudice was. It always made her angry when Mom said that. Elizabeth knew her mom was wrong. The people at school were pretty cool, but she had even observed racism there. Last month, the new boy from Alabama called her friend, Grace, that 'n' word. It made Grace cry. They never told Mom or Dad, but Charlie beat the boy up after school. He told him people shouldn't denigrate other people over the color of their skin, no matter if they are black, white, or red with yellow stripes.

Dad - Rick - would talk to her about racism still existing in America more than Mom would. He told her how hard it was for his mother to cope with being biracial as a child and as an adult. Liz could understand, although she realized her path would be easier today than when his mother was growing up. Elizabeth did not intend to fall prey to drugs, as Katherine Winslow did.

Yes, she thought, racism still existed, even though it was not the same as way back when Kirk and Mom first walked the earth. Slavery ended long ago, but from its ashes arose the Klan and Jim Crow laws. Black kids still often couldn't go to the good schools, which were usually built in wealthier, white neighborhoods. Blacks were given the right to vote after the Civil War, but with the rise of the Klan and Jim Crow laws, many blacks couldn't vote for years after slavery ended. They couldn't sit where they wanted on buses or in restaurants until after Rosa Parks. They even had to use separate restrooms and water fountains. Gramma O told her about getting spanked for drinking from a 'whites-only' water fountain when she was little. She told how blacks used to have to buy food from restaurants at the kitchen door, and eat outside or take the food with them. She told Elizabeth about all of those things, and explained those were dehumanizing treatment intended to keep blacks and persons of color 'in their place.' Elizabeth knew it took another hundred years after slavery ended for blacks to gain the vote, for schools to be desegregated, to be able to sit where they wanted on buses and in restaurants, and for the Civil Rights Act of 1964 to be passed.

Gramma O also told her how hard it was as a black woman to marry a white man in the south back in the '60s when she married Ronan Roberts. It was still illegal in many places for blacks to marry whites then, just like Kirk was saying about Barbados. That was why Gramma O and Grampa Ronan moved to Boston. It was a more diverse town and more accepting of their mixed marriage than Atlanta would have been at that time. And of course, Rick's mom met his dad at Harvard in Boston, where Katherine was able to attend on a scholarship under the Affirmative Action program.

"I guess if you get right down to it, Mom is a woman of color, even though she looks white," Elizabeth mused.

Kirk nodded. "Aye. I reckon all the Winslow family are, as Fancy and Rick reminded me. I'm sorry I'm a relic of an earlier era. What is it you called me? Ah, yes, a dinosaur. One of those big lizards that all died out long ago. I'm sorry I say things that come across as thoughtless. I…"

His voice broke again. Elizabeth's heart lurched as tears welled in his eyes. She reached a tentative hand over to pat her father's back. She reached over and put an arm around his shoulders. "It's okay, Poppa."

He shook his head. "Nay, lass. I'm not sure if it will ever be okay again."

She took a big breath and patted him on the back. "Mom says we are all at least a little broken. She says a famous writer named Ernest Hemingway wrote, 'the world breaks everyone, and then some become strong at the broken pieces.'"

He jerked his head up at her words. "Fancy told you that?"

Elizabeth nodded. "She tells us that all the time. She's pretty smart, you know. She says the Japanese repair things with a process they call Kintsugi. They repair broken pottery with a strong adhesive and sprinkle it with gold dust. The repaired piece is stronger, more beautiful, and more interesting for having been broken and repaired. Daddy says people are a lot like those Japanese vases. He says we can all become stronger, more beautiful, and more interesting when we become repaired after we are broken. Instead of trying to hide our flaws and cracks, we should all accentuate and celebrate as our flaws are mended and become the strongest part of us."

Kirk looked stunned. "Really? Richard said that?"

Elizabeth nodded, her excitement growing as she shared the concept with Kirk. "He really did. Mom says mosaics are made from broken pieces, but they fit together to create beautiful works of art. She says we are all works of art created from broken pieces. It's even in her books—"

She broke off, shocked as she realized she had opened a can of worms which probably should never have been opened.

Kirk tilted his head at her. "Books? You mean her school books?"

She gulped. "Uh, yeah, her school books. I think she must have read about it in college."

Good lord, Elizabeth thought, what would Pops think if he got hold of a copy of *Diary of the Reluctant Duchess*? It didn't paint Kirk in the kindest light. He came across like a sexual predator in Mom's book, which was the real reason Liz called him a pervert when they first met him at the Beech Bottom trailhead when he was dressed in that ridiculous loincloth thing. Mama was kinder in her words about him in *My Wee Duchess*, her second book, but Elizabeth thought it still painted him as a not-so-very-nice person who took advantage of vulnerable women. For heaven's sake, he *bought* Mom! Both of the books she wrote were on the bookcase in the house. How would Kirk react if he read them? Mom said he had a bad temper 'back in the day.' Elizabeth hadn't seen it since he came here, but she remembered the fights they used to have. She worried about the volcanic eruption of anger to come if he realized what Mom wrote about him, in not just one, but two books about her life Before.

They sat and talked for hours. Elizabeth told Kirk about the difficulties she had as a child when they first came here from Before. He laughed as she told how she got in trouble once for telling schoolmates that her Mommy used to know George Washington. Mom quickly diffused that one, explaining to her teacher that she and Dad used to participate in re-enactments at Williamsburg and Mount Vernon. She told the teacher Elizabeth probably remembered meeting an actor who played the role of our first President. Later, Mom stressed she should never tell they came from Before because people would think they were lying or crazy.

"I tried to argue with her, but you know that will get you nowhere fast. She insists we shouldn't lie, but she also says we cannot tell where we came from. Still, I know Aunt Dee and Uncle Dan know. So do Uncle Jim and Aunt Sue. Aunt Bay knows, too."

"Why do you call her Aunt Bay? She's not kin," Kirk asked.

Elizabeth shrugged. "We always called Dee and Dan 'Aunt' and 'Uncle.' Of course, Dad – I mean Richard – works with Dan. It always seemed like a polite thing to call them Aunt and Uncle. Mom says it's a Southern thing. And of course, Bay is Dan's sister, and she's Baylie's Aunt. I guess it was just kind of natural ..."

Her voice faded off.

Kirk's heart lurched. "I didn't mean anything negative by it. I was just curious. It's good to have people around to whom you feel close. Bay seems a bit odd, but Dan and Dee seem nice enough."

Elizabeth laughed. "You got off on the wrong foot with her. Were you really her slave? What was that like?"

Kirk stood up, shook his head, and cleared his throat. "I don't think you're old enough to hear about such things, lass. It's getting late. We had best head back to the house, or your Mam will be angry with me. Again."

Elizabeth nodded. "You're probably right, but remember: her bark is worse than her bite."

He grinned. "With you, perhaps, lass. As I recall, she can get pretty angry with me at times."

They walked back to the house in comfortable silence. Neither had realized they had walked nearly five miles earlier. Elizabeth felt worried as they entered the house. They had been gone for hours, and she forgot to take her phone when she ran after Kirk. Mom would be dishing out a good tongue lashing tonight.

Mom and Bella appeared to be deep into a conversation when Kirk and Elizabeth walked in. Mama stopped mid-sentence, looked up at them, and frowned. "Where have you been? You missed dinner, and you didn't answer your phone."

Elizabeth felt her face redden. As she started to stammer, Kirk interrupted her.

"You've raised quite a girl here, Fancy. When I took off after Bay left, Elizabeth realized I was upset and came after me. We walked for miles before we sat down by a pond and talked. I don't think either of us was aware it grew so late until we started back. Elizabeth was going to call you then, but she realized she left her phone here. I'm sorry I kept her out so late."

Mama blinked a couple of times before she nodded. "Okay. Next time, tell me what's going on. I was afraid you two headed to the Corner to go back in time."

She tried to laugh. Elizabeth rushed over to her to hug Mama. "I would never just take off like that. I'm sorry."

"For God's sake, Fancy, use your common sense. Surely you knew we wouldn't just take off," Kirk fumed.

"Well, you know what Mom always says," Bella said.

Kirk's head snapped towards her. "No, what does she say?"

"If common sense were lard, most people wouldn't be able to grease a pan."

Kirk started laughing. Fancy cut her eyes at him in a warning Kirk well remembered from the past, which only made him laugh harder.

Richard walked into the room with a quizzical look. "What's up?"

Kirk was laughing so hard he couldn't speak.

Fancy glowered at him. "Oh, shut up." She looked over at Richard. "And don't you start. Not right now."

Richard stared at her for a minute before he shrugged. "Whatever, sweetie."

Kirk began laughing all over again. Richard stood with his mouth gaping open, his head tilted as he tried to comprehend the situation, and he blinked repeatedly. Kirk thought Richard looked for all the world like his poor brain could not comprehend the magnitude of Fancy's anger. What did Johnny call that? It wasn't confounded. Ah, yes. "Richard, ye look as though yer tardfounded by all this."

Fancy let out a little screech as she threw a shoe at Kirk's head. "Watch your language!"

He managed to duck as the shoe sailed past his head. "Ah, darlin', you still need to learn to control that temper."

"Eff you, O'Malley," she snapped.

He raised an eyebrow at her as his grin grew wolfish. "Gladly, *mo leannan*. It would be my pleasure. Just say when and where."

Richard's eyes grew wide as Fancy threw the second shoe at Kirk. "Oh, bad move, O'Malley."

As the shoe hit its mark, Kirk let out a yelp.

"You go eff yourself, asshole," Fancy said through gritted teeth as she clinched and unclenched her hands into fists while she ground her teeth.

Kirk stood rubbing his head where the shoe had struck. "And to think you used to say I had a bad temper. Where did a nice girl like you learn language like that, Fancy?"

"Ooh! Men!" She turned and stormed out of the room.

He looked at Richard. "Ye could have warned me about the second shoe."

Richard shrugged. "Hey, like my Mom always said about dog shows: 'you pay your money, you take your chances.' If you make that woman mad enough to throw the first shoe, you are taking your chances. She picks up the second shoe and aims it at you, and chances are you are gonna get hit. Dad and I knew decades ago to duck if a woman grabbed the second shoe. I'm surprised you didn't already know that."

Richard was laughing as he left the room.

Chapter 10
Fancy - Beyond

I took a deep breath. I would deal with the incorrigible 'Son of Satan' later. I decided it was time to read Marc's letter.

Marc wrote quite a bit about the fact he was the one who killed the Chickamauga warrior who tried to kidnap me years ago. He told us that when he was here before, but he was especially remorseful in the letter. He felt they needed to leave McCarron's Corner to avoid further trouble between the Cohutta tribe and the Chickamaugas. I figured that must be about to kill him. He loved the Cohutta Wilderness with an endless passion. He wrote about the murder of the Cohutta Eagle warrior, the tribal outrage when the warrior's body was found, the subsequent declaration of war against the Chickamauga, the battle, the resulting capture of the Chickamauga prisoners, and how Kirk came to be Bay's slave. I laughed at the idea of proud Kirk O'Malley enslaved by the Cherokees until I read what the women did to him. It horrified me to learn how the women sexually assaulted him while bound and helpless. Heck fire, it sounded mighty close to rape to me, in fact, far too close for comfort. I chastised Kirk for keeping me as his sex slave, and now I learned the Cherokee women did the same thing to him. I could well imagine the degradation and shame a proud man of the 18th century like Kirk felt to be sexually exploited in that manner.

I felt like I was there with them as I read how it all happened. I long ago realized while Marc would rather not talk, he loves to write. He is a true wordsmith. I suspect he could have been a great writer if he had been so inclined. I like to think I get my storytelling ability from him. I felt like I was there with them during that fateful battle. While I was thrilled Baylie rescued Kirk from the Chickamauga, like Marc, I was more than a little surprised she did. To be blunt, white men do not hold a warm and fuzzy place in her heart. Hmm. Why did she rescue Kirk?

And then, my eyes widened with surprise as the last packet fell into my hands. I opened the old journal, and my heart leaped. It was the diary of my grandmother, Meara McCarron, beginning when she was eighteen years old. Inside the cover was a note from Lily explaining they thought I might make good use of the journal and write another novel based on the story of Meara and Micah. And then, suddenly, I was not worrying about Kirk O'Malley or Baylie Smith anymore. I was lost in the story of how Meara met Micah.

June 3, 1721. I can barely contain my excitement! For the past months, I have hoped against hope that Da would relent and allow me to go to court. I was fair sure he would never let me near London after the Jacobite Rising of 1719, especially considering the capture of the Eilean Donan Castle by Captain Boyle of Worcester. Da was well-advised not to participate in that ill-fated fiasco, which fair ruined the Jacobite attempts. Apparently, he had a change of heart now, and he decided he will allow me to go.

Da told me this morning that my mother's brother, Seamus Tolbert, will escort me to London in four short weeks on his ship, the Sea Sprite. I have much to do to be prepared to go by then. I will stay with Aunt Sylvia and him at their residence in Hampstead until I am accepted officially as a lady in waiting by good Queene Caroline. Da already warned me Aunt Sylvia's sister-in-law, the Honorable Jacqueline Innes, usually called Jacqui by friends and family, will be trying her best to marry me off to an Englishman. She'll have no luck at that ploy. I'll not have an Englishman to wed and bed. Hopefully, Aunt Sylvia will know a nice Scot or two. Even one of those wild Irishmen would be better than a stuffy English stick.

Mam is a bit aggravated with Da and keeps saying he should have had some consideration for her in all this. We will have to work our fingers to the bones night and day to prepare my clothing for the trip. We are cutting down three of Mam's pretty silk court mantua gowns for me. They should do quite nicely, even for make-overs. We have four day gowns in the process as well, two make-overs, and two brand new. Both of the new ones should be quite fetching. We are making a new mantua of blue watered silk with a floral tapestry underskirt and stomacher. I always love a pretty blue gown. We are also making a beautiful green mantua. Mam says it will look stunning with my red hair and green eyes. I should be quite elegant for a country lass from the Isle of Skye in the wild Scottish Highlands when I arrive in London.

Of course, Mam says I may buy new gowns when I arrive in London, but I know money is tight, and I fear there is not much money to waste on fripperies for me at Court. I will save my shopping budget for special events. Mam promised she would send me with several more mantuas to remake once I arrive there. I'm hoping we can manage to update a few more of my gowns, which still fit for everyday wear. We figure six to eight day gowns, and the court mantuas should do for a start.

Mam is sure I'll meet a man I will love as much as she loves Da. I laugh and tell her that it isn't possible. How could I possibly fall in love with an Englishman? But, in any event, I'm going to London!

I laughed at Meara's youthful exuberance as she prepared for her first solo foreign trip. At eighteen, I made a trip, too, from Belle Rose to McCarron's Corner in Indian Territory with my infant daughter. I went with great trepidation and more than a little fear of the unknown. Thank God I had Will to take me there, and Marc and Lily to help me. Thank God Sassy took me in, and we became fast friends. My heart ached with old longings to see my family again. And then, I grew quiet as I remembered my first trip solo, twelve years ago, when I left Bermuda with my children to head out in search of Daddy and Lily after the Dreadful Hurricane.

That was when I learned Kirk and his crew died in the hurricane.

I put the journal and the harp aside and helped Bella transcribe music for a couple of hours. She loves to find old music manuscripts to transcribe for the piano. She plans to study musicology at Trinity. We were surprised she did not take the scholarship offered to Juilliard. She insists she wants to study the history of music, and she claims that she lacks sufficient talent ever to be a successful concert pianist. We think she is wrong, but it is her choice and her life.

She recently found some old music for sale on Amazon and wanted to transcribe it for piano. I transcribed an ancient plainsong chant. I find the work challenging but tedious. As I tired, I pushed the old music aside, picked up the diary again, and settled back down onto the couch in the sitting room to resume reading.

June 8, 1721. The most wondrous thing has happened. Old Master O'Carolan showed up today. M'God, he's older than Da. He must be 50 if he's a day! He had not visited McCarron Manor in recent years, not since I was a wee child. Today he arrived only weeks before I am due to leave.

Da surprised me this evening when he asked me to play his Queene for Master O'Carolan. It's quite intimidating to play for the man known far and wide as the most celebrated harper in all the world. I realize there may be excellent harpists in Europe who play those big, gut-strung, pedal harps which are all the fashion on the Continent now, but no one plays the wire-strung *clarsach* like Master O'Carolan. Afterward, Da announced he intends for me to take the Queene with me to London. His announcement stunned me speechless.

Then I received an even greater surprise. Master O'Carolan announced he composed a new tune for me. He will teach it to me before I leave.

I tried to explain it can take me weeks to learn a new song from the beginning to the end. Master O'Carolan laughed and said, "You will do fine, Meara lass, you will do fine. Trust me."

I'm not a Master on the harp as he is. I'm a young woman headed to London. I am not quick at music. May the Good Lord guide my fingers and help me memorize the notes.

I was most considerably relieved when his assistant, young Master Will Canolan, came to me later to assure me he would write out the melody line for me. I pray he will do that before I leave. I can add the harmonization on my own if I have the melody line scripted out for me. Hopefully, I can memorize how Master O'Carolan plays it and learn to do the same.

I was astonished. I knew O'Carolan wrote *Hewlett* for Meara's father, Hewlett McCarron, but I had no idea he ever returned to the manor house, much less that he wrote other tunes for family members. Here was an unexpected twist to the story I never anticipated. Did she win my Grandpa's heart with her music? I read on with eagerness.

June 9, 1721. My head is paining me something terrible. Master O'Carolan drilled me on the blasted song all day. Mam is fussing. We should be sewing, and we need to do dress fittings. Tis a lovely tune, but it is more challenging to learn than his usual tunes, mayhap because I usually know the tune when I sit down to learn it, and this one is brand new.

He calls the tune *Planxty for the Queene*. He refuses to specify whether it is for Queene Caroline or for the harp he dubbed the Queene years ago. He knows Da is allowing me to take the Queene with me on my journey. The harmonics in the piece are exquisite, but I fear I will not get it all written down the way he wants me to play it. What if I canna remember it all?

I began to read with avid interest. And then, as I turned the page, I thought my heart would burst from my chest. There, folded in two, was an old piece of music. I carefully unfolded it, and gasped as I read, *Planxty for the Queene*, by Turlough O'Carolan, and Transcribed by his Student, Will Canolan, 1721.

Fingers trembling, I ran to Bella. I grabbed her by the hand and dragged her back to my room to the old harp and the delicate sheet music. She gasped as she gently touched the old sheet music. She pulled the harp to her shoulder and worked her way through the tune.

"Mama, I swear this is a previously unknown O'Carolan Planxty. I never heard this before. It's gorgeous. I would remember it," Bella said in awe.

An hour later, Bella and I agreed Meara McCarron was correct. It was a beautiful piece with an ethereal, haunting melody. The harmonics were different from anything we previously heard by O'Carolan, but Bella remembered his pieces matured as he grew older. His later pieces were often intricate and complex. One might even say his later tunes sounded rococo, typical of the music of the era in which he wrote. We also suspected Will Canolan's hand was in the piece, in the rich harmonics, if nowhere else.

"You still sure you don't want to study music as your major?" I teased.

She looked uncertain. "This might motivate a change in my plans, although musicology is such a wonderful blend of music and history. I sure wish Grampa Owen was still alive. Where's a good historian when you need him?"

I laughed. "Just remember, if Owen were still alive, Sassy would never have gone back in time to marry Will. And I would never have met Richard."

"And we wouldn't be here now. Wow. Good points, Mom. Hopefully, my musicology major will combine my love of music with my love of history. You know you must write a book about Meara, Micah, and the harp."

I nodded. "I thought the same thing. *Conversations with Gramma O* comes out next week. My publisher is already after me to write something else. Pre-sales are out the roof, and Kirkus gave it a fabulous review."

"Kirkus always loves your books. I saw the review. Of course, it was well-deserved. *Planxty for the Queene* would be a killer title. The new house will be right by Trinity. You could research at the Chapman Library. It's on the edge of campus, just down the street from Suarez House. Or you could research in the Music Department." Bella squeezed my hand.

I nodded. "Or both. Hmm. Yes, this might be the next book. I had been thinking about writing about Elizabeth Selk and Thomas Ranscome."

"Another excellent idea, once this one is finished. And who knows? Maybe you will luck out and find Elizabeth's journal, too," said Bella.

I laughed. "That would be almost too much to even hope for, but it sure would be a fabulous find. So, what am I going to do about Kirk?"

"Beats me. I never dreamed he would like it here. I'm still concerned Daddy and he might kill each other. What was Daddy saying about inviting Kirk to Fight Club?"

I cringed. All I needed was the two of them at each other whole hog in a mixed martial arts fight. Kirk has Richard beat with muscle mass and length of limbs, but Richard is a damned good mixed martial arts fighter. He slacked off it for a while, due to time constraints, but the stresses of the last six months sent him back. He swears it is great at burning calories, cardio conditioning (always a big deal to a cardiovascular surgeon), and it is the best stress relief he ever found. He lost most of the weight he gained after we learned about Sara by going to Fight Club three times a week. It was hard for me to say whether Kirk or Richard would win that one. "Yeah, it wouldn't be pretty, but Richard does know various fighting techniques. He can kick some ass with that Muay Thai and Krav Maga stuff, whatever those are."

"Muay Thai is Thai-styled fighting while Krav Maga is Israeli kickboxing. Muay Thai focuses on hard kicks and superlative upper body strength. Krav is a combination of styles developed for the Israeli Defense Forces and Israeli security forces. It's derived from a combination of techniques from boxing, wrestling, aikido, judo, and karate, along with realistic fight training. At least, that's what Daddy says. And don't forget Daddy won that regional MMA competition last month. He may not be as big or as bulked up as Kirk, but he damned sure knows how to kickbox."

I nodded. "That's what Daddy says. My land, girl, you could write ads for the Fight Club!"

She winked at me, and then we both laughed.

My Richard runs ten miles a day and has kick-ass, strong, quad muscles. He has knocked more than one guy out with blows to the jaw from those powerful legs. I would hate to have him put me in a clinch hold in a real fight. I've seen him in action at Fight Club. It's tough enough when he is horsing around at the house, and he puts me in a clinch hold. I decided it was time to change the subject. "So how are Liz and Kirk getting along? Is she still calling him Conan? Oh, no, I forgot. The latest is Macho Man, right?"

Bella laughed. "No, that's what I call him. Liz is not acting so mean to Kirk anymore. She seems to be enjoying his stories about Ireland and Barbados. She seems to be enjoying all of his stories about the past."

"I didn't realize he had been telling those stories."

She nodded. "Yes, in fact, I heard her call him Pops today."

I started laughing, as well. "Pops? I wish I could have seen his face over that. How did he react?"

"He grinned. I think he liked it," she replied.

"Hmm. I guess it's a far sight better than calling him Conan." I snickered, and then I grew somber as I remembered pointing out to Kirk, he bought me from Tarleton long ago in Baltimore. It was true, but I knew it was hurtful to remind him that our 'relationship' began with me indentured against my will to be his sex slave.

Why did I feel a need to hurt him? I am not usually mean spirited. I sighed and shook my head. *Dammit, Fancy, what was it Sassy always told Richard? Oh, yes. How could I have forgotten?*

Don't make permanent decisions based on temporary feelings.

Chapter 11
Baylie - Now

I took a big breath and squared my shoulders before I pushed the door open. "Hi, I'm Baylie Smith. I have an appointment with Dr. McClintock. Mrs. Winslow recommended her."

"Of course, Mrs. Smith. Let me show you to the examining room. The doctor will be right with you. Did you bring the urine specimen?"

I laughed, awkward, and self-conscious. "Oh, yes. How could I have forgotten to hand you this? But it's Miss Smith. I'm not married."

The young nurse was calm and polite in her response. "Of course, Miss Smith. Now, I'll go run the test, and then Dr. McClintock will be right in."

I gulped. "I'm pretty sure it's positive. I collected the urine first thing this morning. The home test was positive. In fact, all three of them were positive."

About fifteen minutes later, the young ob-gyn whizzed in. "Hello, I'm Dr. Kathleen McClintock. My friends call me Kate. It's a pleasure to meet you."

After the pelvic exam, Dr. McClintock nodded. "Looks like the home tests are correct. Today's urine test and my exam both confirm you are pregnant. My estimate is you are about ten weeks. First baby?"

"Yes. That's what I figured, too." I sat, chewing my lip. I was worried.

Dr. McClintock reached out to pat my hands. "Are you worried about this?"

I forced myself to focus on the pretty, young doctor. "Um... a little. I was married for fifteen years and no baby. Now, I've been with this man for a few months. I didn't think I could get pregnant, especially at my age."

My laugh sounded anything but funny.

"My dear, you are not too old to get pregnant. But you don't have to have this baby. Your body, your choice, you know that."

I felt shocked. "Oh, that's not my concern. But, I'm in my 40's. Am I too old?"

My voice broke as I struggled not to cry.

Dr. McClintock handed me a tissue. "Here. Blow. Everything will be okay. Well, being older puts you at higher risk for certain congenital disabilities."

"For Down syndrome." My voice was soft, but the tone did not disguise the horror in my voice.

"That is the most common defect. About one in every 600 births in this country has Down syndrome. Does that scare you?"

Unable to speak, I nodded my head as I dabbed the tissue at my eyes. "Damned eyes are leaking again."

Dr. McClintock gathered me into her arms for a hug. "Eyes do that in here sometimes. There are several tests we can run to see what we have here. I usually start with a simple blood test that measures two proteins in a mother's blood serum. We can also do a special ultrasound scan in the second trimester. It's called a nuchal translucency test. A second blood test is done then, also, to evaluate four other substances in the maternal serum. The combination of the first and second-trimester screening is called integrated or sequential screening. Integrated screening can detect 94-96% of babies with Down syndrome. It is considered the most accurate noninvasive screening available today. I would recommend we start with those first."

"I thought physicians usually perform an amniocentesis." I took a deep breath as I tried to calm down and regain my composure.

Dr. McClintock nodded. "The amniocentesis is an invasive diagnostic test. A needle is inserted into the uterus to withdraw a sample of amniotic fluid. The sample is used to check for chromosomal abnormalities. It's usually done in the fifteenth week of pregnancy, or about five weeks from now. I don't usually do that unless the other tests are positive. The amniocentesis is invasive and has been known to cause fetal injury and death."

Accuracy?" I whispered.

"Ninety-nine percent accurate. But again, I don't usually recommend it due to the dangers inherent in the test. Baylie, do you want this baby? I mean, if you don't, we don't have to jump through all these hoops."

I felt horrified. "No, of course, I want my baby. I'm just scared what kind of life it would have if it's a Down syndrome baby."

"DS babies used to have very short life spans. A sizable percentage are born with heart abnormalities. The advent of open-heart surgery helped lengthen the lifespan of many DS children. The average life span today for a Down syndrome child is 60 years."

I took a deep breath. "I didn't realize that. My brother is a cardiovascular surgeon."

She smiled. "Well, it sounds like that would not be a problem."

I nodded slowly. "I read a book years ago about a DS baby. Sh-she died."

"Angel Unaware? Yes, Dale Evans was an enormous blessing to the DS community. She humanized the children who had been stigmatized and often rejected and institutionalized before her book. Of course, poor little Robin died when she was so small from complications from mumps. Can you imagine a child dying from mumps in this day and age?"

"But, what quality of life *do* these children have today?" I blinked back tears as I struggled not to begin crying again.

Dr. McClintock stared at me for a minute before answering. "My dear, DS children are special. They are sweet, loving, and kind. They are often described as angels, just as Dale Evans called Robin her angel in disguise. But yes, many have cognitive defects, some mild and some more severe. It can be a challenge to raise a child with this condition. However, many DS children lead normal lives these days. They get married, drive cars, and hold jobs. Some go to college, but I will admit, many require a sheltered work environment. We hear of DS men and women accomplishing remarkable things. One young DS woman I know designs beautiful clothing and jewelry. Several are quite accomplished actors and models. I believe one DS man was nominated by the Academy Award for best actor a year or so ago."

I smiled at the doctor's words. "Really?"

She nodded. "Really. Now, I suggest we run the first two tests. If they look positive for DS, you can decide if you want the other blood testing and the amniocentesis." She frowned. "Have you talked to the father?"

I shook my head. "He's not in the picture."

Dr. McClintock frowned again. "I still urge you to talk to him. This is his baby, too. Tell him you are expecting. Unless, of course, you decide to terminate the pregnancy."

I struggled to hold back tears as I nodded. I couldn't explain that Wolf was hundreds of *years* in the past any more than I could tell that disabled babies in that culture were usually put out to die.

The practice made me sick to my stomach. When I first went back in time, I was impressed to see there were virtually no disabled children, until one day I found a baby left out to die in the forest. Horrified, I asked but one question: why? I was told it was easier that way.

I knew I would never forget the pathetic cries of that poor, dying baby the rest of my life.

I wasn't sure if I could go back again. I doubted that I would go back if my baby carried a genetic defect. I would never be able to leave my baby to die, abandoned, cold, and alone. It seemed the cruelest death imaginable.

But could I bear not to return to Wolf, even if my baby had Down syndrome?

Chapter 12
More Unexpected Surprises

"So, we will meet there at about 7, if that works for you." Stephan grinned as he patted Kirk on the back.

Melanie grabbed Kirk's arm. "Are you going out with Stephan?"

Kirk looked puzzled. "Aye. He asked me to go out for a couple of beers. He says it's an Irish bar in Blue Ridge. I want to see if it's authentic. Why?"

Melanie dimpled as she grinned up at Kirk. "Sara's going to be with Rick this weekend. How about I drop her off at their house and then tag along with you guys?"

He smiled down at her. "That's, um, what do they call it? A date?"

Mellie dimpled again. "Exactly. A date. To the Brian Boru."

His eyes lit up. "Ah, ye ken the place?"

Millie's eyes narrowed. "Ken the place? Oh, you mean, do I know it? Yes, Stephan has mentioned it before."

Dr. Stephan Holzmann grabbed a file from Mellie as he walked back into the office. "Are you coming, too, Melanie?"

She nodded. "Oh, believe me, I wouldn't miss it."

"*Bien*. Wear something sexy." He winked.

Melanie laughed as she shook her head. "Of course, Doc. Kirk, Stephan says to dress sexy."

Kirk gave her a blank look. "How do I dress sexy?"

"Dress like you always do. You always look sexy," said Stephan with a wink at Kirk.

"Wear your leather pants and Rick's leather jacket," Melanie suggested.

"Oui, with that black shirt and your boots." Stephan grinned. "You'll look like an Irish pirate."

Melanie laughed. "Hate to tell you this, but he *is* an Irish pirate, Doc."

"Even better, we take the Irish pirate to the Irish pub." He handed her another file, winked again, and walked into another examining room.

Three hours later, Melanie arrived at the Winslow house with Sara in tow. Kirk let out a low whistle when he opened the door. "I'm not sure I look sexy, but you most definitely do, Mellie, *mo ghràidh*."

She tilted her head at him. "*Mo ghràidh*? I never heard that before. What does it mean?"

He blushed. "Uh…"

"It means 'my darling," Fancy said as she entered the room. "My, my, you two look gorgeous. Hot date?"

"Dr. Holzmann asked Kirk to go to the Brian Boru tonight for a couple of beers. I invited myself along to go with the two big, handsome men." She grinned at Fancy.

Fancy giggled. "Stephan Holzmann asked Kirk to go to the Brian Boru? Oh, my God, I want to go, too. Well, you both look wonderful. I love the way your little black dress hugs your curves. You look perfect next to our big, handsome privateer. Have a great time."

Mellie laughed. "Oh, we will. I'm the designated driver. I'll try my best to keep the boys out of trouble."

"With those two? Good luck. Take lots of pictures!" Fancy shook her head as she struggled not to laugh. Kirk O'Malley at the Brian Boru? Who would have dreamed Stephan could get Kirk into the most infamous gay bar in North Georgia? What she wouldn't give to be a little fly on the wall tonight!

. . .

"You look gorgeous tonight, Mellie. And I'm delighted you offered to come along with us." Kirk suddenly felt as nervous as a schoolboy.

She smiled as she eased the sleek little red Sportster out to head north on 76 towards Blue Ridge. "Well, I about gave up on waiting for you to ask me out, so I decided I would invite myself to come along with you guys. But, Kirk—"

"Wait, you mean you *wanted* me to ask you out? I'll be honest, with all you ken about me from Fancy, I'm surprised you would give a bloke like me the time of day."

Mellie gave him a sharp look. "Why would you say a thing like that?"

He shrugged as he struggled to look as dashing and debonair as he wanted to appear to this beautiful woman. "Ah, well, ever since I found those blasted books on their bookshelf, I have to admit, Fancy's description of me, sure enough, rattled me."

My gosh, he's blushing, Mellie thought with a start. "Writing *Diary of the Reluctant Duchess* was cathartic for her. She was in a bad place emotionally back then. I personally always thought she was rather hard on you. But, have you read the sequel, *My Wee Duchess*? She is much kinder to you."

Kirk tried to laugh. "Truth be told, I was afraid to tackle that one after the first. It was quite a shock to realize she viewed me as a rapist. I was afraid to ask you out."

Mellie looked over at Kirk, shocked by his words. "Oh, Kirk, I don't think she felt that way about you. Fancy says she grieved terribly when she thought you were dead. She realized what she felt for you was more than mere lust. She realized she loved you."

"You think so?" he asked.

Mellie's heart lurched at the raw anguish in Kirk's voice. She reached over with a tentative hand to pat his arm. "Yes, I think so. At the same time, I know there is a difference in loving someone and being in love with someone. Rick loved me in his own way. Back then, he guarded his emotions. He was never in love with me."

"Fancy said that, too. What's the difference?"

Her smile was bittersweet. "Rick and I weren't meant for each other, like Fancy and he are. On one level, it's not true love if you don't both feel it. He could never commit to me. In fact..."

Her voice trailed off. Kirk glanced over, surprised to see her cheeks burning bright red. "In fact, what, *mo stor*?"

She glanced over at him and smiled. "I like it when you call me that. I don't think anyone other than my mother ever had a pet name for me before. Um, I knew I was pregnant before he left. I was so angry he was leaving that I wouldn't tell him. It was wrong of me, but I didn't want him to offer to marry me out of pity. I want it all. No halfway measure. If I couldn't have his heart, I didn't want him. Does that sound crazy?"

Kirk sat gently stroking her hand. "No. Not anymore. At one time, I would have thought it did, but now, what is it Elizabeth would say? Ah, yes, 'I think I got it.'"

"Exactly." She eased the sports car into a parking spot. "We're here."

Kirk lifted her hand to his lips and kissed her fingers before he leaped out of the sports car to hustle around to the other side to open the door for her. As she stepped out of the car, Stephan called out to them from the outdoor balcony.

"*Bon soir, mes amis*! Up here!"

Laughing, hand in hand, Kirk and Mellie hurried up the steps to enter the bustling club. Located in the center of town, the Irish-styled pub had a great menu, excellent beer on tap as well as its microbrewery, spirits, and the best wait staff in town. They told the hostess they were meeting Stephen Holzmann and started through the crowd towards the balcony where they had seen him. About halfway there, Stephan met them, hugging each before he kissed them both on their cheeks.

Mellie was a little surprised that Kirk did not seem offended by Stephan's kisses. She bit back a comment as they hurried back to the table Stephan had staked out for them.

Stephan led them back to a table where several other men were already sitting. He introduced everyone. They all sat chatting as they waited for the waitress to bring a round of the microbrewery's most popular brew.

One man could not keep his eyes off Kirk. "Oh, Stephan, darling, where did you ever find this gorgeous specimen? He's simply scrumptious."

Stephan laughed. "Kirk used to be married to Fancy Winslow. He's visiting his daughter."

Kirk nodded. "Aye, but I love the area. I may stay awhile."

Kirk scanned the crowd, surprised to see so few women. "Mellie, it looks like a woman's jackpot. You're one of only a handful of women here tonight."

The men laughed. Melanie smiled and leaned closer to Kirk and laid a hand on his arm. "I'm happy to be here with you."

The other men laughed again, but Stephan frowned. "*Non, non, ma cherie*, I thought Kirk was my date tonight."

"Well, you know what they say, Doc." Mellie grinned.

His eyes narrowed. "No, what do they say?"

"*Sea lo que sea.* Whatever will be, will be." She smiled again as she took a sip of her Coke.

"*Tres bien*, Melanie! Well said!" Stephan laughed out loud at her witty comeback.

Kirk alone looked lost. "I must be missing something."

That set off another round of laughter.

Mellie grabbed his hand. "Come dance with me. I'll explain it."

As they approached the dance floor, Kirk stopped abruptly. "What in the blazes are they doing? And why are men dancing with men and women dancing with women? Has the world gone topsy turvy?"

"Just move with the music. I'll explain the rest later."

She swung him onto the dance floor, where she snuggled up close to him. As they rocked back and forth to the music, she began to talk. "Kirk, do you realize Stephan is gay?"

He chuckled. "Well, aye, he always seems quite happy. Why?"

"Oh, boy, this is going to be awkward. Not that kind of gay, sweetheart. Uh, you see, Stephan and his friends prefer the company of men."

Kirk gently lifted a strand of her hair from her face and tucked it behind her ear. "Well, there are times I like to be with the boys, too. And other times? I prefer the company of a beautiful woman."

Mellie opened her mouth to respond, only to realize Kirk had dropped his head to kiss her. Suddenly, she had no idea what she had been about to say to him. Her hands crept up to pull him closer.

As the kiss ended, he grinned. "You were saying?"

"Hell if I know, big boy. How about you kiss me again?"

He laughed as he pulled her into his arms again. As the kiss ended, she reached up to stroke the side of his face. "You make my knees go weak."

"Good." He laughed as he twirled her around and around.

The music changed, and a group of men moved to the dance floor to begin a popular line dance. Melanie laughed and clapped her hands as the men danced the complicated steps to the country-western tune.

Kirk dropped his head to kiss her again, winked, and then joined the crowd of dancing men.

'Do the hoedown and get into it
Take it to the left now and dip with it
Gon' throw down, take a sip with it
Now lean back, put your hips in it...'

Mellie howled with laughter as he ground his hips lasciviously while he grinned at her. It was clear he was dancing for only one person in the room. Melanie beamed. Standing on the sidelines, she mimicked the moves in response to the fun song.

As the song ended, another popular song began. Kirk rushed over and grabbed Mellie by the hand to swing her out onto the dance floor. "Damn, I love this song. 'I'm gonna take my horse to the old town road, gonna ride til I can't no more...'"

She laughed. "You love that the Cowboys came through that hole in time with their horses."

He grinned as he spun get around again. "'Can't nobody tell me nothin', you can't tell me nothin'...'"

At the end of the dance, they returned to the table, laughing.

"So you like a little Billy Ray Cyrus?" Stephan took a swig of his beer.

Kirk nodded. "I love the remix video, where they fall through the hole in time from the old west to the present."

Stephan nodded. "Ah, if only such things could occur. It would explain the enigma you are, you big, glorious example of manhood."

Kirk choked on his beer at Stephan's words. "Say what?"

"*Ah, mon cher, tu etes tres adorable.*" Stephan laughed, shaking his head. He looked at his friends. "He is so innocent. It is as if he does not understand..."

"*Il ne comprand pas, commes tu sais.* You know he doesn't understand. Quit teasing him." Mellie sounded angry and protective. She leaned towards Kirk and placed her arm across his shoulders.

"Ah-ha, so the claws come out on the little *chat*," Stephan smirked as he looked from Kirk to Mellie, and back to Kirk.

"I'm sitting right here between *la petite chat y tu, mon ami, y je comprands le francais*. You know I speak French, Stephan. You should both realize that by now, as many times as I conversed with Stephan in French at the office." Kirk sounded annoyed. "Come on, Mellie. Let's dance again."

Stephan's eyes narrowed as they went back on the dance floor.

"I think you may have misjudged him." His friend, Carlton, punched him on the shoulder.

"Perhaps. Perhaps not. We shall see how long *la petite chat* keeps his interest. Fancy hurt Kirk badly and he lost a lot of his trust in women."

"That does not mean he would be interested in a same-sex liaison, *mon ami*." Terrence grinned at Stephan.

Stephan smiled. "But if she breaks his heart, too? We shall see."

"Hmm. I'd be interested in riding that horse down the old town road," said Terrence.

They all nodded in agreement.

"So would everyone in this club tonight, male and female. Look at the hungry stares, even from the lesbians." Carlton wiped a little bit of drool off his lip.

"Care to wager a little bet on who will ride that horse first?" Terrence pulled out $100 from his wallet. "My money is on *la petite chat*. That man is straighter than straight, Stephan. You are going to have to give up that pipe dream."

"But, of course, I will put my money where my mouth is." Stephan grinned as he pulled out another $100, which they both handed to Carlton. "If *la petite chat* betrays him, as Fancy did, he'll be mine yet."

. . .

Kirk lead Mellie outside so they could cool off from dancing.

"Explain to me now what you meant by 'he's gay.'"

"As I said before, he enjoys being with men. I can't complain. I do, too." She winked at him as she rubbed down his well-muscled arm.

Kirk caught her hand to raise it to his lips to kiss it, and then stopped halfway there. "You mean ... like this?"

She nodded. "Yes. Stephan is sexually attracted to you, Kirk."

"Oh, God. He's a great guy, but I'm not into that. I mean, I knew men on ships that turned to other men on long voyages, but I never…" His face turned beet red. "What do I do? I like him. He's a great guy, but I don't want to have sex with him."

"Forewarned is forearmed. Just know Stephan lusts after you. I mean, I understand. You are a very lust-able specimen."

He grinned and slowly trailed his fingers down her arm. "Do you lust after me, Mellie?"

"What do you think, big lug? 'Gonna take my horse down the old town road, gonna ride, til I can't no more.' Don't you understand why that song is so popular here?"

He shook his head. "No. Why?"

"They are all envisioning riding a big strong horse like you til they can't ride no more." She winked and licked her lips.

"Is that what you want to do, Mellie, my love?" His voice grew husky with unspoken desire as he pulled her closer to him.

"Oh, sweetie, I'm not that easy. I'll make you work for that ride," she teased. "But I will say, it's been a long time since I was in the saddle. I would definitely be interested in this ride."

Kirk grinned at her as his head dropped back to hers for a long, deep kiss. "So, you want to ride til ye can't no more?"

She trailed her fingers down the side of his face. "Well, one of these days…"

He pulled her close for another long kiss.

Chapter 13
Prom Shopping

"Mom, you really aren't going with us Saturday to shop for our prom dresses?" Liz sounded shocked.

I looked up from the recipe I was preparing, surprised by the question. "No. We already had this discussion."

She shrugged. "Come on, Mom. You said you would think about going. You have better taste in clothes than Dad does."

I shook my head. Bella and Elizabeth were both invited to the Junior-Senior Prom.

Liz was a junior, dating a senior, Dave Kozlov, a local boy. Dave's family immigrated from Russia some years ago. There is a sizable Russian émigré population in Atlanta and North Georgia. Dave is tall, slender, blonde, with blue eyes. His looks contrast beautifully with Liz's darker complexion and dark hair. They dated off-and-on this year, but the real reason they chose each other for the prom was that Dave is Liz's dance partner. They have danced together for a decade now. They dance like dreams together, even if they do argue like cats and dogs at least half of the time they aren't dancing. They either love each other or hate each other, with no in-between.

Bella was a senior, dating a young man already in college. She met Miguel when we went to San Antonio last year to visit Trinity. Handsome, dark-haired, dark-eyed, Miguel Vargas was assigned to show us around the campus. He's a bio chem student with a particular interest in music since he also plays the piano. That was why he was assigned to show Bella around. They hit it off right from the first. They wrote to each other ever since, and he came to visit a couple of times.

Bella visited his family over part of Christmas break. He has called her every night since Christmas. Bella was delighted Miguel could come to Georgia for the prom. Miguel will help out at the new clinic in San Antonio this summer.

The girls were excited they could attend this dance together. At first, they wanted me to make their dresses, *Outlander* and *Poldark* style. I know how to make gowns like those, and I began working on Bella's indigo-blue version of Claire's infamous red gown, and a snappy eggplant-hued zoned dress for Elizabeth. That girl must have been a queen in another life because she sure loves the color purple.

But no sooner than I had cut the patterns and begun sewing than their dress plans changed. Bella came running in with a picture of dresses based on books. "Look, Mom! Couldn't you make this instead?"

I sighed. Oh, wonderful. Now, they wanted corseted tops. There is nothing I hate to sew worse than stays and corsets. I could not manage to convince them to make the dresses with the same fabric, so Bella's gown transitioned in design to be a vibrant, chocolate brown with a corseted top made of material printed with the book cover from *The Diary of the Reluctant Duchess* and Liz's would be dramatic black, with a corseted top made from fabric printed with the book cover of *My Wee Duchess*.

I ordered fabric made with the book covers they wanted. But no sooner had the fabric arrived and I began working on the boning of the corseted tops than they changed their minds again.

"Uh... Mom, we want to discuss the dress designs again. We want to go a different route—" Bella began.

I let out a sigh of exasperation. "Why?"

"It turns out all the girls are wearing short dresses. These are a lot more formal than everyone else would be wearing."

I stared at her, still not quite believing what I was hearing. "You can't be different? What if we make these with short skirts?"

Bella shook her head as she nibbled on a finger. I noticed she could not quite look me in the eye. At least she had the decency to look embarrassed.

I pushed back from the sewing machine. "Fine. Then you guys get to look for styles you like and make an appointment to go to Atlanta to see dresses one Saturday."

Elizabeth blinked. "Aren't you going to make them? I mean, no one sews like you."

"Oh, hell, no, girl child. The third time *is* a charm. Your mama now resigns as prom dressmaker. You girls are getting ready-made now."

They took me at my word. They searched the internet and decided which shop they wanted to visit. They each made a list of favorite dresses and emailed their lists to Richard and me. After we made a couple of peremptory strikes on the basis that way too much skin showed, we all agreed on the dresses they each wanted to see. The girls emailed the shop their favorites and arranged an appointment.

I told Richard he could take them. He initially fussed, but he finally caved in. It would be a father-daughter shopping trip to Atlanta. The girls were excited because we all know Richard is looser with the purse strings than I am, but they also know I am better at the color, style, fit, and design than he is.

I shook my head. "No. We already decided. This is a father-daughter event. Dad will take you. You guys have a fun day. I'm doing something with the other kids that day."

She frowned. I bit back a chuckle as she assumed The Liz Pose, hands on her hips as she stamped her foot. "But, Mom..."

I shook my head. "No. Dad will take you. Have fun."

She frowned again. "You don't understand. If you go, Daddy won't fuss that I want Kirk to come, too..."

I blinked, and my voice softened when I spoke. "You want your Poppa to come?"

She nodded, as she nibbled on her upper lip.

"Then tell your Daddy. He'll say yes. And, then ask Kirk, but I'm not going. Charlie, Dara, Ronan, and I are meeting Baylie, Melanie, and Sara. We're all going out on the lake."

She frowned. After a minute, she turned to go talk to Richard in his study. I bit back my laughter. Call me a snoop, but I followed along behind her to hear their conversation.

"Well, sure, baby. If you want Kirk to come with us Saturday, that would be fine. We four can shop and then have a nice dinner in town before we come home."

Elizabeth threw her arms around his neck. "Oh, thank you, Daddy!"

I bit back the laugh as she planted a big kiss on his cheek before she turned to run out again to look for Kirk. "That was sweet. Can you cope with him?"

He shrugged. "Sure, why not? We have been getting along pretty well of late. At this rate, I may not have to take him to Fight Club to whup his ass. I'll take him and unleash the Beast of Ireland on my fellow Fight Club members. We'll be shopping for the girls. It will be fine."

I leaned over, wrapped my arms around him, and kissed my husband. "You're a good man."

"I'm a sucker for my pretty girls, as you well know, but yes, we'll be fine." Richard pulled me onto his lap, where we were still kissing when Elizabeth came running back in, dragging Kirk behind her.

"No, I mean it, Poppa. He said it's fine, and I really want you to come with us. It may be the only time I'll ever be able to have you shop with me for something special."

Kirk's heart lurched as he gathered his daughter into his arms. "Ah, lass, it will be fine. You'll have both of us there to help ye decide on the right dress. And besides, what makes ye think I'm planning to leave soon? I have to see this Juilliard School you want to attend, right Richard?"

"Absolutely. We're all going to check it out soon. We have to be sure it's good enough for our girl." Richard tried to smile. He was not stoked on the idea of sixteen-year-old Elizabeth going off to NYC to attend The Juilliard School. He could see that going south in no time at all.

"Who said anything about me leaving anytime soon? I'm afraid you're stuck with me, lass." He bent over to kiss Elizabeth's hair.

Oh, great, Liz thought. *Now he wants to stay? I love having him here, but Bay will have a cow! Hell, Mom may, too.* But she beamed with joy that she and her Poppa were finally getting to know each other.

She never dreamed she could love him this much.

Saturday morning, the girls and their dads headed out for Atlanta bright and early. They planned to get some breakfast on the way and then would show Kirk around Atlanta a little before their appointment at the dress shop. I soon received photos texted to me by Richard, first of them eating breakfast in Canton, and then photos at the Square in Marietta, with Kirk sitting with the girls at the beautiful fountain. It's an excellent place for photos. The next photos were from the Atlanta History Center and showed a stunned Kirk staring at the ultra-contemporary building. I then received more pictures of Kirk studying exhibits about the founding of the city, the impact of railroads on urban development, and the Civil War. From there, they went to the elegant little dress shop down the street.

Mrs. Linley had already pulled the dresses the girls wanted to try on. Richard videoed them as they oohed and aahed over the gorgeous dresses. Mrs. Linley helped them both into dressing rooms while their Dads waited in the luxurious waiting area, sipping white wine.

"I had no idea dress shopping was so refined here," Kirk marveled as he sipped the delicate Chardonnay. "I could get used to this."

Richard laughed. "Please don't. This shop is way too expensive to frequent very often."

Elizabeth came out first in a figure-flattering white outfit, with bare shoulders, short sleeves, and lace covering the top. Her bare midriff showed through the lace. The short, white skirt ended just above her knees.

Richard laughed when Kirk literally spat some of the wine when she walked out in the ensemble. "Ye mean to tell me you would actually wear something this revealing to a ball?"

She bent over and kissed his cheek before she pirouetted to show the outfit off to her Poppa. "It's pretty, Kirk. Admit it. You love it."

Kirk shook his head. "I don't know, darlin'. What do you think, Richard?"

Richard laughed. "Let's see the others, honey. This is lovely, but I know you were pretty crazy about the purple outfit."

She bent to kiss Richard, pirouetted again, and hurried back to the dressing room just as Bella came out in her first choice, a charming, hot pink gown with a fitted bodice and very full, very short skirt.

"Is that the one you like best, sweetie?" Richard winked at her with an approving nod of his head.

"It was my first choice before we came, and I like it, but I want to try them all on. I want to love it, not just like it." She stood examining her reflection in the mirror. "Right now, I just like it. I'm not feeling the love."

"It fits beautifully. I'm sending pictures to Mom."

"I don't know, Daddy. I think it's too young."

"You *are* young, Bella. Revel in your youth. Enjoy it. Don't be in too big of a rush to grow up."

She smiled, blew Richard a kiss, and turned to hurry back to the dressing room.

"My God, Richard, are all the dresses this short? Would you let them wear these outfits in public?" Kirk sounded horrified.

Richard laughed. "Hate to tell you this, but yes, they are. You better prepare yourself, because every dress Elizabeth picked out except one has a bare midriff."

Kirk looked shocked. "You are joking, right? They can wear things this bare?"

Richard laughed. "Sorry, old man, I'm quite serious. It's not the eighteenth-century any longer, Kirk. Francesca checked with the school for prom dress requirements. We sent it to Mrs. Linley to be sure the dresses would be acceptable. Bare midriffs are okay as long as there is not 'excessive skin or too much cleavage exposed'. After the girls made their preliminary choices, we also sent the photos of them to the school for approval. Every one of these dresses met with the high school's dress code for prom dresses."

"My God, what is this world coming to?" Kirk shook his head, clearly stunned.

Elizabeth came out next in a sassy little gold number with a sweetheart neckline, sheer illusion around the waist, and a pleated skirt. The dress was heavily overlaid with gold lace. Illusion was above the neckline and gold lace circled the neck.

Kirk nodded in approval. "I like this one. Much more appropriate."

Richard snickered. "Turn around, Liz."

Elizabeth turned around to reveal an almost bare back, held together with a single button at the neck. The daring back dipped to her waist.

Kirk groaned and put his head in his hands. "Oh, sweet Jesus…"

About then, Bella came out in a purple strapless gown trimmed with Swarovski crystals covering the bodice. The dress was cut empire-style, with the short skirt falling in tiers from the raised waist.

Elizabeth huffed up. Hands on her hips, she said, "Hey, that's supposed to be one of my dresses."

Bella shrugged. "I wanted to see it in pink or navy. They only had the purple in my size. I like it. What do you think, Daddy?"

Kirk nodded his head. "I personally like it a far sight more than the others Elizabeth has tried on."

Richard stifled his own laughter. "It's quite pretty, honey. Elizabeth, how would you feel about wearing the purple and your sister wearing it in pink or navy?"

Elizabeth frowned. "We are not twins. We are different people. I want my own dress. Keep it if you want it. You ruined it for me now."

She flounced away to go back to the dressing room.

Bella waited until Liz was out of earshot. "This one is too little for her anyway."

Kirk groaned as he shook his head. "Figures."

Bella looked embarrassed. "I'm sorry, Kirk."

The men sat chatting quietly as the girls changed their outfits.

"Are all the clothes they wear like these, Richard? They seem so … so…"

"Sexy? Yes, I agree. And the school approved these. You should have seen some of the dresses that weren't approved!"

About then, Mrs. Linley refilled both their wine glasses. "You two are so cute. Your daughters must really appreciate their dads doing this."

Richard laughed, his eyes twinkling. "Oh, I think they do appreciate us. Even though poor Kirk is rather stunned by the overt sexiness of the dresses."

"How long have you two been a couple?"

Elizabeth walked out as Mrs. Linley asked her question. As Kirk first choked on his wine and then began stammering, his cheeks burning bright pink with embarrassment, Richard could not resist putting his arm around Kirk's shoulders. Liz leaned over to place her arm around both of them. "Not very long, but they really do make an adorable couple, don't they?"

"My daughter jests. Richard is married to my ex-wife. We get along pretty good, all things considered, and the girls wanted us to bring them shopping." Kirk cut Richard and her a dirty look as Mrs. Linley walked away to check on Bella. "There is something not right in your heads. Why on earth would you say something like that? And why does everyone seem to think I'm gay?"

Elizabeth dimpled as she giggled. "Oh, chill out, Pops. There's a lot worse in this world than being gay. Dr. Holzmann is one of the nicest men we know."

Kirk groaned again. "Oh, lord, I may never recuperate from him takin' me to that gay bar last weekend."

Liz tousled his hair like he often did to hers. "And now you know 'gay' means more in this day and age than just 'happy.' So, the man thinks your sexy? We all know Daddy and you are both straighter than straight. Don't get your knickers in a twist. Now, what do you think about this one?"

She pirouetted again so he could see the cute brown ensemble from all angles. The top had a modest, high neckline, with slight cap sleeves. Like the gold dress, the back was bare, as was the midriff above a solid brown, gathered skirt.

Poor Kirk groaned again. "I like the neckline. The back and middle are so... so bare. You look half naked."

"I like the gold more, honey. It's more elegant. I think Mom would agree." Richard winked at her.

About then, Bella came out in a black dress with a sweetheart neckline, fitted waist, and flirty, short, full skirt. Sheer, black illusion fabric filled in above the sweetheart neckline right up to her collarbone, with lace trim around the neckline and across the bodice.

Richard let out a low whistle. "Very pretty, honey. Very elegant and quite chic. It's got my vote so far."

'Why can't Elizabeth pick anything this pretty?" Kirk muttered.

Richard bit back the laughter. "Liz picked out pretty dresses. She is a dancer and she is very body conscious. Let's face it, your girl has a killer body. In contrast, Bella is a musician. She is more accustomed to dressing a little more conservatively. She has a pretty shape, too. Don't get me wrong. But she is very slender and lacks some of that well-defined musculature Liz is so proud of having. A musician does not want her clothes or her body to be the focus. She wants her music to be the focus. A dancer wants her body to be the center of attention."

Kirk arched his eyebrows and sniffed in disdain. "Hmm. If you say so. But the dresses show off Bella's lovely figure without being, well, without showing off too much."

"I agree. Ah, here comes your beautiful daughter now."

Elizabeth came out in a black strapless dress with a sweetheart neckline. The 'fit and flare' skirt swung to and fro as she walked. The small, white polka dots covering the black fabric were close together on the bodice, and then spread out on the skirt, giving an ombré effect. A narrow, black patent belt accented her tiny waist.

Kirk's eyes softened. "Ah, darlin' you look like an angel."

"I agree. It's very flattering, Elizabeth. Mom would like this, too." Richard smiled at her. "You two could both wear black dresses, and look completely different."

Liz sniffed. "I don't know. Quit trying to twin us up, Daddy. We aren't twins. We are two very different girls. Anyway, I still want to try on the purple one."

Bella blinked in surprise. "I thought you said you didn't want it anymore after I tried it on."

Elizabeth smirked at Bella. "That's not the only purple dress on my list. You know purple is my favorite color. I'll try that one on before I decide. It's my fave, at least on paper. I saved it for last. Now, I'll see if I like it when I put it on."

Kirk groaned as she flounced back to the dressing room. "God only knows what this one will look like."

"Oh, it's pretty, Kirk. You'll love it. Daddy, did you send the pictures to Mommy?" I really don't know which I want." Bella frowned.

"I sure did, sweetie. Want me to call her?"

She nodded. "Yes, please. I guess I'll go get dressed. I tried the other one on back there and I didn't like it."

Richard frowned. "Why don't you look and see if you like something else? To be honest, you haven't seemed totally stoked on anything, although this little black number is my top pick so far."

She sighed. "I tell you what, Daddy. How about you guys look for me? I really wanted something grown-up enough to take to college and not look like a high school prom dress. The black dress is probably the best. I'm just not sure. I wish Mommy would answer the phone."

"Well, we knew they were going out on the lake. She probably has no reception out there."

"I guess so." She sighed and turned to go back to the dressing room.

"Okay, old man, you heard our marching orders. Help me find Bella a dress she will think looks more grown-up. After all, she's dating a college man and she's going to a top-notch college next year."

The two men walked over to the designer racks to peruse gowns. As they looked at dress after dress, Mrs. Linley came back in, and frowned. "What's the problem?"

Richard chuckled, his face reddening at being caught rifling through the expensive gowns. "Bella wants us to look a little for something that won't scream 'high school prom' at college next year. She's dating a young man wo will be going to med school next year. His dad is retired from the Air Force as a full-bird Colonel, and they go dancing at the Officers' Club at one of the bases fairly often. She decided the pink and the purple are too youthful. The black is still in the running but she is not completely convinced."

Her face softened and she nodded. "Ah, I understand. You know, come to think of it, I have something in the back she might just like. Bella did say she would prefer a dark blue. It just came in yesterday, and we pressed it this morning. I think it would fit her. I'll go take it to her."

Kirk's brow wrinkled as he wondered what the next dresses would look like. "Is it always this hard?"

Richard looked startled. "What?"

Kirk laughed. "Shopping with daughters. Is it always this hard? I will admit it was much easier with Fancy. I bought the fabric she desired and she made the dresses the way she wanted. They were always beautiful."

Richard smiled as his face softened. "Yes, she is always beautiful. I'll give you that."

Kirk frowned. "Give me what?"

"We both have damned good taste in wives."

Kirk shook his head, frustrated, and then chuckled as he thought of Mellie. "Aye, we do seem to be attracted to the same sort of women."

About then, Elizabeth came out wearing the dark purple ensemble. The cropped top was heavily beaded front and back. It showed off her shoulders and her well-toned dancer's abs. The high neckline and the covered back were probably unexpected by Kirk at that point.

The fit and flare skirt was long.

Richard grinned. She had the picture of this prom-worthy outfit pinned up in her room. Francesca was sure she would choose it. They were not sure if she would wear it long or if she would want the skirt shortened.

Richard looked over at Kirk in time to see his eyes grow wide. Kirk rose from the comfortable chair and strode over to his beautiful daughter. He took her by one hand, and walked around her. "Oh, darlin', you look so much like your mam in this. I canna' believe how beautiful you are."

His voice broke as he pulled her into his arms. As their hug ended, Richard could see tears in Kirk's eyes.

"This is my dress. I love it." Elizabeth sounded exultant.

"How will you wear the skirt? Short or long?"

She grinned mischievously. "It's a surprise."

Just then, Bella came back out in an exquisite confection of midnight-blue, slubbed, raw silk. The strapless gown had an asymmetrical neckline. The fitted bodice accentuated her slender figure and tiny waist. The skirt gently belled out, falling gracefully from her hips. The hemline, short in front, fell longer in back. It was a sophisticated gown for a young woman about to go to college and commence her adult life.

Richard smiled as he blinked back the tears of pride. "What do you think, pumpkin?"

She lifted her eyes to him. "I love it, Daddy, but ..."

"But what?"

"It's nearly twice as expensive as the others. What will Mommy say?"

He chuckled. "Mommy will say it's perfect."

And she will fuss at me about cost, he thought. *But you only have one senior prom.*

She rushed over and threw her arms around his neck. "Thank you, Daddy."

Richard took photos of both girls in the dresses they selected and texted them off to Francesca. She texted back one word: Perfect.

Mrs. Linley measured the girls to order the dresses, and assured them the gowns would arrive in time to make any last-minute alterations before the prom. She helped them pick out shoes, but both girls declined her offer to help pick out jewelry.

"Our Mom has exquisite jewelry. She promised we could borrow some."

Mrs. Linley smiled. "That's wonderful, girls. Just remember that we have some lovely selections if you change your minds about the jewelry."

As they walked outside, Elizabeth grinned at Bella. "Dibs on the pink tourmaline."

"Works for me, but you ought to wear the amethysts with that dress. I want the sapphires." Her blue eyes twinkled as she beamed at her sister.

They fist bumped as they gushed on about their dresses. The girls sat in the back of the SUV and giggled all the way to Kennesaw, where they ate at Provino's, their favorite Italian Restaurant. As the men dug into enormous plates of spaghetti carbonara with garlic knots, the girls ate their salads chock full of cheese and meats in addition to a multitude of veggies. Later, they all splurged calories and enjoyed the homemade spumoni ice cream the restaurant makes daily. Richard snapped numerous photos of them all enjoying their dinner, although his personal favorites were of Kirk as he ate his first bites of the spaghetti.

"I don't think I've ever felt so full in my whole life," Kirk lamented as he pushed away from the table. "My God, their food is evil. I never devoured anything quite so delectable before in my entire life!"

Richard laughed. "We say that every time we eat here. Francesca loves this place."

Kirk tilted his head at Richard. "Why do you call her Francesca?"

Richard laughed. "Well, it is her name. Why?"

He shrugged. "Everyone else – all her family as well as her friends – call her Fancy. I just wondered."

Richard grew serious. "I think that's why I call her Francesca. It's a beautiful name, for a beautiful woman. Plus, this way, it's the special name I call her that no one else does."

Kirk's surprise showed on his face. "Huh. I never thought of that. Dammit, you are a clever man. Do you think we could get some more of that spumoni stuff?"

They all laughed as Kirk ordered four more bowls of the delectable treat.

Chapter 14
Shadow Wolf - Before

"It has been two months since she followed him Beyond." Wolf stood staring out the doorway of his daughter's asi.

Bright Star nodded without looking up from her weaving. "Yes, Father, it has been two months. Are you sorry yet you made her go?"

Wolf's head jerked back towards his daughter. His lips narrowed in frustration more than anger as color deepened on his copper burnished cheeks. "I did not *want* her to go. You know that."

She sniffed in disdain and shrugged as she passed the spool back and forth, weaving the thread spool through the warp threads. "Well, you certainly *let* her go alone. How do you feel about that now? Do you still think it was the smart thing to do?"

"No, I did not think it was the smart thing to do when she went. You know how I feel. Why are you doing this to me?" He snapped the words at his favorite child.

Star shook her head and frowned. She sat the shuttle down and looked her father straight in the eye. She did not want him to miss a single word she was about to say. "You did not even remind her that you love her, that you wanted her to come back—"

"Shut up, woman!" He snapped. Wolf sighed as he walked back outside to stare at the darkening sky. "I told her I love her before she left. I told her to come back to me. Dammit, I was sure she would be back by now."

Star shook her head again as she picked up her spool and began weaving again. "And yet, as you see, she is not. Happy?"

Wolf cut his eyes at her. His frustration was evident to his daughter. "No, I am not happy. You know I am not happy. I am miserable. Now, what do I do to fix this mess?"

"I don't know what you will do, but if the one I loved had been sent Beyond on an impossible task, I know what I would do." She passed the spool through the warp threads again.

His face brightened. He leaned towards his beautiful daughter. "What would you do, my daughter?"

She sat the shuttle down again and smiled at her father. "I would go after the one I love and bring my love back."

He frowned. "But daughter, the council—"

"To hell with the council. You are the chief. Act like one. Take charge. Go after your woman. Bring Guider back. We need her. You need her. You are incomplete without this woman. O'Malley is a grown man. He can make his own decisions about his life." She battened down the latest pass with a definite slam of the comb. "I could care less if he creates chaos there, as long as he is not creating it here."

Wolf glanced around, as if worried they might be overheard. "But he is the *Tsul Kalu*."

Bright Star let out a most unladylike noise. She sat the spool down crossed her arms across her chest, and glared at her father. "Nonsense. He is a mortal man, like Michael or you. He grieved over the woman he lost. Who, might I add, he went right after when given the chance. Unlike someone I could mention, Father."

Wolf stood up. He started for the doorway to the *asi*, and then stopped and turned back towards Bright Star and shook a finger at her. "Do not mock me, daughter."

She bit back the chuckle. "Of course, Father. So, when will you leave?"

"I need proper clothes. And money. A map. And I lack a communicator-thing like Guider had."

Star's fingers stopped weaving as she looked up at her father. "Her phone thing?"

He nodded. "Yes. They hold big magic. With one, I could call Guider when I get there. I know not how a person can speak into that little box and another person can hear them, miles away, but she swears it works."

Bright Star nodded. "I remember. Marc left some of his clothes from Beyond here for you. I shortened the pants and shirt sleeves. They left you a bit of cash, a map, and a compass as well. Oh, I almost forgot. Lily left her phone. It has Guider's number and Fancy's number in it."

His eyes lit up and then almost as quickly, he frowned. "Why did they leave these things?"

Star frowned at her father, impatient with his stubbornness. "Really, Father? They were sure you would follow after her. It is past time. You need to go after your woman. The sooner, the better. We do not know how much time may have elapsed there."

He sighed. His shoulders slumped as he nodded. "Guider taught me how to read maps and to use the compass. But I cannot read words. How will I know her name in the box?"

She tossed the little box to him. "No, but you know numbers. Fancy is Number 1."

He held the little phone as if it were a precious treasure. "And Guider?"

"Look there on the front. Lily called that the screen. What do you see?"

His eyes lit up. "The mark for an eagle's track? Lily marked Guider's number for me with the symbol for an eagle track?"

Star laughed, the corners of her eyes crinkling as she did. "The old man can be taught new ways. Yes, Guider's mark is the eagle track. This will guide you on your path to find your eagle. Tomorrow is full moon. That means the best time for you to pass is—"

"Now." He grabbed the clothes, the cash, and the other things and started for the doorway. Halfway there, he turned back, and quickly grabbed his daughter and pulled her to him for a quick kiss. "Thank you."

She smiled and hugged her father close before she patted his back. "Bring her back. I don't care what you do about O'Malley."

He laughed and kissed her again. "You should be the Chief."

She smiled up at him. "That could be arranged. After all, I am—"

"Our Bright Star of Hope. And now, my daughter, you have given me hope for *my* future with the woman I love." He hugged her tight again before he strode inside the *asi* to prepare for his trip Beyond.

Chapter 15
Kirk Lands a Job

Mellie and Kirk often visited the Brian Boru, with Stephan as well as by themselves. Kirk made friends with the owner, grey-haired, rotund, diminutive Grady Sullivan, who hailed from County Sligo. Grady was every bit of 5'4". Grady proudly told Kirk he looked like Mickey Rooney when he was a young man. Grady was fast approaching 70, or as he put it, he was 'getting up in years and didn't move as fast as he once did.' He admired Kirk's strength and courage. Grady was especially impressed with both after an incident when Kirk took care of a problem for Grady one evening.

It had been a reasonably typical evening if anything is ever routine in a gay-friendly bar in North Georgia on a Saturday night. Kirk and Mellie snuggled close together as they nibbled on buffalo wings and sipped cerveza at the counter, while Kirk and Grady chewed the fat. Suddenly, a disgruntled client approached Grady and slung a barbecued poor dog on the bar.

"What the hell is this slop? I ordered a Pedro con carne, and the damned wait staff brought me this pile of crap instead."

Kirk wiped a bit of food splatter from his face, looked at the man's plate. "That is a barbecued poor dog. Looks pretty damned good to me."

The big brute glared at Kirk. "Did anyone ask for your opinion?"

Kirk smiled. "You asked a question. I answered you. Either send it back or eat your food and shut up. You're boring people."

The man's face, already red, turned purple. He reached to grab Kirk by the collar, but before he could reach him, Kirk grabbed the man's arm in midair. "I don't think you want to be doing that, my boyo."

The man tried to shake free only to find Kirk had him in a chokehold. As the man began to sputter, Kirk bum-rushed him to the door. Kirk kicked the door open and shoved the man outside. He pulled out a twenty-dollar bill and handed it to the waiter. "Is that enough to cover his dinner?"

"Oh, yes, sir, Mr. O'Malley. Thank you, sir," gushed the nervous young man.

Kirk walked back to the counter, grinned at Grady, and shook his head. "As you were saying, Grady?"

Grady's eyes narrowed and nodded at the Irishman. "Hmm. Nicely done, lad. I'd been wondering if you might like a job here, Kirk."

Kirk grabbed a handful of boiled peanuts. "Mayhap. What would it entail?"

He smiled. "You would be my assistant manager. You would handle the disgruntled customers like you just did."

Mellie laughed. "Who would? Kirk? Aren't you afraid he'd run off all your business, Grady?"

"Only the bad customers, like that one. What do you say, Kirk?"

He nodded as he grabbed another handful of peanuts. "Sure, Grady, it sounds great. Oh, look. Your asshole returns for round two. I reckon I'd best begin earning my salary, whatever it may be since we've not yet discussed it."

He took his time as he stood up and dusted his hands off before he sauntered over to the hostess and the disgruntled customer.

"That's him! This creature pitched me out of here like he owns the place. Who do you think you are anyway?" The furious customer screamed at Kirk, with drool running down his chin.

"I think I'm Captain Kirk O'Malley, sir, and I'm the assistant manager of this establishment. I told you to leave and not return tonight. Why have you come back despite my politely worded instructions?"

The man snorted. "Politely worded? Oh, that's a laugh. I've got half a mind to whup your ass."

Kirk shrugged and flashed his crooked smile as he winked at the hostess. "Well, sir, if you find the other half, you are welcome to come on over, and you can damned sure try."

And then, as Mellie later put it, the fight was on. However, it was almost over before it started.

Mr. Angry Client pulled back his arm, intending to lambast his fist into Kirk's face. Kirk grabbed the man's arm again and forced the man down to his knees. The next thing anyone knew, Mr. Angry was on the floor, blubbering like a big baby with Kirk's size 12 foot planted in the middle of his chest.

"You need to learn to listen, sir. Your manners are atrocious. Unless you learn some better self-defense skills, you need to learn to listen, and to control your temper." Kirk kept his voice low and calm as he smiled down at the man.

The big man nodded as if afraid to utter another word.

Kirk smiled. "Good. Now, you've had a wee bit too much to drink tonight. I understand. It happens. When you sober up, you are invited to return to this pub, *if* you can control your temper and your mouth. However, I'll not put up with you coming in and acting a fool again. Do you understand?"

Tears began to slide down the big fellow's cheeks. He nodded.

Kirk tilted his head. "I'm sorry, sir. We could all hear your vociferous complaints earlier, but no one heard your response to my question. Do you understand?"

The man nodded again. "Yes, sir."

"Excellent. Then let me help you up. Dottie, please call this gentleman a cab to take him home. No, no, sir, the ride is on me tonight. I don't want you driving in an obviously impaired condition. You would have to be impaired to try to take me on. Now, wait right over here. The cab will be here shortly. Dottie will fetch you a cup of coffee, and if you like, we can get you a Pedro con carne to go."

Kirk strolled back to the counter and winked at Grady and Mellie.

"Well done, lad. Well done indeed. I think you'll be worth every penny I pay you."

Kirk laughed. "Oh, Grady, I'll be worth at least twice what you pay me, or I'll be cheating you."

Chapter 16
Prom Approaches

"Hey, Mom, I need a tux. I'm going to the prom." Charlie picked up an apple, polished it on his shirt sleeve, and chomped into it.

Fancy's hands stopped kneading the dough she was preparing as she turned to stare at her older son. "What did you say? Charlie, you're a sophomore. You can't go to the Junior-Senior prom."

He grinned. "Mom, as you should know, I became a junior in January. Amy broke up with her girlfriend. She still wants to go to the prom. She has her dress and the tickets. I just need a tux. Well, and some flowers for Amy."

Amy has been Charlie's best buddy as long back as I can remember. They climbed trees, rode horses, river rafted, fished, rescued animals, you name it, they did it, except for sex. Amy has a definite preference for female companionship romantically, or I would have expected him to take her to the prom from the 'get-go,' as they say.

I shrugged. "As long as it's okay for you to go. Call around and see if you can get a tux."

He nodded. "I already did. Tucker's Tuxes reserved a couple for me to try on this afternoon. Can you drive me there?"

I shook my head as I finished pounding my dough. "Going to the prom and doesn't even have his driver's license yet. Okay. Give me fifteen minutes to finish the bread and to clean up, and we can go."

He leaned over and pecked a kiss on my cheek. "You're the greatest, Mom."

My little boy. It seems like he was born yesterday. Now, he towers over me and is taking his best friend to the prom. I shook my head as I finished preparing the dough, divided it, and put it into the loaf pans. I could bake the bread when we returned home from renting his tux.

It's so different shopping with boys than with girls. In less than an hour, Charlie decided which he wanted, ordered it, and they measured him.

"Did you say he's 6'1"?" I asked the clerk.

Mr. Tucker nodded. "Yes, ma'am. He's going to be tall."

I shook my head. He's already taller than Calvin at 15. I thought again he resembled a kinder, gentler version of the father he never knew.

He also ordered black patent shoes and quickly paid the man (with my credit card, of course) before we headed to the florist.

"I hadn't thought about what kind of flowers she would want, Mom." He sounded nervous. I glanced over at him and saw him chewing on a thumbnail.

My answer was simple. "Call her."

"What color is her dress, young man?" The florist peered over his glasses at Charlie.

Charlie was on the phone with Amy as the man asked the all-important question. "Just a minute, sir. It's red and black. She's giving me my marching orders on the corsage."

Amy requested a corsage made with red roses and baby's breath and a red boutonnière for Charlie. I rolled my eyes at the cost of the flowers as Charlie handed the man the plastic again.

He grinned at me. "That wasn't so bad."

"No, not at all. You guys will have a great time." We were out $500, but that was a drop in the bucket compared to what the girls spent, and Charlie did this for his best friend. I leaned over and kissed my son, amazed once again that Calvin Hobbs produced a boy this sweet and thoughtful. He resembles Calvin physically, but that is where the similarities stop. Thank God Calvin did not have a hand in raising my sweet Charlie.

Soon, it was time for the prom. Richard and Bella drove into Atlanta to pick up Miguel at Hartsfield-Jackson International on Friday afternoon. A few hours later, they came in, bubbling over with excitement about the weekend.

Miguel is a good-looking young man, with his coal-black hair and chocolate brown eyes. I told Bella the first time I met him that his eyes reminded me of her father's eyes. Calvin may have been an ass, but he was a handsome man. As they entered that Friday evening, Miguel handed me a bouquet and bowed to kiss my hand. "Thank you for having me back, Mrs. Winslow. I appreciate your hospitality."

I sniffed the flowers. His romantic, debonair attitude always impressed me, although once again, I worried Miguel was too polished, suave, and sophisticated for my sweet and innocent Bella. "Now, how did you know that blue irises are my favorites?"

He grinned. "Oh, a little birdie might have whispered that into my ear."

He pulled Bella close for a hug as she giggled.

I served homemade lasagna with a beautiful green caesar salad and garlic bread for supper. Richard brought home spumoni he picked up from Provino's for dessert on the way home from the airport.

"That was great, Mrs. Winslow. I appreciate you guys having me this weekend." Miguel beamed at me again.

Charlie and Miguel met Dave, and the three guys went to the tux store the next morning to pick up their tuxedos for the prom. Amy came over with her dress, and then the three girls went to the hairdresser for their prom 'do's, nails, and makeup. They would all leave in the limo Richard rented from our house later that evening. That way, no teen would be driving.

We chuckled as three handsome young men all dressed in what Richard called 'James Bond tuxes,' with white dinner jackets, black ties, white shirts, and black tux trousers, appeared in the foyer. Miguel leaned up against the railing to the stairs, looking for all the world like a dashing young 007.

"Shaken, not stirred?" I struggled not to laugh.

He grinned, pleased I knew a bit of Bond lore. "Absolutely, my dear."

We all laughed at his attempt at an English accent.

About then, the girls came down the stairs, one by one. Amy appeared first, in an attractive, figure-flattering red and black outfit with red lace around her neck, over her shoulders, and extended down across the torso of the dress. The short, black, lace-covered skirt ended just above her knees. Her black hair was styled in an elegant French twist that showed off the ruby-colored chandelier earrings perfectly.

Charlie grinned as he fastened the corsage around Amy's wrist, and then bent over to kiss her cheek. "You look great."

She beamed at him. "So do you. Very handsome and dashing."

Next down came Elizabeth in all her purple splendor. As I expected, she had the skirt cropped short to show off her long, gorgeous dancer's legs. She wore her long, dark brown hair pulled high in a complicated swirl of voluptuous curls with tendrils framing her face and trailing down her nape. She opted to wear a pair of my antique amethyst pendant earrings instead of the pink tourmaline she initially claimed, and an amethyst and jet bracelet she bought in Atlanta on a recent shopping excursion adorned one wrist.

Kirk leaned over to me, with a worried frown. "She looks way too sexy in that. Isn't the skirt obscenely short?"

"It's fine, Kirk. Behave," I whispered back as I struggled not to laugh at the big lug. "She looks lovely."

He made a rude, snorting noise. "Yeah, sure."

Tall, blonde, and handsome Dave stepped forward with a grin and fumbled to fasten the white, mini calla lily corsage onto Liz's wrist. The corsage was an altogether modern look when combined with the purple dress, perfect for our edgy Elizabeth. "Gee, Liz, you look hot."

She dimpled at his words. "Thanks. You look pretty great yourself."

And, then, my Bella appeared at the top of the stairs in the elegant midnight blue gown. She accented the gown with a dark blue velvet ribbon around her neck, to which my twin hearts brooch was attached. The brooch had a rose-cut diamond in one heart, and a sapphire in the other. She wore earrings of sapphire hearts surrounded by tiny diamonds. Calvin gave me the set long ago for our first anniversary. I never wore them much, but Bella cherishes all the jewelry her father gave me. A pretty gold bracelet with a single sapphire and two small diamonds adorned one wrist. She had her dark auburn hair pulled back in a loose French braid, with sprigs of babies' breath tucked into it. My heart lurched as I realized my little girl was a child no longer, but an exquisite, beautiful, young woman.

She took her time walking down the stairs.

Miguel kissed her hand when she reached the bottom. "*Tu eres hermosa, como siempre, mi amor.*"

"*Muchas gracias, mi corazon,*" she replied, her accent flawless.

Richard and I glanced at each other, surprised by the exchange in Spanish. He told her she was beautiful and called her 'his love.' Bella thanked him and called him her 'heart.' We knew she was studying the language and made excellent grades. She always did. Now we understood her motivation to learn Spanish.

Miguel attached the corsage to Bella's right wrist. Made of purple dendrobium orchids and delicate pink calcynia, it was a perfect contrast to the navy dress. Bella seemed thrilled with the beautiful corsage. My eyes widened as Miguel arose and pulled Bella into his arms for a kiss.

Richard cleared his throat. "Uh, Miguel, she might not want you to mess up her makeup before you guys leave for the dance. She paid a pretty penny to get her makeup done for tonight."

"Looks like I should have been cleaning that shotgun after all," Kirk whispered.

"Behave," I whispered back. I tried not to giggle.

"You ought to be worried about those two behaving." Kirk glared at Miguel.

I realized Kirk was dead serious. I glanced at Richard, who nodded in agreement. I gulped and nodded as well.

They broke off the kiss, with Bella laughing at Miguel's embarrassment over Kirk and Richard's correction. Miguel leaned towards her again to wipe a tiny smear of lipstick from where it had smudged beyond her lip.

"Take our pictures, Daddy."

Richard snapped pictures of the three couples, as individual couples and of the six together. He and Kirk then spoke to the young men in low voices before they escorted the girls out to the waiting limo.

"What did you say to them?" I asked as we watched the limo pull away.

"I told them to mind their p's and q's, keep the girls safe, and to remember the girls' dads all know how to shoot."

Kirk came up beside us then. "I told Dave he'd best not be taking liberties with my girl, or I'd be gutting him like a hog."

I started laughing. "What did you tell Miguel?"

He grinned. "*Te dare' de comer a los cerdos si le rompes el corazon.*"

Richard began laughing as well. "You told him you'd feed him to the pigs if he breaks her heart? Well done, old man. It sounds like something Will would have said. Well done, indeed."

Kirk grinned, flashing those gorgeous pearly whites as he did. "Well, now that you mention it…"

I chuckled. It was something Will said to Kirk about me at Waterside the night before they left to go back to Belle Rose. I wondered if it was the last thing my big brother ever said to Kirk.

. . .

"Whatever led you guys to go with the white dinner jackets? Heck, I hear a lot of the boys are wearing regular suits." Bella snuggled close to Miguel.

"It was Dave's idea. Besides, we aren't boys, my love. We are young men." Miguel dropped his head to kiss her again. "Gosh, you look gorgeous tonight. I love your dress."

She beamed at him and laid her head onto his shoulder. "Thank you. I wanted something that I could wear next year at Trinity, too."

Charlie nodded. "We started to all wear evening suits, but Dave said Liz and he had a dance routine in which he wore a tux like this, and he thought it was uber cool. He sent us pictures, and we decided we could all look 007 fantastic without stealing the limelight from you girls."

"Well, it was a great idea. We'll be the best-looking group at the prom." Liz grinned as she envisioned their entrance. She already knew it was going to be a fabulous night.

The kids had been dancing for about three hours when Miguel slipped over to the band. He handed the bandleader a twenty-dollar bill and requested they play Unchained Melody. Miguel knew Bella loved the song. As they began to play it, he led Bella back onto the dance floor, where he swept her into his arms as if she were made to fit there. When they reached the middle of the dance floor, under the big flashing disco ball, he sank to one knee and pulled out the ring. Bella threw her hands up to her mouth as he extended the ring to her.

"Bella, *mi amor*, I love you more than life itself. Will you do me the honor of marrying me?"

Eyes sparkling, Bella nodded as she pulled him up into her arms. "Oh, yes, Miguel!"

All around them, kids began snapping pictures of the happy couple. Miguel slipped the antique sapphire and diamond ring onto her ring finger. Everyone clapped as he dipped his head to kiss her again right there on the dance floor.

The principal groaned and shook his head.

The assistant principal laughed. "Oh, relax, Martin. It's romantic."

He shook his head. "The boy flies in from San Antonio for prom, and just happens to have an expensive engagement ring in his pocket? I'm not buying it. Neither will her dad."

"They will break up by summer's end, Martin. Just chill out."

He sighed. "It happens every year. Some guy asks a girl to marry him under the light ball at prom. It's become a Blue Ridge tradition. But really, Meg, Dr. Winslow is going to have a cow."

The pretty assistant principal slipped her arm through the crook of Martin Sayer's arm. "Nah, he'll be okay. The Texan kid needs to worry about her step-dad. My gosh, you'd think he's her father. He's possessive, protective, and he's got one heck of an Irish temper. I bet he will be cleaning the shotgun when they get home. Well, next year, we can announce no engagements will be tolerated at prom."

He snorted again. "Oh, yeah, Megan, like that's going to work."

In less than five minutes, the pictures and videos were all over Instagram, Snapchat, YouTube, and Facebook. Less than ten minutes later, Amy's mom, as well as Dave's dad, called to tell Fancy and Richard that Miguel asked Bella to marry him at the prom. Mellie arrived minutes later as Kirk prepared to clean the shotgun from Richard's study.

They were watching the engagement video taken by Charlie and posted on his YouTube channel when Bella, Miguel, Charlie, and Elizabeth came in after the prom. The kids had already dropped Amy off at home, and Dave left them outside to head to his house. Amy and Dave chose to avoid the storm of parental anger, sure to come inside the Winslow house. The excited chatter stilled at the sullen stares of the four angry adults sitting in front of the television, the shotgun in front of Kirk, where the video was being shown on the late-night newscast.

"Uh… I think I'll head to bed." Charlie started up the stairs, two at a time.

"Hold it right there, mister. I think you've got some explaining to do, young man." Fancy's voice quivered with anger.

Charlie turned back, feigning surprise. "Who, *moi*? I just took the video…"

"How did you know to record it?"

Charlie winced. Richard's voice was low and controlled, but Charlie could hear the clear-cut anger Richard barely kept under control. "Now, Dad, I was filming lots of stuff…"

"Bull crap, Charles. This video is the only thing you posted about the prom on your channel. If you filmed all evening, there would be a bunch of new videos instead of only one. Oh, there are lots of photos of all the kids, but this is the only video you posted. How did you know to be filming when Miguel dropped to one knee to propose to Bella?" The anger in Fancy's voice was palpable.

"Mama…" Bella began.

Fancy cut her off as she brushed a tear off her cheek. "I'll get to you in a minute, young lady. Answer us, Charles Ranscome Hobbs Winslow. How did you know to videotape right then?"

Miguel stood up. "This is all my fault. I asked Charlie to videotape us. I didn't tell him why."

The three adults stared at the four young people. Finally, Kirk spoke up. "I call bull shit. Young man, I don't know how they raise men in Texas, but where we come from, a man asks the young lady's father for her hand in marriage before proposing to the young lady."

Miguel swallowed hard as the color began draining from his face. "Sir, I meant no disrespect—"

"Then, you should have spoken to her father first." Kirk glared at Miguel.

"Mama, people don't do that anymore. I'm eighteen. I'm graduating from high school in two weeks. This isn't fair." Bella winced as her trembling voice began to get higher in pitch. It did that when she was nervous or scared.

Fancy shook her head. "You two barely know each other. How do you plan to live? Love won't pay the rent. You're both going to be in college, with tuition of $43,000 a year. Miguel has years of med school and residency ahead of him. How the blazes do you think you two will be able to live?"

Bella cringed as her mother's voice broke.

Richard pulled Fancy into his arms. "It will be okay, sweetheart. Elizabeth, Bella, why don't you girls help your mom get to bed?"

The girls hesitated.

"But, Daddy—" Bella began.

"Help your Mom, Bella Boo. This has been a pretty big shock for her. Help Mommy."

She still hesitated. "But, Daddy—"

"Bella, you may be eighteen, but you still live in my home. Please do as I asked and help your mother."

Fancy frowned as she shook her head. "Knock it off, Richard. This is important. I'm not going anywhere. I may have been born in the eighteenth century, but it's the twenty-first century now. The little women don't have to meekly go to our rooms any more while the menfolk handle the problem. I am not some frail, delicate, little flower of femininity. I intend to stay and be part of this discussion. After all, I *am* her mother. I'm the one who gave birth to this child."

Bella's eyes flashed. "Well, that's my point, Mother. It *is* the twenty-first century now. I am a modern woman. I am 18, and I can say 'yes' to Miguel's proposal without approval from my parents. It would be nice to have it, but we would manage without it. It's not like we're planning on getting married right away."

Richard rubbed his forehead, trying to will the oncoming headache away. "Well, I guess that's something. Miguel, what the hell are you thinking? You always struck me as a young man with a good head on his shoulders. This blows me away. Why on earth did you feel the need to ask her to marry you tonight? Are you that insecure about her coming to Trinity? Why now? Why not wait until, oh, I don't know, until sometime in the future when maybe you could support her?"

Miguel flinched at the anger in Richard's voice. He took a big breath. "Dr. Winslow, Bella is an exceptional young woman, and I fell really hard when I met her last year. We corresponded ever since, and you know from her phone bills we talk every day. When she came during Christmas break to meet my family, my *Abuelita* – my Grandmother –"

"I know what the word means," Richard growled. "I've spoken Spanish longer than you have been alive. My mother is Hispanic."

Miguel paused for a second. He took a big breath and then continued. "Well, my *Abuelita* told me, 'that girl's a keeper, Miguelito. Don't let her get away.' And she gave me the ring my *Abuelito* gave her 50 years ago to give to Bella. I waited until now."

"Miguel, she had to know about that ring before tonight. I'll concede it's a beautiful ring. Her dress compliments it perfectly. She wore my sapphire and diamond twin hearts brooch, along with sapphire earrings, even a sapphire and diamond bracelet that are all perfect compliments to the sapphire and diamond ring you gave her. She had to know this ring was coming tonight." Fancy spat out the words like they left a bad taste in her mouth.

Miguel swallowed hard and licked his lips. He forced himself to look Fancy straight in the eyes. "Yes, ma'am. I asked Bella to consider becoming engaged at Spring Break. I told her to think about it because it was a big decision. She said she didn't have to think about it. She knew she loves me."

"I do love you," Bella interjected. "With all my heart."

He smiled down at her. "And I love you, *mi amor*. My *Abuelita* sent the ring with me, and I showed it to her. We agreed we should wait –"

"Just not very long? What? - a month? You couldn't even wait until she got to San Antonio next month? Fine. Whatever." Fancy spat out the last word as she flipped her hand in the air.

All the men cringed.

"Now, Mother, be reasonable. You got married when you were seventeen…" Bella sounded frantic.

"No, I didn't, Bella. I was 20. You were nearly two before your daddy and I married."

Bella blinked, surprised by her mother's comment. "I thought you were 20 when you married Richard."

Fancy shook her head. "Nope. Wrong again. Twenty when I married Calvin. He died when I was 21 and pregnant with Charles. I married Kirk when I was 22…"

"You used to be married to Mr. O'Malley?" Poor Miguel looked more and more confused.

"We're divorced," said Kirk as Mellie rubbed his neck, struggling not to laugh.

Fancy glared at Miguel. "And I married Richard when I was 24. In the glen up by the cabin. That was twelve years ago. You know that, Bella."

Suddenly, Miguel looked like a light bulb had been switched on. "Wait a minute. Did you say you were born in the eighteenth century?"

Chapter 17
The Gig Is Up

Fancy turned to stare at Bella. "You didn't tell him?"

Bella huffed up at her mom. "You stressed to all of us not to ever tell anyone. Remember the fuss when Liz told her teacher that you used to know the Washingtons?"

"Not even the man you say you love? The man you say you want to marry and spend the rest of your life with?" Fancy smirked at Bella.

"You said *never*, Mother. I took you at your word." Bella spat the words out as she glanced nervously at Miguel.

"We don't need to be discussing this right now." Richard looked stressed. He rubbed his hand across his forehead again. "Oh, God, I'm getting a migraine."

"Well, actually, Doc, I'm kinda interested in this whole eighteenth-century stuff. The Washingtons, huh? Yes, I'd like to talk about it some more." Miguel sounded fascinated.

Bella threw her hands up in the air. "Fine. Whatever. What do you want to know?"

"How about we start with when were you born? *Bellissima, mi corazon, digame,* in what year were you born?" Miguel's voice was soft as he coaxed her to reveal her secret.

Bella glanced at Fancy, who threw her hands up in the air. Richard sat, rubbing his forehead. Kirk looked like he didn't know whether to laugh or cuss. Finally, Bella's shoulders sagged. "I was born in 1778 at Belle Rose Plantation, in the Commonwealth of Virginia."

Miguel shook his head. "No, no, Bella, no. That's not possible."

"You might be surprised to learn all sorts of things are possible, Mr. Vargas," Fancy snapped.

He stared at her for a minute. "How?"

"Time travel," Richard replied. "They came through a portal from then to now."

"A portal?"

"Yes, like a door through time. Miguel, you look bumfuzzled, to say the least." Bella leaned against him, one hand stroking his hand.

"You were really born in 1778? And your family knows – knew – the Washingtons?"

She nodded. "Martha Washington is my godmother."

"And actually, you were born at Mount Vernon, not at Belle Rose." Fancy sounded defiant.

"*Aye, Dios mio*, think if people from then could use time travel to the present for medical care." Miguel's voice sounded reverential.

Fancy looked surprised and glanced at Richard.

He nodded. "Go ahead. Tell him. Hell, why not? What difference would it make now?"

Fancy's smile was tremulous. "Well, Miguel, I believe God let me come forward in time for that very reason."

Miguel tilted his head as he studied her. "What do you mean, Mrs. Winslow?"

"I had two heart murmurs, one on my aorta, which is called aortic stenosis, which I was born with, and one on my mitral valve from rheumatic fever when I was a child. Of course, the rheumatic fever was untreated by antibiotics. We didn't have antibiotics in the eighteenth century. When I came forward in time, Richard and Dan were able to operate on me and replaced both valves."

His jaw dropped in stunned surprise. "Wow!"

"Wow indeed. Plus, because of time travel, I found and fell in love with the man I was destined to meet. Okay, I think we've been tough enough on the young'uns for one night. What say we all turn in? Kirk, put that blasted shotgun back in the study. It's late, and we can talk more about all these surprises tomorrow. Unless, of course, you two are planning to elope?"

Miguel looked horrified. "Oh, no, Mrs. Winslow, we would never do that. Bella wants a big wedding. You know, Bella has been in classes in high school with dual credit for college. She will start Trinity with 24 hours of credits, all straight A's. Since they were honors classes, she already has a 6.0 GPA for the first two years of college. She should graduate in no more than three years, max. I start med school this fall. We figured we would get married the summer she graduates from Trinity."

The three adults all looked relieved.

"And I know you're worried about my being able to support Bella while I'm a resident. That won't be a problem. I know you look at the Mexican boy and probably thought, how will the kid from the barrio manage? Dr. Winslow, my Dad is a doctor in San Antonio. I guess you didn't realize he was a doc in the military before he retired from the Air Force. My *Abuelito* is a doctor, too. They have a pretty lucrative orthopedics practice in San Antonio. I hadn't mentioned it before, I don't talk about it much, but I have a very comfortable trust fund. My folks always stress not to talk about money, but it seems like maybe I should right now. My Dad pointed out to me money won't be a problem for us. We'll be okay, even if we decide to get married sooner."

"So, why didn't you kids wait a year or two before this big announcement?" Kirk asked as he scratched his head and stifled a yawn. He reached around Mellie and pulled her to his chest.

Fancy shook her head. "We can talk more tomorrow. Just let me say that calms a lot of my concerns, Miguel." She reached over to hug him. "And since you're going to be part of the family, you can call me Mom. Unless you prefer to call me Fancy, *m'hijo*."

Miguel's face softened. "*Muchisimas gracias*, Mommy."

Chapter 18
Baylie's Worries

Dan Smith looked worried. "What are you going to do, Baylie?"

I held up my hands in frustration. "I don't know, Dan. O'Malley seems perfectly happy here. He does not want to go back. He says he likes this world we live in, and he loves being around Elizabeth. I think he loves being around Fancy."

Dan shook his head. "I'm not so sure Fancy is the hold on him. He's gone out several times now with Melanie Henderson. They seem quite taken with each other."

I could feel my eyebrows pop up. "With Mellie? Isn't she the new office manager?"

Dan nodded. "Yeah. She's also the mother of Rick's thirteen-year-old daughter, Sara."

"Oh, my God, Dan! What did Fancy say about that?"

"Not a whole lot. Sara was born while Rick was back in time, falling in love with Fancy. He didn't know she existed until a few months ago. God only knows how Mellie kept that secret all these years. Poor Fancy got rip-roaring drunk when she found out and wrapped the Beamer around a tree. Didn't you kinda wonder why they are moving to Texas?" Dan winked at me.

"Well, yeah, but they said it's a fantastic opportunity..." I knew I must look as stunned as I felt.

Dan nodded. "It is. But I doubt Rick would have seriously entertained the idea if he hadn't learned about Sara. This discovery caused significant turmoil in their lives. My lord, that girl looks enough like Dara to be her twin sister."

"So, what do I do if O'Malley continues to refuse to go back?" I resumed chewing on a hangnail.

He shrugged. "Knock him over the head and drag him? Or maybe convince Mellie she wants to go back in time with him."

"And then you lose your new office manager." I sighed as I shook my head in dismay.

He sighed. "And then I lose my office manager. It would be better than losing Rick. This whole ordeal has been damned tough on Fancy. I'm going to miss them both something terrible when they move to Texas."

I frowned. "Hmm... I wonder how much Kirk weighs?"

Dan chuckled. "Too heavy for you to drag all by yourself, especially in your current condition."

I walked over to the window and smiled as I looked out at the children playing at the playground across the street. I rubbed my baby bump and took a deep breath before I turned back to Dan as tears began to fill my eyes. "That's not my only concern. I'm 41."

"Hey, kid, don't rub it in. You ought to be 49 now if you had been here for the last eight years, but instead, you were Before for a mere 18 months."

I cringed. "Yeah, well, my doc thinks I am 49. Time travel is crazy hard to explain. Either way, I'm in that older mom risk group for increased birth defects. Oops, my bad. I'm supposed to say 'congenital disabilities.' Do you know women are considered at risk at age 35? In particular, Down syndrome usually affects one in about six hundred births. Among older moms, it's one in two hundred. And among Native Americans? One in one hundred. That's pretty scary, Dan. I understand the rate for Native Americans is the highest in the country."

I struggled not to cry.

Dan looked shocked but quickly covered his shock with his best professional face. "What did you say?"

I nodded, my face bleak. "I said Down syndrome, Dan, and that's just for Trisomy 21. The first test didn't consider the other forms of the disease, Translocation and Mosaicism."

Dan could feel the blood drain from his face. "They tested you already?"

I nodded as tears welled up in my eyes.

"The mosaic variety is not usually as severe." Dan sounded thoughtful.

"That's what I understand, but it is still a handicapping condition, Dan." I dabbed at my eyes with the twisted Kleenex in my hands. "These children have below-average intelligence. They often have serious heart defects."

Dan shook his head. "Valve defects. Yes, I guess it's good your big brother is a heart surgeon. Jesus, Bay, has the obstetrician told you she thinks this baby has Down syndrome?"

I shook my head. "Not definitively. They took the first blood tests five weeks ago when I was ten weeks along. The doctor will do a special ultrasound and a second blood test this afternoon, at fifteen weeks. If those look definitive, she will recommend an amniocentesis."

"Do they do the second batch of tests if the first tests show no DS?"

Suddenly, I could no longer contain my tears. I shook my head as my face crumpled. "She said the tests were inconclusive, but you and I know it means my baby probably has DS. The second tests are about 95% accurate as a diagnostic. If they come back positive, they can do an amniocentesis. They are 99% accurate."

Dan pulled me into his arms. "No wonder you're upset. It'll be okay, baby sister. I promise it will be okay."

"She keeps urging me to tell Wolf. I can't get word to a man living in 1788 that I'm pregnant here. I sure as hell can't possibly explain where Wolf is. Every time she asks, I start to cry."

He chuckled. "She probably thinks he's a real rat bastard."

I nodded. "He's anything but that. He's such a good man. He would be so excited about this baby. So would I, except I'm so damned scared."

"And you just want to go back and share your good news." Dan shook his head.

"Assuming it *is* good news. And I can't go back unless I take O'Malley with me. The council made that crystal clear. Wolf said to come back even if O'Malley won't go, but that would mean we would wind up two Cherokees without a tribe to help us. I'm not that brave. Oh, Dan, what do I do?" I wailed.

"I'm not sure, but I'm leaning towards tying Kirk up and dragging him back to the 18ᵗʰ century. I bet Rick and I could help you do it."

I grinned and then hiccuped as I wiped the tears from my eyes. "I bet you could, even if Kirk is the blasted *Tsul Kalu*. Damned white devil."

"Well, let's get through these tests and see what she says. You may be getting yourself all worked up for nothing." Dan kissed the top of my head and handed me a Kleenex.

I blew my nose. "If it's DS, I can't go back. I can't take her back."

Dan looked startled. "Why not? My God, you would give up your role in the prophecy for a DS baby?"

I shook my head. "No, I would give up that life for *my* baby, who happened to have DS. She'll be a human being first and foremost, Dan."

Dan grinned at me as he pulled me into a big hug. "Good for you, sis. Hey, did you say 'she'? Do you know the sex yet?"

I smiled. "Well, maybe I'm just hoping. The doc suspected she's a girl based on heart rate. She said we would be able to tell for sure from the ultrasound they are doing today."

I paused for a minute as I nibbled my lip and then took a deep breath before I continued. "There's something else."

"What is it? Well, spit it out, sis."

"As I said, the Cherokees think O'Malley is the *Tsul Kalu*, the slant-eyed white devil. If my baby has DS, I would be afraid—" My voice broke.

"Oh, my God, DS babies have almond-shaped eyes. They might think O'Malley fathered your slant-eyed baby. Yeah, that would suck." Dan looked rattled.

I nodded. "Yeah. Big time. And I swear, I never engaged in sexual relations with that damned Irishman. Why would I? I had Wolf. He's all I will ever want. Hell, he's all I ever wanted."

I blinked the tears back from my eyes. I squared my shoulders and gave my big brother a tremulous smile. "Okay. Let's go get these tests done." He pushed open the door to my doctor's office and we walked inside.

Kate looked up from the papers she was studying as we entered the waiting room. "Come on in, Baylie. Let's get these tests underway. Oh, hi, Dan. I didn't know you were coming today. I'm glad you could attend this appointment with your sister."

Dan nodded. "I'm in full support of Baylie, Kate. I want to be with her when you give her the results."

"Of course. Come on, Baylie. Let's get this show on the road."

My skin paled beneath my coppery tan. I gulped and then nodded as I stood up to follow the doctor into the room for the ultrasound.

Dan grabbed my hand. "It will be okay, honey. No matter what it shows, it will be fine. Your big brother is here for you."

I tried to smile as I nodded. "I know."

I turned to follow the doctor into the ultrasound room.

Three days later, Dan and I sat in nervous silence as Dr. McClintock reviewed the test results.

Finally, the doctor looked up from her laptop. "First things first. Baylie, you were right. This baby is a girl."

My face alit with happiness for a moment. I squeezed Dan's hand. "And? What about the test results?"

Dr. McClintock looked grave. "The results appear definitive for Down syndrome. Are you sure you want to go through with this pregnancy?"

Tears welled up in my eyes. I glanced at Dan as I nodded. I squared my shoulders. "Yes. I'm sure. This is the only time I will ever have a baby. I refuse to kill her because she is imperfect. We're all imperfect. We are all broken at least a little bit. I am not the Great Spirit, who let me conceive this child. Who am I, to say her imperfection merits her to die?"

• • •

Rick walked out of the examination room, handed a file to Melanie, and then frowned. "Hey, aren't you supposed to be gone by now?"

She shrugged. "Kirk picked up Sara from my house and took her to your house. He's coming to pick me up here. Why?"

Rick blinked and then grinned. "Well, alrighty then. You know, he could have brought her here and dropped her off with me. You two have big plans for the weekend?"

Her cheeks flushed pink. "You might say so."

She walked away to put up the file, humming a popular tune. Rick chuckled. The new Billy Ray Cyrus song went viral. He even heard Kirk singing it lately. The damned tune would be stuck in his head all night now.

Five minutes later, Kirk sauntered in, dimples flashing as he gave Mellie his lop-sided grin. She smiled at him, grabbed her purse, and waved to Rick, who was making notes to a file. Rick glanced up long enough to smile, shake his head, and wave goodbye to them.

When she reached Kirk, he pulled her close for a long kiss.

"I missed you." He dipped his head to kiss her again.

She stroked the side of his face as she sighed. She grabbed his hand, kissed him one more time for good measure, and then urged him towards the door. "I missed you, too. Come on, darling, let's go. I want to change my clothes."

He held out the garment bag to her. "I figured you would change here."

"Oh, you clever man. Give me a minute and I'll be right back."

Mellie hurried into the ladies' room where she donned the pretty dress she would wear that evening. She touched up her makeup, quickly pulled her long blonde hair into a messy bun, and spritzed on the fragrance she knew Kirk loved. Minutes later, she came out in the sexy, white halter dress that showed off the tan she developed at the lake with her new man.

Mellie smiled. Her new man. She hadn't had a man in her life since Rick. He and Kirk were so different. She no longer regretted letting Rick get away. Kirk thrilled her more than Rick ever did. She never imagined any man could make her feel the way Kirk did.

Not that they hadn't hit a few bumps along the way. After all, he was pure, unadulterated, eighteenth-century male. He could be pretty bossy – no, downright misogynistic – at times. However, she had never seen the temper Fancy claimed he had with her. Kirk was loving, caring, protective, adventurous in bed, and best of all, deeply in love with her. He was, as Sara put it, all that and a bag of chips.

"Do I look okay?" She pirouetted when she walked out, swishing the skirt about her long, shapely legs.

He pulled her close to him again. "No, *mo ghaol.* You do not look 'okay.' You look, what is it the kids say? You look drop-dead gorgeous."

She sighed as she reached up to wrap her arms around his neck again. "How do you always manage to say to the right thing to me?"

He beamed at her. "It must be love."

She pulled him close for a quick hug. "It must be."

• • •

Rick shook his head as he picked up the phone. Things went to hell in a handbasket this afternoon. They always did if Dan took off early, and this was the second time Dan bugged out early this week. It was almost seven and way past time to head home. "Dr. Winslow here. How may I help you?"

"Richard, you have to meet us at the Riverside Restaurant as fast as you can get there." Cessie sounded frantic.

He frowned. "Why, sweetie?"

"Mellie's mom called. Mellie and Kirk are getting married there this evening. I have the kids in the car, and we are headed there now."

"Jesus, Cessie, are you sure? I can't believe they wouldn't even take Sara."

"Well, Sara is going to be there. Get your hustle on. We're crashing this wedding. They'll have family and friends in attendance whether they like it or not."

"Well, I guess Kirk won't make any more snide comments about me stealing you. I'm on my way." Richard laughed and quickly dialed Dan's number. "Hey, Dan, you aren't going to believe this…"

• • •

Kirk helped Mellie into the little sports car and quickly headed north towards Blue Ridge. Fifteen minutes later, he eased the car into a parking place outside the Riverside Restaurant. They both loved the place, and he reserved their favorite table for two outside overlooking the river. The hostess led them down the steps to the table set up right beside the river. Little lights twinkled in the night air, giving the spot a magical feel Mellie adored. Rose petals covered the floor around their table, and a small arrangement of roses and heather decorated the table. "It's beautiful, darling."

"No, you're beautiful. But the place looks pretty damned good."

A few minutes later, a waiter brought out a beautiful bouquet of roses. The waiter blushed as he handed the flowers to Mellie. "I'm sorry, ma'am, we were supposed to have these waiting for you when you arrived."

She smiled graciously as she took the flowers. "No problem. Thank you, young man. And thank you, darling. They are beautiful, too."

"Are you sure you want to do this tonight?" Kirk raised her hand to kiss her fingertips.

She nodded. "Absolutely. Never more sure of anything in all my life."

He beamed at her and kissed her hand again.

Minutes later, the manager came up to them.

"Mr. O'Malley, everything is ready, sir, if you two would like step over here by the river."

Kirk looked over at Mellie. For just a second, his heart lurched. "Are you ready, my love?"

She nodded and leaned across and kissed him again and then quickly picked up the bouquet of roses. She giggled as Kirk growled.

He reached across, took her hand, and pulled her up from the chair. "Then come on, *mo ghaol*."

"*Mo ghaol?* Now, what does that mean? You said it earlier, and I meant to ask then. I was just getting used to you calling me '*mo ghràidh*.'"

He blushed. "It means 'my love.'"

She smiled as she nodded and took his hand. Together, they walked to the waiting Justice of the Peace.

"We are gathered here tonight in the sight of God..."

Just then, the sound of footsteps rushing down the stairs caused everyone to look up. Mellie's eyes widened in surprise. "Sara! Rick, I-I-I can explain—"

Sara ran up to stand between Kirk and Mellie. She took each one by the hand. "We thought you needed a flower girl."

"And a best man." Rick grinned at Kirk.

"Speak for yourself, grasshopper. We thought you needed two best men," Dan growled. "We couldn't catch Stephan. He already left when we learned what you guys were doing."

"And Mellie now has two bride's matrons," Fancy and Dee chimed in.

Mellie's mom joined the crowd. "And of course, you meant to invite the mother of the bride."

Tears welled up in Mellie's eyes. "Are you all sure? How did you all know?"

"I spilled the beans. You didn't think I would really let my daughter run off and get married without all of us there, did you? My land, child, you should know me better than that." Her mom grinned ear to ear, her eyes shining bright with unshed tears of pride and joy for her only child.

"I love you, Mom." Mellie hugged her mother tight.

"I love you, too, honey. I hope you aren't mad at me."

Mellie shook her head. "Oh, no. I just didn't want to cause poor Baylie any more grief than she is already feeling."

"Don't worry about Baylie. What will be will be." Dan patted her on the back.

"Who is Baylie?" The JP looked worried.

"My baby sister. She had some bad news this week. It's not related to these two. She would not want to ruin their wedding."

"Well, she might try to get them to go back—" Fancy began.

"—to Ireland. Hey, Kirk, maybe you guys should go to Ireland sometime this summer. That would be a cool honeymoon." Charlie winked at his mom.

The justice of the peace beamed as well. "Wonderful! Well, let's start over. We are gathered here tonight in the sight of God, family, and friends, to join these two in holy matrimony..."

Later, everyone hugged and kissed Mellie and Kirk. Staff quickly brought out more tables to seat everyone beneath the twinkling lights, beside the river. Dan ordered bottles of Dom Perignon, and they all ate trout almandine by the rushing waters of the Toccoa River. The chef brought out a lovely wedding cake at the finish of the meal.

As Fancy looked at Mellie's ring, Mellie swore she couldn't remember anything else of the ceremony after they all rushed in. "It scared me at first when you all rushed in. I knew someone intended to object."

"We left Baylie at home," Dan drolly replied.

"Yeah, well, I was kinda afraid she might raise some Cain if she knew." Mellie blushed.

"Baylie's fighting her own cross-eyed bear right now with the news she received this afternoon, but you two are not among the bears she fights. She will be happy for you, but yes, this had been a damned hard day for her."

Wordless, Mellie nodded.

"Mellie, you can take a couple of days off now if you want. We won't give you that whole week until later this summer, but Rick and I figured a four-day weekend would be a better mini-honeymoon than a mere two days."

Mellie threw her arms around Dan's neck to embrace him. "Oh, thank you, Dan!"

"Don't thank me. Fancy will be there to run the office. It was her idea."

Mellie turned to beam at Fancy.

Fancy cleared her throat. "Mellie, I'm happy to do it. Your rings are beautiful. Where did you get them?" Fancy traced the Celtic knotwork pattern around the exquisite, heart-cut, diamond.

"Kirk says it's a posy ring. It's got a message inside like old fashioned wedding rings."

"Oh, show me!" Fancy exclaimed.

Melanie smiled and slipped the ring off to show Fancy the engraving inside.

"Oh, how sweet. 'My love I give thee freely and of my whole heart.' It's beautiful. I'm so happy for you two." She blinked back tears of happiness for them and handed the ring back to Mellie.

Mellie smiled as she slipped the ring back on her finger and then extended it for everyone else to see it. "Kirk found them. His ring matches, without the diamond, of course. The same thing is engraved in his ring. I think he contacted the same jeweler who made your rings to make these for us. They are pretty, aren't they?"

"Very pretty." Fancy hugged her again. "But what matters is that Kirk makes you happy."

"Here, here! To happiness!" said Charlie.

Rick shook his head. "No, son. Here, here, to a long life filled with much love and happiness."

Everyone nodded as the chimed in, "Here, here!"

Soon, the musicians moved outside of the bar. Mellie and Kirk fell together laughing as they began to play 'Old Town Road.' Everyone joined in as they sang Kirk and Mellie's favorite C&W tune. As the evening ended, everyone pelted them with rose petals and birdseed as they ran to the little convertible to slip away for a quick honeymoon.

"Are you happy, my love?" Kirk asked.

She nodded as she pulled his hand from her lap to her face. She gently kissed his big hand and then smiled. "Immeasurably. And I am most definitely in love with my big, sexy husband."

He pulled her to him and kissed her again. "Me, too. Thank God Baylie told me about the portal, and I was able to come here and find you. I must be the luckiest man alive. I never dreamed I would come here and find the woman I was always meant to love."

"We're both pretty lucky." She laid her head on his shoulder.

Later, Mellie swore she could not remember much of the actual ceremony after everyone crashed the wedding. She was too busy struggling not to cry. Melanie insisted all she could remember was the love shining in Kirk's eyes as he slipped the ring onto her finger. She had never felt quite so loved before.

Chapter 19
Wolf - Beyond

The sun sank below the horizon as the man rode up to the visitor's station at the Beech Bottom trailhead. The rangers stared in stunned disbelieve as the tall, slender, Native American man dismounted from his horse and tied the reins to the railing in front of the cabin. Not many people rode up to the ranger's shack at the trailhead on horseback these days.

"Uh, may we help you, sir?" Todd Rickert asked as he scratched his head.

The handsome stranger smiled at the ranger. Even though outfitted in jeans and a red plaid, button-up shirt, with the sleeves rolled up, the braids and moccasins shouted the man's Cherokee heritage. The ranger's eyes grew wide as the man removed the slouch hat to wipe the sweat from his brow. He had not seen many Cherokees with facial tattoos before.

"Yes, thank you. I missed my turn somewhere." He frowned as he studied the map. "I meant to take the Jacks River Trail."

"Oh, you missed it about four and a half miles back. You should have kept heading south at the Falls along the river. You probably made the loop. Lots of people do that. Now, you need to backtrack if you want to go that way. Where are you headed?"

"Could you give me directions to the town called Blue Ridge? I believe it is supposed to be here." He pulled out his map and pointed to Lake Blue Ridge, which was circled with blue ink, and handed the map to the ranger.

"Oh, of course. Have you come far?"

He smiled. "Yes, it has been a long journey. It looks like Blue Ridge might be another 40 or 50 miles from here. Am I correct?"

The ranger nodded. "Yes, but it's a pretty rugged ride, cutting across through some rough stretches in the Cohutta Wilderness. It will take you three or four days to ride there on horseback."

Shadow Wolf nodded. "I expected it would take at least three. If you can show me the trail, I can get there on my own. I want to surprise my wife."

Todd looked perplexed. "Well, I can assure you, sir, she is going to be surprised when you ride into town on that gorgeous horse. But honestly, can't I call someone to come and get you? It's a two-hour ride by car compared to a four-day trip by horseback. You could be with her tonight."

Wolf smiled. "I prefer to ride through this part of the world a while longer. I have not seen this country in many long years. I am sure it has changed considerably. Besides, I have a phone. I can call her if necessary."

The ranger frowned and shook his head. "Sir, you don't understand. Cell phones don't usually work in the Wilderness. I'd feel a lot better about this if you let me call someone to come up here to get you."

"I will be fine without a phone. I assure you I can manage the Cohutta Wilderness without one." Wolf laughed, his dark eyes twinkling as he accepted a cold drink of water from the ranger. "Ah, thank you. The cold water tastes good."

The ranger looked unconvinced. "Well, maybe so. Uh, why don't you spend the night here, sir? You could get a fresh start in the morning."

Wolf smiled again. "The Falls are only a little over four miles from here, you said. I should have no problem making that far tonight."

"Well, sir, no overnight camping is allowed with horses at the falls. You need to stop at the meadow before the Falls. It's the four-mile point on the way to the Falls."

Wolf nodded. "Then, I will head to McCarron's Corner."

He untied his horse and prepared to mount up again.

"Oh, you know Doc?" Todd looked relieved.

Wolf stared at the man, startled by the question. His eyes narrowed. "Yes, I know Rick and Fancy Winslow. I will head to their cabin, and I will leave from there in the morning."

"Well, sir, they aren't up here right now—" the ranger began.

"I do not think Rick will mind if I spend the night camping outside their cabin. We are old friends." His answer sounded calm, unruffled, and yet adamant. He swung onto the saddle, and he gathered the reins into one hand. "There is a well at the cabin, so my horse and I will have fresh water."

"I don't believe I caught your name, sir." The ranger looked flustered.

"I am Shadow Wolf, of the Cohutta Cherokees." He tipped his hat and pulled back onto the Beech Bottom Trail.

The ranger stood scratching his neck as another ranger came outside the log cabin that served at their shack. "What's up, Todd? Who was the Indian?"

"He said he's Shadow Wolf, of the Cohutta Cherokees." Todd stood scratching his head as he stared after Wolf.

"Why do you look so puzzled?" asked the second ranger.

"The last remaining Cohutta Cherokees were forcibly removed from the area in 1837 during the Trail of Tears, although most of the tribe moved out years before," Todd replied as he watched the lone horseman ride down the trail.

"Huh. Maybe he's descended from them. And maybe he's full of bull."

Todd watched until Wolf and the horse were out of sight. "Maybe so, Willard, but I have a feeling that man was the real deal."

Wolf quickly rode the four miles to the meadow by the McCarron cabin. The changes Rick made to the cabin impressed him. Marc had not mentioned they used the cabin while they were in the future. He smiled. *Not the future now. I managed to go Beyond. I am in their current time.*

He dismounted and unsaddled his horse. He eased the bridle off the big Appaloosa stallion as he murmured to the horse softly in Cherokee. He then hobbled the animal to keep him from wandering too far from the meadow. The stud began to graze on the plentiful native grasses as

Wolf bent over to start a small fire in the fire pit he found near the creek. Soon, he was cleaning a fat trout he speared in the stream as his water heated in a leather pot over the fire. Wolf roasted the trout while his potatoes and corn boiled in the leather pot. He raised his eyes heavenward and gave thanks to the Great Spirit, and then he pondered his actions for the next few days.

The ranger tempted Wolf to call Guider at the ranger's building, but he was not yet sure what to say to her. At the ranger's insistence, he tried to call Fancy and Rick once he got to the cabin, but as the ranger had warned, he got no answer. That was probably just as well, for he did not know how they could carry his horse to their abode in one of the strange conveyances he saw near the ranger's shack. He sighed. He needed these next few days to begin to adjust to this strange, new world. He realized he would not mind staying at the cabin a day or two. He brushed the dirt off his hands and straightened up. *No. You must find your woman. It is now or never.*

Oh, Great Spirit, guide me in my quest.

• • •

"Hmm, I got another call from that unknown number. No message." Fancy frowned.

"Probably someone was trying to sell you insurance. Or maybe an extended warranty for your car." Richard winked at her.

"No, they usually leave a message and a number. They want to make their sales quotas." Fancy looked thoughtful as she stood tapping her forefinger against her temple.

"Well, probably a wrong number then. Come on, sweetie, let's get home. It's late. Ronan fell asleep at the dinner table." Richard swept his sleeping eight-year-old son up into his arms to carry him out to the SUV.

She shrugged. "I dunno. Probably. My poor baby boy must be exhausted. Come on, kids, let's go home."

Mellie's mom went home with Rick and Fancy to give Kirk and Mellie some much-desired privacy at the Carter's Lake house on their first night as man and wife.

. . .

Kirk carried his bride over the threshold of the house an hour later, kicking the door shut as he again kissed his beautiful wife. As he sat her feet to the ground, she began to unbutton his shirt. They somehow managed to continue kissing as their clothing dropped to the floor in a messy line to Mellie's bedroom. Soon, they were entangled on the bed, and as Mellie promised, she took the lead to once again ride her wild, Irish stallion until she couldn't ride anymore. They collapsed together in a tangle of limbs to sleep soundly until the alarm went off bright and early the next morning.

Mellie groaned as the clanging alarm woke her. "Do we have to get up this early?"

She trailed a finger down Kirk's rock-hard abs, as she watched another part grow hard as well.

He groaned. "Rick slipped me the key to the cabin before we left last night. We don't have to camp out unless you want to. And they gave you two extra days off. So, maybe we could wait a wee bit..."

She laughed, the sound sultry as hot sex, and pulled him over to her. "Well, just for that, I guess I should reward you, big boy."

His eyes grew wide as she slipped beneath the sheets. "Ah, Melanie O'Malley, be gentle, my love."

An hour later, both bearing smug grins, they finally headed out for the Cohutta Wilderness.

. . .

"Hurry up, O'Malley!"

Melanie slung the backpack down into the porch of the ranger's cabin and turned to grin at the big Irishman lumbering after her. "Kirk, you look like you've been rode hard and put up wet."

Kirk caught up with her and pulled her to his chest. "I'll show you 'rode hard,' lass. Just you wait until we get to the cabin." His head dipped to claim another kiss from her.

Mellie giggled. She pushed the door open seconds before Kirk caught up with her, where he wrapped her in his arms for another loving embrace. They entered together and approached the ranger. "Officer Rickert, I would like to introduce you to my husband, Kirk O'Malley."

Todd beamed ear to ear. "Mr. O'Malley! I am delighted to see you again, sir. I wondered what happened to you. It looks like you are doing well."

Kirk began to blush. "Yes, I'm doing quite well. It has all turned out amazingly well, and I met and married a wonderful woman."

Todd laughed. "I wondered how Dr. Winslow reacted, but he's a great guy."

Kirk nodded. "Aye, he is. Richard explained many things to me. We've become pretty good friends."

"Did Rick explain how the cow ate the cabbage, darling?" Mellie asked, her voice droll.

Kirk nodded as he bit back laughter. "Exactly. We're headed to the cabin for a few days. The Winslow's loaned it to us."

"Well, great. By the way, there was an Indian fellow headed there yesterday. He took the wrong turn headed for the Jacks River Trail. He swore he was going to ride his horse to Blue Ridge."

Mellie noticed Kirk turned pale despite his tan. "Did he mention his name?"

Todd nodded. "Yes, ma'am, he said his name is Shadow Wolf."

Shit, thought Kirk. *I willna go with him.* "Riding a horse, you say? Interesting. Did he say why he planned to ride his horse to Blue Ridge?"

"He said he wanted to surprise his wife." Todd resumed tidying up the cabin.

Kirk cut his eyes at Mellie. "Aye, it should surprise her to see him ride into town on horseback. Is he still riding that big Appaloosa stallion?"

Todd shrugged. "Oh, you know him. I didn't get close enough to the horse to check it's gender, but it was a gorgeous animal."

"I'm calling Fancy," Mellie said. "Someone needs to let Baylie know—"

"Hell, don't call Fancy. Call Dan. She lives with Dan and Dee. She's his sister," Kirk said as he pulled Mellie outside. "But I tell you, I'll not go back with him. Not now. I found my future, here with you. He'll not deprive me of it."

Melanie beamed at him. "I love you, Kirk O'Malley."

He pulled her into his arms again. "I love you, too, *mo ghaol*. Well, let's head to yon cabin and see what problems await us there."

Mellie hugged him. "It'll be fine, darling. You found your destiny here. Surely that will be all that counts."

Kirk smiled. "Aye, love, surely it will."

Kirk kissed the top of her head. *It had damned sure better be, for I'll not leave this woman. I'll die before I leave her.*

Mellie tried to call Dan, but got no answer. She left a message that a Native American man riding an Appaloosa was seen headed towards Blue Ridge. "He said his name is Shadow Wolf, Dan. Could he have come to help Baylie? Call me back. We're headed to the cabin now."

They headed down the trail, and in a little over an hour, they arrived at McCarron's Corner. Kirk stood agog at the dramatic changes Richard had made to the log cabin over the years.

"My lord, it looks like a mansion now," he marveled. "It must be as big as Belle Rose."

Mellie nodded. "I never saw Belle Rose, but they fixed the cabin up beautifully. Wait until you see inside."

As she began to put the code into the digital lockbox, Kirk swept his bride into another kiss. As the kiss ended, he swung her into his arms and pushed the door open.

"Ahem."

Kirk looked towards the sound and paled. He lowered Melanie to the floor and pushed her behind him. "I'll not go with you, Wolf. I found my destiny. I intend to stay here with my wife."

Wolf stared at him for a minute before he answered. "You gave up on Fancy, then?"

Kirk nodded. "Aye. She is very happy with Richard, just as I am with Melanie. They have a good life here. We intend to have a great life here, as well. I will not go with you. Our lives are here."

Wolf nodded. "So be it. Then, I will find my wife, and we shall return home."

Kirk blinked. "B-b-but Guider told me the council insisted I had to return."

Wolf nodded. "That is their desire. I desire to ensure that the will of the All-Seeing One is done. I believe it will be done if you found your rightful place. My goal now is to find my Guider and take her home. Her place is with me, just as your place is where your heart is."

Mellie tapped Kirk on the shoulder. "Put me down, darling. Chief Shadow Wolf, there might be a problem with Baylie – um, I mean Guider – going back home with you. Come in. I'll make us a big pot of coffee. We need to talk."

Wolf reached out for her arm. "What is the problem? Please, tell me."

Mellie pulled Wolf into the cabin to the table. "Sit down. This is complicated."

Wolf grabbed her hand. "Is my Guider sick? What is wrong?"

Mellie shook her head. "No, she is not sick, unless it is heartsick because she has been separated from you. Oh, my, this is complicated—"

"Perhaps *she* needs to be the one to tell him these things," Kirk said, his voice full of unspoken warning.

"What is wrong? Tell me, woman. Now." Suddenly, the easy-going demeanor of the handsome Native American disappeared, to be replaced by the irrefutable honed steel of the warrior chief.

Mellie frowned. "Wow, way to channel your inner chieftain, sir. Okay. She's pregnant."

Wolf's face alit with joy. "How is this a problem? This is wonderful news."

Mellie sighed. "Well, maybe. There are complications, Wolf—"

Chapter 20

Wolf headed towards Blue Ridge the next morning. O'Malley's bride talked to him for hours about Guider's concerns. He had to admit he felt concerned as well. His face showed new creases from worry about Guider and their unborn child. It now appeared more creased from anxiety than it had been lined from exposure to elements over the preceding five decades. Wolf believed the tribe would accept the baby; at least, he prayed they would accept her. But, what quality of life would a mentally challenged child have, living in the Indian Territory in the 1700s, far from quality medical care and education? Or would such a child fit in better with the Cherokees, who had no written language at that time, than here in the modern world? Guider assured him a Cherokee man would soon create what she called a syllabary, by which Cherokees could learn to read and write, but it seemed like a pipe dream to Wolf. He could neither read nor write any language, and he spoke several. Could such a thing as the development of an alphabet for the Cherokee language indeed come to pass?

He looked around and sighed. While much of the Cohutta Wilderness remained pristine, as he remembered it Before in his own time, he saw some changes when he traveled to the location of the ranger's cabin, including the strange machines Mellie called 'cars.' She told him the people of this time travel in those cars. He also saw many fascinating creations from this new world in the cabin, ranging from running water, the cookstove, and the magic box that kept food cold, which Mellie called a 'fridge.' His amazement over the many modern conveniences seemed endless.

His concerns also seemed endless. How could Cherokee children ever be expected to keep the old ways in this new world filled with such tantalizing conveniences? He would be sorely tempted to live in the comforts he saw in the renovated cabin and to never return to the past.

Except for his duty to the prophecy.

He and Guider had never discussed the last part of the prophecy. No one understood it, so why consider it? Now, it finally made sense. "And after the Path of the Guiding Light shall come to lead her people to the new lands, Faith shall be sorely challenged, and yet, Faith shall prevail with renewed Charity towards all."

Ginny told him, 'Faith, Hope, and Charity' was a Christian concept. He told her he did not believe Christians were the only group who believed that faith, hope, and love could unite and guide a people and that the Cherokees believed in those concepts.

His people knew the travel westward would be difficult. The difficulties ahead terrified some of his tribe. They knew their faith would be tested. But, was it possible the Faith mentioned referred to a person rather than their spiritual beliefs?

Or could it mean both? Might the birth of their daughter herald the beginning of the difficult times for their people? And might the strength and courage of one girl, mentally and physically challenged as she might well be, inspire his people to accomplish the impossible task before them?

He had heard Christian friends, and even his beloved Ginny say, 'a little child shall lead the way.' Ginny swore Bright Star was the child who would come to lead the way. Wolf knew Star would be able to persuade their people to move again. He was never sure she would also be the child to give his people faith in themselves to tackle the journey. Wolf thought Guider would provide them with the faith to tackle another move. It had not occurred to him the faith Guider would provide might be through a child, or that they might name their child, go hi yu di, Cherokee for Faith.

He talked to Rick on the telephone device at the cabin. Rick was excited he came to find Guider. He resisted the urge to let Rick meet him with what Rick called a horse trailer and to take him straight into Blue Ridge. Wolf needed time to think. Too much was happening too fast. He could not, what was the word Guider used? - oh, yes, he could not assimilate it all. He could not take it all in. He had much to discuss with Guider, but first, he needed to organize his thoughts.

Wolf pulled up his horse and stared across the mountains deep in thought. His woman expected a child. Not merely a child, but his child. Their daughter would be sorely challenged, but she would inspire their people.

He smiled and kicked the horse into a canter. Yes, one daughter to be the promised Bright Star, and another daughter to be called the Faith of the People.

"Hey, Mister, where are you headed?"

Wolf pulled up his horse and smiled at the eager young man. "I am riding to the town called Blue Ridge."

The young man's eyes grew wide with surprise. "Wow! That's a good forty miles from here."

Wolf nodded. "So, I understand. I travel to find my wife."

The young man chuckled. "Did you lose her, Chief?"

"No. She has been visiting her family. I missed her. It was time I came."

They talked for about a half-hour. As Wolf rode on down Old Highway 2, the young man muttered, "Damn. Not a very impressive first interview for my paper. I've got a dude riding down an old country road like it's the most normal thing in the world. How could I forget to ask his name or his tribe?"

· · ·

"You've been pretty quiet this weekend, Sis. What's going on in your head? Are you going to have the amnio?" Dan pulled Baylie close for a hug.

I trembled and clung to my big brother for a minute or two and tried to smile. "No. I decided the tests are already 95% accurate. Why spend more money on another test? Besides, there are dangers inherent in the amniocentesis. If done incorrectly, it can kill a baby. I made up my mind. I don't need to keep second-guessing myself."

Dan's face softened at her words. "It'll be okay, kiddo. You know we will support your decision, no matter what it is. We're here to help you."

"I know." I nodded as tears filled my eyes. I pulled away from Dan, embarrassed to again be crying. "Damned leaky eyes."

Dan chuckled and hugged me even tighter, but no laughter lit my eyes.

I walked outside to stare out over the bustling lake, yet I barely noticed the crowds of people enjoying the water. All I could think was 'my baby has Down syndrome.' Dr. Kate talked to me again about terminating my pregnancy when she gave me the news. I swore for the past month that was not a possibility, but now I was having second thoughts. How could I fulfill my role in the prophecy with a handicapped baby?

I knew it was politically incorrect to call my unborn child 'handicapped' or even to call a child with Down syndrome 'disabled.' I considered myself to be a progressive thinker, and yet it was proving difficult for me to think of my unborn child as 'different-abled' rather than 'disabled.'

I knew my baby would more than likely face intellectual, cognitive, and developmental challenges and stood a good chance of being born with a heart abnormality. Did I have the right to curse a child to such a life simply because I wanted to be a mother?

Dr. Kate kept telling me that many women chose to terminate pregnancies of their unborn babies who were diagnosed with DS. She reminded me again on Friday that it was my body and my choice.

It might be my choice. But we weren't talking about my body. We were discussing the body and the life of a little, unborn child who was dependent upon me. My eyes filled up with tears for the millionth time as I cradled my baby bump with my hands. Great Spirit, what should I do?

Of course, Dr. Kate thought I was 49, not 41. Dr. Kate told me again on Friday that she was concerned for me, not just my baby, but also me, due to my age. I had not attempted to explain that I time-traveled back to 1787 when I was 40, stayed there a year and a half, and when I returned here, eight years had elapsed. I could not explain time travel and the anomalies regarding the time-space continuum, as I called it, to my Ob-Gyn. Plus, raising this baby would be hard with a supportive spouse, and I was a single woman.

I realized I needed to decide where I would work. I knew I needed to find a job to support the baby and myself, but I also knew I probably would not land a decent job until after the baby was born. I sighed. Could I handle a high-pressure job at the BIA again, or did I need to hang a shingle out in Blue Ridge? And if I returned to the BIA, could I stand the endless monotony, not to mention the sexual harassment? I smiled. Hell, I was a warrior woman now. I might deck any guy who tried to proposition me again. But, could I bear to work for the agency again?

I sighed, my shoulders again sagging. What should I do? How could I make a decision this enormous on my own? *Oh, Great Spirit, help me make the right decision.*

I slumped against the rail on the deck overlooking the lake. "I'm so tired," I whispered.

Dee came over to me and wrapped an arm around my shoulders. "Why don't you take a nap, hon? It will help you clear your mind."

I shook my head. 'No, I'm not just physically tired. I'm so tired of crying, Dee. I'm tired of being sad. I should be happy now, and all I feel is sad. And angry. I'm so tired of feeling angry. One in a hundred Native American women have a pregnancy with a baby carrying Down syndrome. That means ninety-nine out of a hundred don't have it, so why me? Why my baby? Why the one baby I will ever have? Why?"

Dee pulled me into her arms as my tears began to flow again. "It'll be okay, hon—"

"No, Dee, it won't. I miss Wolf so much. I need him here with me. I'm tired of being alone. Oh, I know I have you guys but, I want my Wolf. Dammit, I want the life I can never have now."

Dee frowned. "Why do you say that, Baylie? You can go back."

I shook my head. "The council said I couldn't go back without O'Malley. He'll never go back now. He's happy, married to the woman he loves. Oh, Great Spirit, why can't things ever work out for me? I finally got rid of Brian, and I went back to help our people. In the process, I fell in love with a great guy. I thought I found my place with Wolf. I expected to spend the rest of my life with him. And now? I'll never see Wolf again. I thought the Great Spirit let me bring a part of him with me, but my baby, my poor baby. I'm tired of wishing for a life I can not have. I'm tired of missing people. I'm tired of feeling empty inside. But you know what I am most tired of, Dee?"

"No, hon, what?" Dee leaned forward to hear me.

I took a ragged breath. "I'm tired of it all. I'm so tired of being sad all the time. I ought to be happy now. Excited, like you were when you were expecting your babies. But, I'm just plain tired of being tired."

I stared out over the water of Lake Blue Ridge as if suddenly oblivious to Dan and Dee as they hovered nearby.

"What do we do, Dan? How can we help her? She's so broken right now," Dee whispered.

He shook his head. "I don't know, honey. I've never seen her like this, not even at her lowest during her divorce with Brian."

"Well, Daniel, she's never been 49, pregnant and alone before," Dee snapped.

"Well, Dee, technically, she is 41," Dan said.

Dee frowned. "Oh, for the love of- we have to help her, Daniel. What do we do?"

"Fancy says something about everyone is broken. What is it?" he asked.

I looked up, surprised I had even heard him. "Oh, I forgot about that. It's a quote from Hemingway. 'The world breaks everyone, and then some become strong at the broken pieces.'" I answered, my voice calmer than it had sounded in weeks. "I had completely forgotten about it. I remember Fancy told me we could become human Kintsugi, like Japanese pottery, mended and made stronger, more interesting, hell, more beautiful because of the repair. I was bound and determined to be better every single day when I first went back. I guess I forgot that somewhere along the way. Although I'm not sure if enough gold exists to fix me right now."

"Well, Fancy certainly got a lot better," Dee said. "I'll never forget the hot mess she was that awful Fourth of July."

I nodded. "God knows she got better. Dan, maybe I need to talk to Fancy. Or maybe I need to see her therapist. His name was Dr. Tamaguchi, or something like that. I think he might be a Japanese American. He knew that whole Japanese pottery thing."

"Brian Tanakawa. He's a wonderful psychologist. He just opened an office here in Blue Ridge. Want me to call him for you?"

I tried to smile. "Yeah, I think that would be a good idea. Have I mentioned lately you're a pretty wonderful brother?"

Dan pulled me into his arms and kissed my forehead. "You're a pretty wonderful sister, too, kiddo."

"Even if I'm just your kid sister, Bay, and I'm not the Guider?" My voice cracked.

"Even so, kiddo. But, don't dismiss your role for our people just yet." He kissed my forehead again. "After all, I remember something in that old prophecy about faith being challenged would create the faith that would prevail in the face of all odds. You gotta keep the faith, sis, about your baby and your role in the prophecy."

I tried to smile. "Keep the faith, huh, bro?"

He nodded. "Yeah. Keep the faith."

Chapter 21
The Proposition

Tuesday afternoon, after Kirk and Mellie returned from the Cohutta Wilderness, Kirk went into the Brian Boru to help Grady Sullivan set up for the night. Grady stood tidying the bar area when Kirk entered the pub. Grady prided himself on a well-kept Irish pub. Customers loved the elderly gentleman and his never-ending stories about 'the old sod.' Likewise, the big tall Irishman managed to quickly finagle a place in the hearts of the regular patrons. Kirk greeted a half dozen by name as he came in. He eased behind the bar, picked up a towel, and began wiping up a spill.

"Hey, man, did you have a nice little honeymoon?" Grady asked as he wiped the sweat from his face. "I didn't expect to see you back here until tomorrow night."

Kirk grinned. "We decided to come back this afternoon. We would hate to miss the excitement. Has the Indian arrived in Blue Ridge yet? We saw it on the news."

Grady shook his head with a puzzled look on his face. "An Indian? I don't know what you're talking about. Look, man, I meant to talk to you—"

Kirk paled. "Jesus, Grady, are you goin' to fire me?"

"Oh, hell, no. Quite the opposite. Let's talk in the office. I want to throw an idea past you and see what you think. Come on. Hey, Sue, cover for us a few minutes."

The waitress smiled. "Sure, boss."

Kirk started after his boss only to balk at the door to the cluttered office. Grady had spreadsheets opened across his desk and had more pulled up on the computer. The office was always organized chaos at best, but this seemed to have some rhyme to the usual illogical reasoning. Kirk's eyes narrowed speculatively. Grady was cagey as a fox and one of the most astute businessmen Kirk ever met in this era or Before, as Fancy called the past age they came from. What could the old man have up his sleeve this time?

"What have you got in mind? You look serious."

Grady grinned at Kirk. "Aye, it is. I've been thinking about this for a month or so. I've looked over the spreadsheets at least a dozen times, and I talked to my accountant about it again today. Lad, I have a business proposition for you…"

. . .

The next morning, Kirk brought Mellie to work. Instead of dropping her off with a kiss outside, he parked the sleek little convertible and walked inside with her. "Hey, Rick, you got a minute?"

Rick never looked up as he continued writing a note on a patient's file. Finally, he laid his pen down and grinned at Kirk. "Sure. What's on your mind?"

"A couple of things. First, has our friend showed up here in Blue Ridge yet?"

Rick shook his head. "Not yet. I'm starting to get worried."

"Ah, he'll be fine. I'm surprised Baylie hasn't spotted him on the news. He's been on Channel 3, out of Chattanooga. That young guy has bird dogged Wolf for the better part of three days now."

Rick shrugged as he signed off on the next file and then handed it to a nurse. "Please give that to my wife so she can schedule the patient's surgery."

"Right away, Doctor."

Rick waited until the young nurse left the area. "Yeah. Fancy is so excited he came that she can barely sit still. She wants to take Bay out Old Highway 2 towards the Jacks River Road to look at that acreage Bay wants to buy. You know as well as I do that she is trying to engineer a meeting somewhere out there."

Kirk laughed. "Sounds like her. I can almost see the wheels turning in that pretty little head of hers. That reporter would love to catch the reunion on film. I need to talk to you. Grady offered to sell me the Brian Boru. I've been helping him at the club, and he says he likes my management style. I've been working as his assistant manager for months now. What do you think?"

"Are you kidding? Heck, I knew you were over there a lot, but I didn't know you were management. I will say the club has been more fun since you showed up. I noticed the patrons seem to love you. I was surprised you guys didn't get married there."

Kirk blushed. "We talked about it, but Friday nights are too busy, and we wanted to be able to have the weekend for a honeymoon."

"I guess that makes sense. This opportunity is the chance of a lifetime, Kirk. That club is the hottest spot in North Georgia. How much does he want?"

Kirk grinned and handed Rick a spreadsheet. "Here are the numbers. What he wants for the club, and how much it earned per month over the past five years. It looks like a profitable venture to me."

Rick frowned. "Why does he want to sell?"

Kirk shrugged. "He says he's turning 70, and he wants to move to Savannah to be near his daughter and grandkids. You know he has a bar there as well, so he will still have an income, plus what I will be paying for the Brian Boru. Anyway, I thought you might know an accountant who could, what is it?... crash the numbers?"

Rick struggled not to laugh. "I think you mean crunch the numbers, old man. Sure, I'll email it to my accountant this afternoon. Now, let me ask: how do you plan to pay the down payment?"

Kirk looked flustered. "Well, Grady said he would work with me about that. Why?"

Rick smiled. "Let's get the evaluation back from the accountant and see if this club is as financially remunerative as it appears on paper."

Kirk's brow knitted together in a combination of confusion and worry. "Wait, you don't think it is worth this much?"

"Rick shook his head. "I didn't say that by any means. Look, I don't know if you would be interested, but if this is as good a deal as it looks on paper, I thought you might like a silent partner who would front you the down payment."

Kirk's mouth fell open. "Are you serious?"

Rick chuckled. "Well, if the deal is as golden an opportunity as it looks here, then yes. I would be very interested."

"*Ai, Dia*, Rick, that would be grand. Thank you. I don't know what else to say."

Rick laughed and clapped Kirk on the back. "Who would have dreamed we would ever get along this well, huh? Glad I took you to Fight Club?"

Kirk looked embarrassed. "Aye, it was certainly a male bonding moment for us, that's for sure, and it's a great way to work off some steam. Dammit, Rick, I should have let her go with you in Barbados."

Rick shook his head. "Nah. We would probably have stayed there, Before, Ronan would never have been born, and Francesca would be dead by now."

Kirk nodded. "And I would never have found my Mellie."

Rick nodded. "Exactly. It took me a long time to get here, but it was meant to happen the way it did."

· · ·

That afternoon, my big brother and I walked into the Blue Ridge office of Dr. Brian Tanakawa, a clinical psychologist. I paced back and forth in front of the big picture window as we waited for Dr. Tanakawa.

"Oh, look! That dreamy Indian guy is being interviewed again. Karen, come quick, look at this. He's riding his horse in from out near Cisco. He says he's going to surprise his wife." The receptionist bubbled on and on.

"Ooh, he's so handsome! This is so romantic!" gushed the secretary.

I tapped my foot impatiently. "Can you believe they are watching television during work hours? Not very professional," I snapped. "I'm here to see Dr. Tanakawa if you can break away from your precious television long enough to tell him I'm here."

"Aw, kiddo, don't be too rough on them. I heard about that guy yesterday at my office. It is pretty romantic," Dan said.

I made a rude noise. "Yeah, sure. My life is falling apart, and Mr. Romance is riding into town on his valiant steed to sweep his lady love off her feet."

Dan laughed. "Bay, you crack me up. I'm surprised by your reaction. You are usually such a romantic. I figured you would have seen this guy on the news by now. It's been broadcast a couple of times."

"I don't care, Dan. I don't care. I have other things on my mind." I rubbed my forehead. "I have such a horrible headache."

About then, a slender Asian American man stepped into the doorway. "Miss Smith, I'm Brian Tanakawa. Would you like to come to my office? Hello, Dan, would you like to join us for a few minutes?"

Dan reached over and shook Brian's hand. "Good to see you. It's up to Baylie. Do you want me to sit in with you at first, or would you prefer to talk to Brian alone?"

I stood there, pale and trembling, as I reached over and grabbed Dan's hand. "Uh, I think I would like you to stay, Bubba."

Dan pulled me close and hugged me tightly. "Girl, you made my heart lurch. You haven't called me Bubba in at least 30 years. It'll be okay, Sissy. I promise. We're all here to help you."

I was acutely aware of my discomfort as we took our seats in Brian Tanakawa's office. How could I explain this enormous jumble to Dr. Tanakawa?

Brian Tanakawa cleared his throat. "I spoke with a former client a while ago to see if I could discuss certain things with you. Let's just say I also know Fancy and Rick, and I know Fancy's story."

I blinked. "Then, you know where I've been."

He nodded. "I know a little, from your brother, in addition to my work with Fancy Winslow, so I know about the whole time travel thing. Does that help move things along a little? Maybe break the ice?"

I nodded. "Yes, it certainly does. Um, eight years ago, I went back in time to help fulfill an ancient Cherokee prophecy. I was there about a year and a half before I came back."

He frowned. "I thought you said you left eight years ago?"

I chuckled. "Yeah. Imagine my surprise to have been gone for a year and a half and get back to learn eight years had elapsed here. So, technically, I'm 49, but I have lived 41 years."

Dr. Tanakawa let out a low whistle. "I didn't see that one coming. So, Baylie – may I call you Baylie?"

I nodded. "Of course."

"And feel free to call me Brian or Dr. T, or whatever feels right. So tell me, what brought you back?"

My eyes clouded with new tears, and I rubbed my forehead as if to ease my tension. "Thank you, Brian. I appreciate that. The tribal council sent me back after I told Kirk O'Malley where Fancy was. He went running off and was carried forward in time without adequate preparation. They told me that I had to bring him back or not to return to the village."

Dr. Tanakawa blinked. "Wait a minute. — you somehow sent Kirk O'Malley here? Fancy's Kirk O'Malley, right?"

My laugh mixed with a sob that slipped from my lips. "Exactly. Only Fancy is happily married to Rick. I hoped he would go back with me, but no such luck. He is the most difficult man I ever met."

"Worse than Brian?" Dan asked.

"Pretty close. Brian's my ex-husband," I explained to Dr. Tanakawa.

"What did O'Malley say when you asked him to go back?" asked Dr. Tanakawa.

I grimaced and shook my head. "Damned Irishman said, 'you aren't just missin' a screw, girl. Your whole toolbox must be missin' even to suggest such a thing. Why would I go back?' Anyway, O'Malley began establishing a relationship with his daughter, Elizabeth. And then he started seeing a woman here."

Dr. Tanakawa looked surprised. "Oh?"

I struggled not to start crying again. "Yes. Kirk and Melanie married last Friday. But that wasn't the worst news I got Friday."

Dan reached over and placed a protective arm around me. "It's okay, Sissy. Take a deep breath."

I tried to smile. I took a deep breath, as Dan suggested. "I'm 16 weeks pregnant. Friday, it was confirmed that my baby has Down syndrome. I'm feeling pretty overwhelmed right now. Huh, maybe this is why the Great Spirit let O'Malley come forward in time, and the council insisted I had to come after him."

"Wow, that's a lot to be hit with at one time." Brian Tanakawa looked rattled.

"Yeah, well, they always say that when it rains, it pours," I replied.

"Why was O'Malley your responsibility? Why did they send you after him?" Dr. Tanakawa asked.

I sighed. "Well, you see, Kirk was my slave—"

Brian Tanakawa's eyes bulged at that tidbit of information. "Wait a minute! Did you say Kirk O'Malley was your *slave*? How did that happen?"

I flipped my hand in the air dismissively. "Long story. I don't want to go into it right now."

Brian Tanakawa shook his head. "Oh, no, no, no, Baylie. Please, tell me. I am too invested in the story of Kirk O'Malley. Tell me, how did he become enslaved?"

I sighed and shook my head, frustrated. "Oh, gosh. We raided a Chickamauga village, and he was their prisoner. We took him in the raid. I claimed him, thinking I could free him and send him merrily on his way. Ha! No such luck. When the council awarded him to me, I could only free him in a council approved method. He could become a member of the tribe. He refused. He could marry into the tribe. Several women wanted to marry him, but he rejected his suitors. He could agree to leave the Indian Territory and never come back. He refused to do that unless he knew where Fancy and the children went so he could go after them. Or, I could sell him to someone else, like Fancy's father, Marc McCarron, who might subsequently free O'Malley once they were out of Indian Territory. Marc refused to own a slave even temporarily until they left Indian Territory."

I took a sip of water as Brian waited.

"I argued that we should tell him she came forward in time, found Rick, they married, and were living happily ever after in the Beyond, as we call it there. The council was mixed in their opinions, but Wolf agreed we should tell him."

Brian frowned. "What went wrong? Why did they send you after him?"

I sighed, clearly exasperated. "Yours truly here told him Fancy went through a hole in time to the future, and Rick and she married. But then, being the fool I am, I also told him I went back in time, to what my people call the Before, to help fulfill a prophecy. So, of course, he decided he could go forward in time, too. He rushed to the portal location, and low and behold that dratted white devil came forward in time."

Brian shook his head. "Okay, I'm missing something. They wanted to be rid of him. What was the problem?"

"I agree, but you see, Kirk was not, um, appropriately clad when he came forward. He had been dressing a deer, and wore only a loincloth."

Brian gawked at me. "A loincloth?" As I nodded, Brian began laughing. "Oh, that must have been something to see when he got here."

"So, I understand from Fancy. Add to it, when she showed up at the ranger's hut at the Beech Bottom Trailhead in Tennessee, Kirk thought her daughter, Bella, was Fancy, grabbed her, and kissed the girl right on the mouth. Yuck! Kirk freaked Bella out."

Dan raised an eyebrow and grinned. "Oh, I hadn't heard that."

I nodded. "Yep, I'm not sure the girl will ever recover from that traumatic experience. Anyway, the council jumped my butt for 'letting' him go forward in time without adequate knowledge, clothing, or supplies, and they sent me to fetch the white devil back."

Brian sat laughing. "Unbelievable."

"Yeah, I'm lucky you know about time travel, or you would probably be wanting to hospitalize me right about now. Then again, a vacay, even in the hospital, might be okay. If I could stop worrying so much…"

My voice trailed off.

Dan cleared his throat. "Uh, Bay, tell Brian about the *Tsul Kalu*."

She rolled her eyes again. "You cannot imagine how imbued in superstition the *AniYunwiya* were then—"

"The what? I don't know the word," said Brian, as his brow scrunched into a frown line.

"Oops, my bad. 'The *AniYunwiya*' is what the Cherokees have long called themselves. It means the People of Another Language. Anyway, the tribe believes O'Malley is the slant-eyed, white devil called *Tsul Kalu*, or one of the devil's descendants. They believe his devil status was confirmed when he came forward in time. Go figure."

"Aha! That's why you keep calling him the 'white devil,' and they sent you to fetch him back!" Brian exclaimed.

I nodded. "By Jove, I think you've got it. Yep, I am supposed to drag the white devil back before he creates chaos and disharmony here. But, he found love and seems happier than, well, gee whiz, just about any freaking human I know. Dammit."

"Why 'Dammit,' Baylie?" asked Brian.

Tears welled up in my eyes again. "His life is all hunky-dory, and mine is falling apart. I find myself in the twenty-first century, pregnant, unwed, unemployed, dependent on my brother's charity. The man I love, the father of my child, is back in 1788. The council was clear. Don't come back without O'Malley. Now, I learn my baby has Down syndrome. How can I go back, even if they would let me? They don't have the kind of medical care my baby girl will need. And if I don't go back, I cannot fulfill the part of the prophecy I was born to fulfill. Oh, Doc, it's a hot mess."

I covered my face with my hands as I sobbed. Brian handed Dan a box of Kleenex, which Dan passed to me. Brian waited until my tears subsided to speak again.

"Have you explained all this to O'Malley?" Brian asked.

I nodded. "Yes. O'Malley doesn't care. He says if he has to choose between me being happy and him being happy, he's going to win this vote. He even said if I can't understand that, then it's not that I have a screw or two loose, but my whole freaking toolbox is gone. Bottom line: O'Malley likes it here. He intends to stay, especially since he met and fell in love with Mellie. And, even I have to admit, he seems happier, more relaxed, and more at peace than he has been at any time since I met him. I just wish I felt some of that peace right now."

Brian leaned towards me and took my hands into his. "Okay. Tell me what is the biggest, most pressing you have."

I wiped my nose again and took a big breath. "I've sworn for weeks I want this baby. Dr. Kate keeps reminding me I can have an abortion, and I know 90% of pregnancies with a baby carrying Down syndrome are terminated. But, Brian, this is my baby girl, the daughter I always wanted. This baby is my one shot at having a baby of my own. I know she's the girl I always longed to have. She is flesh of my flesh, blood of my blood. But, is it fair to bring her into this world just because I want a baby?"

My tears began to flow again.

"Bay, that's not the only reason you want a baby, and you know it," Dan protested. "Daughters are important in our Cherokee culture. Clan membership follows from our mothers, not our fathers. But this is more than you want a child. This goes to the last part of the prophecy, Bay, and you know it. This has to do with you having faith, and the villagers following your faith to a new home."

"Oh, Dan, I know you think that is the answer. But, can I go back with a different-abled child? What kind of life would she have in the eighteenth century? Would the tribe accept her? Or-"

My voice trailed off, and I began not merely to cry, but to sob again. Big, racking sobs that shook my body.

"It's okay, Baylie. Take your time. This is important," said Brian.

I nodded and took another ragged breath. "Or would the tribe think the *Tsul Kalu* sired my almond-eyed child? Would they think O'Malley is her father?"

My voice broke again. The men waited for me to compose myself again. I took a deep breath and continued. "Would Wolf accept her as his daughter if we went back, or would he think she is O'Malley's child? Because I swear, if he thought that she was not his blood, it would kill me."

. . .

The therapy session lasted well over an hour. Baylie appeared exhausted as they left. Dan paid for the visit and scheduled another meeting for Baylie on Friday. He figured Wolf would arrive by then, and they would need the session.

Baylie was quiet as they pulled out from the professional building parking lot. She sat lost in thought as Dan headed the luxurious Mercedes back towards Blue Ridge until he turned off the Blue Ridge Highway onto Old Highway 2. She looked at her brother, quizzically. "What are you doing? Aren't you going back to work?"

Dan shrugged. "You keep talking about that land on the Jacks River Road. I don't have any appointments this afternoon, and I thought we could drive out there to see it."

Baylie sat up straighter in the seat. "But I thought you said it's too far out of town. Why the change of heart?"

He kind of grinned. His real purpose was to try to engineer an 'accidental meeting' between Wolf and her that afternoon, as Fancy suggested, but he had no intention of telling Baylie. "I wouldn't want you to move out there until after the baby is born, but we could go ahead and buy the land if it is what you want. We could start building you a cabin."

For the first time in weeks, Baylie began to smile. "Oh, Bubba, are you serious? I don't need a big place. I'm accustomed to living in an *asi*, and I would bet they only have about 300 square feet of living space. Even a tiny house would work."

Dan laughed. "My baby sister and my niece are not going to live in a tiny house, but a small cabin would work."

A shaky smile appeared on Baylee's face. "I have about $100,000 here. I can afford to buy the land outright. It could be a down payment on a house for my baby and me."

He nodded. "That was my idea. I saw another nice plot out here, too. It's six acres on Hell's Hollow, right on the lake. I figured with either of those, you would have mountain and water views."

She nodded, her eyes sparkling with excitement. "If you don't mind driving around in the wilderness, both sound great. Thank you, Dan."

Dan chuckled as Baylie began chatting with more animation than he had heard in days, if not weeks.

"Two bedrooms would be plenty. All we need is one bath. I would love an open living room and kitchen. I bet 700 square feet would be plenty big enough. I would love a log home with a wood-burning fireplace, though. Do you think I could afford it?"

Dan laughed. "Honey, I was thinking more like 1400 to 1800 square feet, maybe three bedrooms and two baths. Let's decide on the land, and then we can figure out what Baby Girl and you will live in."

She smiled. "Sounds good."

As Dan slipped a CD into the player, she shook her head. "You always loved jazz. Don't you ever listen to Native American music?"

He nodded. "Yes, sometimes. I was worried it would depress you."

She turned to smile at him. "I'll be okay. I promise."

He smiled at her. "I know. You're Cherokee. We're made from tough stock."

They were almost to the turn to Hells Hollow when he spotted Wolf. "Huh. It looks like we get to see the mysterious Indian riding into town to find his wife."

She sniffed in disdain. "Oh, the guy those women were calling 'the big, handsome, sexy'— oh, my god, Dan, stop the car!"

He pulled up right in front of the man, so close that the Appaloosa reared onto its hind legs. Baylie was out of the car before the car completely stopped. Dan sat back in the leather seat, grinning from ear to ear as Wolf swung down from the horse and pulled Baylie into his arms. They could see the land another day. As Baylie cried clinging to Shadow Wolf, Dan heard the handsome Cherokee chief utter words in Cherokee as he held Baylie close to his chest.

"A tsi lv quo di, gv ge yu hi."

He called her his beloved. He loves her. Dan smiled as he blinked back a few tears of his own. With those few words, he knew Shadow Wolf was the right man for his sister. After all, he came hundreds of years into the unknown future to find and reclaim the woman he loved.

"Gv ge yu hi," Baylie replied to Wolf. "Wolf, my heart, you must meet my brother, Dan."

Before she could introduce them, Wolf shook his head. "Dan will wait. I am holding my wife. It has been too long."

She laughed as if embarrassed. "Wolf, we aren't married yet."

"We will be soon. I came to claim you."

She shook her head as tears welled in her eyes. "O'Malley won't go back. He—"

"I did not come for O'Malley. I came for you, woman. You are all I want. With you, I have everything." Wolf lowered his lips to hers.

As the kiss ended, Baylie stood leaning against him, her eyes closed, her lips parted. Dan could see the anxiety and fear begin to drain from her face. Dan knew they would be okay.

Dad always told them 'sometimes, life doesn't give you what you want. It's not because you don't deserve it. It's because you deserve so much more.'

Dan realized years ago life didn't give him to Lily because they both deserved so much more than they had together. He found his something more with Delia. Lily found her something more hundreds of years in the past with Marc. Fancy found her something more with Rick. O'Malley found his with Mellie.

And now, it seemed his baby sister found her something more with a Cherokee war chieftain, who was so determined to have his own something more that he followed Baylie more than 200 years into the future so he could claim his future with the woman he loved.

Dad was right. The secret to having it all is realizing you already have it all.

Epilogue
Twenty-Six Weeks Later

Wolf stared down at his newborn daughter, awe and wonder written across his face. I smiled as my husband began examining our baby's fingers again.

"Did she grow any new ones?" I asked, tongue in cheek, as I peered over his shoulder to see what he was doing.

Wolf looked up, startled, and then smiled back at me. "No. They are all still here. No webbing. They are perfectly formed. She is perfect."

I laughed. "No, darling, no one is perfect, not even our little girl. She is perfectly imperfect."

Wolf smiled. "Perfectly imperfect. Hmm, I like that."

We bought the land on the Jacks River Road deep in the heart of the Cohutta Wilderness. Like McCarron's Corner, the property was part of an old estate which had never been absorbed by the government when it bought most of the lands in the area. We both loved the spot from the moment we first saw it.

The little log cabin was ready for us to move into it. Bigger than an *asi* and far smaller than Dan and Dee's mansion at Lake Blue Ridge, it would be a comfortable living space while we remained here. It had two bedrooms, a bathroom, and an open living room and kitchen with a big, stone fireplace. Wolf had the plans and intended to replicate it without the indoor plumbing someday when we moved westward with the tribe to what would eventually be called the Arbuckle Mountains of Central Oklahoma. Wolf built a pole barn for his horse. I decorated the cabin for Christmas before I came to the hospital to give birth. I put up a Christmas tree and hung three stockings from the mantle.

We decided we would stay here until our baby had a good start. She could receive the best possible medical care and various therapies at this time, which would not be available in the wilderness when we went home.

We both looked up at the sound of the door opening. "Oh, hi, Dan. What did the echocardiogram show?"

Dan walked into the room and smiled at us. "Pretty decent report. We knew she has a heart murmur and suspected she has an atrial septal defect. The echo confirmed she has one, but it also confirmed the defect is quite small."

My brow furrowed with worry. "What does that mean in regards to possible heart surgery?"

Dan smiled. "It means the defect is mild, and I anticipate it will close on its own over the next few months. I'll keep an eye on it, but I doubt she will need surgery."

I closed my eyes and sighed with relief. "Oh, thank the Great Spirit."

Wolf nodded. "Yes, this is a true blessing. Thank you, Dan."

Dan chuckled. "No need to thank me. I just did the test. Did the geneticist come in to see you?"

I nodded. "Yes. Dr. De Asis stated, based on her physical appearance and the DNA tests, she believes our baby girl has partial trisomy 21."

Dan smiled. "That's what she told me. That means your baby was born with part of an extra number-21chromosome in her cells. That explains why she has fewer physical characteristics than Down syndrome children usually have."

My head bobbed up and down with excitement. "She had a slightly elevated nuchal translucency of 3.11 millimeters in her first ultrasound."

"Exactly," Dan said as he smiled at me. "Just slightly above the cut-off used to help identify potential Down syndrome children."

"And even though she has almond-shaped eyes-" I began.

"Cherokees tend to have almond-shaped eyes. Look at my eyes. The eye shape is not necessarily a marker of Down syndrome in this case," Wolf completed her sentence for my brother and me.

Dan nodded again. "I can tell you guys have been busy studying about this. I heard Wolf say when I came in that her fingers are not webbed."

Wolf lifted a tiny hand and spread the fingers. "They aren't webbed. They are perfect."

Dan shook his head. "No. Her fingers would be perfect even if they were webbed. They would be different, Wolf, not defective."

"I understand. My child is perfectly imperfect." Wolf smiled at Dan.

Dan's jaw hung slack. "Damn, that's the best phrase I ever heard to describe a Down syndrome baby. I'll have to remember it."

Wolf shook his head. "You do not understand, Dan. We are all imperfect. No one is perfect, except in the eyes of their parents. She is just like all other babies. There are some things about her that are different from most babies. She is perfectly imperfect."

Dan's face softened as he smiled. "Yeah. Well, she may have milder developmental delays than other children with Down syndrome with partial trisomy 21. We just have to wait and see."

"Like the heart defect," I said, and my brother nodded at me again. "Dr. De Asis said she isn't demonstrating other physical conditions DS babies often manifest. She thought that was a good sign."

"I agree, Bay, but remember some of those don't usually show up right away." Dan frowned.

I nodded, but I am always the worrier. I began to chew my lip. "So, she's at least a little broken."

"Aren't we all? I know I am," Wolf said.

"Amen, Wolf. Yes, we are all broken in one way or another. Fancy spouts off that quote by a famous author about how we are all a little broken. I can't remember who said it right now," Dan replied.

I looked at my brother, surprised by his words. "Really, Dan? I thought you loved Hemingway. Remember? He said, 'the world breaks everyone, and then some become strong at the broken pieces.' I know I've had my fair share of breaks. I remember being hungry a lot of the time when I was little after Daddy died."

Dan nodded. "That was a rough period for us all."

"Yes, it was. Thank the Great Spirit that grocer took you under his wing and helped us out. I think Daddy's death cracked us all a little bit. I had another break when Mama died." My face reddened, and I began to sniff.

Wolf patted me on the back. "I broke when we were forced to leave Virginia, and I shattered into a million pieces when my Ginny died."

"Shattered, yeah, that's a good description. I shattered when my Mama died, but I sure didn't shatter when I kicked Brian out," I said, my voice tight with emotion. I remembered meeting and marrying Brian soon after our mother died.

I foolishly thought Brian would fill the empty spot my mother left. I realized too late he was emotionally devouring me. I had to go. Dan knew Brian used to belittle me. No one knew Brian used to beat me when he grew frustrated with my success and his failure. I told everyone the black eye I wore the day I left Brian was because I hit my face with the car door. I feared Dan's reaction if he knew I received the black eye when my face collided with Brian's fist that morning.

Hell, I feared Dan might kill Brian if he knew about the abuse.

"No, Brian had already broken you. Brian was a sorry excuse for a man. I never liked him. And, your damned job with the BIA did its part at breaking you, too. She hated that job, Wolf." Dan's voice sounded surprisingly angry and bitter.

Wolf shook his head. "She loved the job, and she also hated it. Brian was always the wrong man for her. It was inevitable there would be pain in their relationship. He was a weak man. To be blunt, he was not strong enough for her."

I smiled at my husband. "Wow, you nailed that one. Rest assured, my love. You are the right man."

He nodded. "And yet, even I have hurt you at times."

I grew quiet as I thought how I felt when Wolf and the council told me that I had to come after O'Malley. Silent, I nodded. I was not ready to talk about that dark time in my life in front of Dan.

I was well aware of the cracks in my shell when I first met Fancy. When the young woman told me about Hemingway's comment, I took it to heart. When Fancy told me about the way the Japanese mend things with epoxy and gold, and how the concept could be applied to people, I was determined to use the Kintsugi method to help repair myself with spiritual epoxy and gold.

Dr. Tanakawa helped me a lot in the past six months. I knew I was finally getting better each day. I hoped I was becoming stronger and more interesting, maybe even a bit more beautiful, as well. Instead of trying to hide the flaws and cracks, my emotional scars would be accentuated and celebrated as they become the strongest parts of me. Like Fancy, I was a survivor. I intended to be a badass survivor. After all, I would need all my inner badass when we returned to the time we called 'Before.'

"So, what are you guys going to name this sweet baby girl?" Dan asked as he picked up the baby and laid the stethoscope on her little chest.

I smiled at my husband. "You want to tell him?"

Wolf nodded his head. "This is the child who will teach our people to be faithful. She will be our faithful angel. If we are faithful, if we keep the faith, the tribe will be invigorated by our faith and will go with us to our new home."

"That's from the prophecy. But come on, guys, level with me. What are you going to name her?" Dan pressed as he handed the baby back to Baylie. "Faithful Angel is a great name for a Cherokee child, but living in this era, she also needs a more Americanized name, like Baylie and I have."

"Someday you must tell me how the name 'Baylie' was chosen," Wolf said with a wry grin.

"Not unless you pick an Americanized name people can call you, Mr. Wolf. Or have you decided on a name for yourself yet?" I teased.

He smiled. "I think I shall go by Max. I like Max Wolf. It is a strong name."

I chuckled and nodded as I looked at the tiny baby nestled in my brother's arms and eased her into my arms. At least he had not insisted on being named 'Dude.' He loved The Big Lebowski. He laughed every time he told me about Sassy calling Will 'Dude.' "Can't you guess? We are naming her Faith Smith Wolf."

Wolf laughed. "Her mother is an eagle, but I believe our little Faith will be a hummingbird, a messenger of the gods."

"So, now we all have Americanized names as well as Cherokee names. Baylie Smith is also Path of the Guiding Light. Max Wolf is also Shadow Wolf. Faithful Angel is our little angel, Faith Smith Wolf."

We all stared at the baby sleeping in my arms. Perfectly imperfect. Perfect for the difficult job ahead of her. Her imperfections would be mended with the epoxy and gold of the gods, just as my imperfections were being mended day by day. I would help my little girl to grow stronger, more interesting, and if such a thing were possible, more beautiful. We would teach our little girl how to lead our people by faith.

I smiled. And a little child shall lead them.

I eased the bit of sage out of my pocket and crumbled it with my fingers before I blew it into the air. I closed my eyes and uttered a quick, silent prayer of thanks, and then I smiled at Wolf. I found my love, my faith, my hope.

I was ready to fulfill my destiny.

Note from the Author

Word-of-mouth is crucial for any author to succeed. If you enjoyed *Path of the Guiding Light*, please leave a review online—anywhere you are able. Even if it's just a sentence or two. It would make all the difference and would be very much appreciated.

Thanks!
Sharon

About the Author

Sharon K. Middleton is a fourth generation Texan. Her first relative to the Colonies came in 1742 as a 12-year-old Irish indentured servant. Her great-grandmother immigrated from Mexico in the 1890s. Sharon is a graduate of Trinity University, Texas A&M, and South Texas College of Law. She is an attorney licensed to practice in Texas. She enjoys writing, quilting, showing and raising Skye terriers. She loves the wilds of North Georgia and hopes to retire there soon.

Thank you so much for reading one of Sharon K. Middleton's novels. If you enjoyed the experience, please check out our recommended title for your next great read!

Beyond McCarron's Corner: Sassy's Story by Sharon K. Middleton

"A tale with an intriguing historical setting and time-travel premise..."
-Kirkus Reviews

www.ingramcontent.com/pod-product-compliance
Lightning Source LLC
Chambersburg PA
CBHW011133100726
47898CB00009B/2967